Dark Whispers

FROM BEYOND

THE CHILDREN OF THE GODS
BOOK SIXTY-FOUR

I. T. LUCAS

Copyright © 2022 by I. T. Lucas

Published by Evening Star Press

EveningStarPress.com

ISBN-13: 978-1-957139-33-3

William

$\sim\!\!\sim\!\!\sim$

Worry about Kaia, her family, and the future of the project had kept William awake throughout the night.

Kaia and her family were being forced to rush into life-altering decisions that might either kill its older members or grant them immortality. And if that wasn't enough, Gilbert and Karen's relationship could suffer irreparable damage.

Karen was running out of time, and even though it was easy to understand her preference to wait for Gilbert to transition first so he could induce her, she might not have the six months it would take for his fangs and venom glands to become fully functional. Karen needed to choose an immortal male to activate her dormant immortal genes, but even though her survival depended on it, she and Gilbert might not be able to get past that and continue as a loving couple.

1

The continuation of the project was less troublesome, but it had many moving parts, and assembling them into a workable solution had also kept William from getting any sleep.

They had only scratched the surface of Okidu's journals, and there was still a lot to be deciphered before William could dismiss the rest of the team and continue just with Kaia. In fact, she would have to do the heavy lifting because he needed to go back to work on the other projects he'd put on hold.

Last night, after they'd made love and Kaia had sailed off on the wings of euphoria, William had called Marcel, and they'd discussed the progress that had been made so far and what Marcel would do with the team in William and Kaia's absence.

The project would continue with them working remotely from the village and Marcel supervising the team of bioinformaticians, but before William introduced his replacement to the team, he needed to discuss with Marcel a few things about managing humans.

Marcel was a sharp guy, but his people skills were even worse than William's, and the guy hadn't dealt with humans since his days as a student at Caltech. That was why William was picking him and the pilot up from the airport instead of just sending a driver for them. He and Marcel needed the time to go over the rules of conduct and what was okay to tell the team of humans and what was not.

It was time to leave, but that was easier said than done.

Standing at the foot of the bed, he gazed at the sleeping beauty sprawled over the covers, his eyes fixed on her gorgeous face and his feet refusing to move.

William would have liked to believe that Kaia's blissed-out expression was his doing, and that she could sleep so peacefully despite yesterday's shocking revelations because he was such an incredible lover, but he knew it was the venom's lingering effect.

Would she be as relaxed when she woke up?

Probably not. As soon as memories of yesterday's events rushed in, she would without a doubt be stressing over her impending transition and the decisions her family was facing.

With a sigh, William forced his eyes away from Kaia and walked toward the door.

"Where are you going?" she asked sleepily.

William turned around and smiled. "I'm going to pick up Marcel from the airport," he reminded her.

Kaia spread her arms. "You can't leave without giving me a kiss."

He couldn't refuse an invitation like that.

Walking back, he sat on the bed and leaned to lightly kiss her on the lips. "You don't need to get up for another two hours. You should go back to sleep."

She yawned. "I want to call my mother and hear her impressions of your village. Do you know if Marcel gave my family new clan phones? If he did, I need their numbers."

"I'm sure he or someone else from the lab took care of that." William cupped her warm cheek. "I'll get the numbers and text them to you, but it's five in the morning, so your mother is probably still asleep, and you should be as well."

Kaia covered her mouth with her hand and yawned again. "No wonder I'm so sleepy. I hope that Cheryl can download Instatock on her new phone. If she can't check her stats every five minutes, she'll get panicky, and she'll demand to leave right away."

That was an unhealthy obsession, but if her mother didn't object, it was none of his business.

"Cheryl can download any application she wants."

"What about your security? All those apps follow people around and record everything they do on their devices."

"Don't worry about that." He leaned and kissed her forehead. "I designed them in a way that makes it impossible for apps to track anything other than what's necessary for their operation."

Kaia grinned. "My genius boyfriend. But out of an abundance of caution, I suggest that you check this particular app."

"Why?"

She shrugged. "Instatock is only six or seven months old, and it's sweeping an entire generation of teenagers without monetizing a thing. There are no advertisements, nothing to buy, and the application is free. I'm suspicious of its motives."

As his chest swelled with love and pride, William grinned. Even when her body was still mostly asleep, Kaia's mind was fully awake.

"I'll check, but I doubt any application can break through my defenses." He kissed her cheeks one at a time and then added one more to her forehead. "I need to go. Max is waiting for me on the bus."

The Guardian had informed him yesterday that he would be tagging along on the trip to the airport to pick up Marcel and Morris. Unsurprisingly, Kian or Onegus had left instructions that William shouldn't be allowed to leave the safe zone without a Guardian escort.

Kaia pulled the blanket up to her chin. "Text me when you get there." She turned on her side and closed her eyes.

"I will." He forced himself to get off the bed and walk out.

He found Max waiting for him outside his bungalow.

"Good morning." He gave the Guardian a tight smile. "Were you afraid I'd give you the slip?"

Max shrugged. "I could have waited here or on the bus, but I knew the driver would already be there, and he would have expected me to chat with him. I don't have the patience for idle chit-chat, and besides, I prefer not to spend too much time with humans if I don't have to."

William arched a brow. "You didn't mind spending time with Darlene."

The Guardian shrugged again, but William caught the wince he'd immediately replaced with an impassive expression. "She's a confirmed Dormant and a god's granddaughter. She was definitely worth my time."

William wondered whether Darlene's lineage had been Max's main motivation to pursue her. If so, he was glad that nothing had come of it. Darlene deserved to be desired for who she was and not for who her grandfather was. But if Max's feelings had run deeper, he felt for the guy.

"I'm sorry it didn't work out between the two of you." William fell in step with Max. "I hoped that Darlene would dump Eric after the weekend and fall straight into your arms, but now it seems that he's a Dormant as well, and they seem serious about each other."

Max's brows dipped so low that they formed a V. "Even if Eric transitions tomorrow, he can't induce her for another six months. She shouldn't wait so long."

William put his hand on the Guardian's shoulder. "She's a big girl, and she makes her own choices. Being Toven's granddaughter helps her chances, so she's not overly concerned."

"Still, it's not wise for her to wait for Eric to transition."

Detecting real concern in the guy's voice, William was inclined to believe that Max cared about Darlene. "Eric might not transition at all, and then she'll have no choice but to turn to you or another Guardian."

A hopeful smile bloomed on Max's face. "That would be unfortunate for Eric, but I can't say that I would be sorry if he turns out to be just a human. I plan to stay very close to Darlene, so if she needs to choose someone else, I'll be the obvious choice."

"How are you planning to do that from here?"

"I'm not." Max grinned conspiratorially. "I'm way ahead of you. I asked Onegus to reassign me to the village, and he approved my request. I'm coming back with you and Kaia."

Kaia

Kaia stretched like a lazy cat after an afternoon
nap and took a deep breath. She'd fallen asleep
right after William left for the airport and had
dreamt wonderful dreams about life in the immortals'
village.

Could it be as beautiful in real life? Would the immortals
be as friendly and smiley as they had been in her dreams?

It was time to find out.

Hoping that William had sent a text with her family's
new phone numbers, Kaia reached for her phone.

She hadn't spoken with her mother since her family had
departed Safe Haven yesterday afternoon, leaving their
phones behind as Kian had demanded, and she couldn't
wait to hear everyone's impressions of the village.

After finding the text with the numbers, Kaia rushed
through her morning routine, made herself a cup of
coffee, and sat on the couch to make the call.

"Good morning." Her mother sounded cheerful.

"I hope I didn't wake you up." Kaia picked up her coffee mug and took a sip.

"I wish. Your brothers wake up bright and early no matter when they go to sleep. I've been up since six in the morning, but I don't mind. I like to start my day early."

Kaia didn't. She loved lazing in bed. "How is the village?" she asked.

"Beautiful, but we didn't get to see much of it yet. When we got here, we were shown the café so we would know where we could get food, and then we were escorted straight to the house that we'd be staying in. Ingrid, the lady in charge of housing here, was kind enough to take a grocery list from me, and this morning, I found everything I asked for on our doorstep."

"Did she get it for you?"

"I don't think so. I think it was one of the Guardians, or maybe Kian's butler. In any case, it was very nice of whoever did that."

"How is the house?"

"It's cute. Much smaller than ours, but Gilbert is happy. He says that everything is built to the highest standards, and he's especially impressed with the soundproofing. It's incredible. Once you close a door, it's like you are in a recording studio. Complete silence. I'm glad that we brought the baby monitor with us so I can hear the boys."

"Did they get their own room, or are they sharing with Idina?"

"There are only three bedrooms in the house, and from what Syssi said, that's the largest model available at the moment, so it's not like we can get something bigger. Idina and Cheryl are sharing a room, which Cheryl isn't happy about, but Idina refused to sleep in the same room as her brothers. When Eric arrives, he will have to share a room with the twins or sleep on the couch in the living room. I hope he can stay with Darlene at her place, but I overheard her say something to William about there being complications. She might have a roommate that is not comfortable with Eric being there."

"I can't imagine Eric separating from her. If Darlene has a problematic roommate, she should ask for a house of her own. William says that they have plenty available."

Kaia had never seen Eric so taken with a woman, but then he'd never brought any of his post-divorce girl-friends home for the family to meet. Perhaps that was how he'd acted with all of them, but she doubted that he'd regarded any of the women with the same adoration as he did Darlene.

"I'm sure they will find a solution. He's really into her."

"I know." Her mother sounded excited. "I'm so happy for him. I'm crossing my fingers that all of this comes to pass. It would be very disappointing to find out that we went through all this hoopla for nothing."

Kaia's gut squeezed painfully. "I'm crossing my fingers as well." She swallowed the lump that had formed in her throat. Forcing a cheerful tone by faking a smile even though her mother couldn't see her, she asked, "What else? Did you get to meet anyone other than Ingrid?"

"Not yet. Syssi promised to introduce us to Nathalie, who has a daughter Idina's age and a brother who's a year younger, so they can play together." Her mother chuckled. "Just to clarify, the two-year-old boy is Nathalie's brother, not her son. These people are something else." She paused and then asked in a worried voice, "Is your phone secure?"

"I didn't get a new one if that's what you're asking, but William said that they reroute all communication from here through their servers and encrypt it. Just to err on the side of caution, though, we should talk around the topic of you-know-what."

"Right. So, it's a little strange how they all look so good. Anyway, later today, we are meeting with Doctor Bridget. I hope she can test whether Gilbert and Eric are related to Syssi."

"Kian said that she can perform basic tests, and William told me that she checked the maternal lineage of other newcomers, so I assume that she can determine whether they are related or not. She probably has the equipment needed for checking mitochondrial DNA. It's a much simpler test than the more robust DNA mapping test, and what's needed to conduct it is not expensive."

"It would have been interesting to get more detailed information on their genetics, and I suggested for the three of them to send swabs with their saliva to one of those genetic testing labs, but it would take too long to get the results back. They quote six to eight weeks, and none of us wants to wait that long. Anyway, Kian said that he was not comfortable with sending Syssi's biological information to an outside lab. I get it, but on the other hand, I can't understand why they don't invest in a proper lab of their own. Having access to that kind of information could be crucial for their survival, and it's not only about finding relatives."

Kaia picked up her coffee mug and leaned back. "The equipment needed for mapping an entire DNA sequence is not cheap, and it requires training that an internist doesn't have. But if they are interested and don't mind spending the money on the equipment, I can help them build a lab. I'm not a geneticist, but I'm sure I can find instructions on the internet for what's needed."

These days, one could build a nuclear reactor from instructions available on the internet. The tricky part was getting enriched uranium, and even that wasn't impossible to procure for the right price.

"It doesn't seem like they lack resources," her mother said. "I'm sure they have the money to purchase the equipment, and I have no doubt that they have the know-how as well. Kian told us about some of the cutting-edge technologies they are working on, so I'm sure they have what it takes to build a proper genetics lab."

Kaia sighed. "The problem is motivation to make the investment. Syssi was the first carrier they discovered, and that was only four and a half years ago. After her, additional carriers were found, but they were few and far between. William told me that Bridget suspects that they are not going to discover anything anyway, and it will be a waste of time and resources. When you meet her, ask her why she thinks that."

Her mother chuckled. "I wouldn't understand her explanation. I'm a system administrator, and I know my way around hardware, but all that genetics stuff sounds like a foreign language to me. When you get here, you can make an appointment with Bridget, and the two of you can talk it out to your heart's content."

"I have a better idea. Can you postpone the meeting with her until William and I get to the village? We can all talk with her together."

"I'll ask Syssi if that's possible and if Bridget won't get upset with us for changing the appointment time. As far as our family goes, right now she's the most important person in the village, and I don't want to alienate her from the get-go."

"We wouldn't want to do that." Kaia did some quick thinking. "William is a council member, which I'm sure gives him considerable clout. If he asks to be present at the meeting, Bridget won't object."

Kian

As a knock sounded on Kian's office door, he got to his feet and opened it for Toven. "Good morning. Thank you for agreeing to see me this early." He offered the god his hand.

"This is not early." Toven shook it. "I've been up since six o'clock. Mia and I went for a walk around the village." He smiled. "Well, she rode her wheelchair. I walked."

"Still, I appreciate you coming to see me on such short notice." Kian led him to the conference table.

Somehow, it didn't seem right to have a god sit on one of the guest chairs in front of his desk. Toven was aloof and not really friendly, and their relationship was more formal than any of the others Kian had with people living in his village.

Then again, Toven was a god, and they weren't related, so the distance was natural. Nevertheless, he needed Toven's help, and he didn't expect it to be difficult to convince the god to grant it.

"You said that it was important." Toven pulled out a chair and sat down.

"It is. I'll give you a quick recap to get you up to speed on what's going on. William recruited several bioinformaticians for a project he's working on, and he fell in love with one of them. Naturally, he suspects that she's a Dormant."

"Congratulations. What does it have to do with me?"

Usually, Kian was the last person to beat around the bush, but he was about to ask the god for donations of his blood, and that required some finesse, which wasn't his strong suit. Syssi had suggested that he should tell Toven about the family first and present them in a positive light, and also mention Darlene and her possible bond with Eric. The god would be more inclined to help his granddaughter's chosen mate and by extension, Eric's family. It wouldn't hurt if he also liked what he heard about them.

"I'm getting there. Despite finishing her PhD, Kaia is a very young woman of nineteen who has a loving family she's very attached to. They came to see where she would be working, and when Darlene met Kaia's uncle, sparks flew."

Toven lifted a brow. "I hope the uncle is the mother's brother. Darlene is supposed to find an immortal male to induce her, but if the uncle is a Dormant, he can be induced first and then induce her. Naturally, it is preferable if her initiator is someone she actually likes and can form a bond with."

Kian sighed. "I would like that for her too, but the problem is that it will take Eric six months until his venom glands are fully operational. We are also not sure that he's a Dormant, and even if he is, he might not make it through the transition. He's forty-two."

Understanding dawning, Toven nodded. "You want me to help him along with transfusions of my blood."

"Are you willing to do that?"

"Of course. Darlene is my granddaughter, and I want her to be happy. I'll help her chosen mate, and when the time comes, I will naturally help her as well."

Kian let out a breath. "Thank you. But there is more to the story. Eric is not Kaia's mother's brother. He's her stepfather's brother. But it turns out that there is a strong possibility of Eric and Gilbert being Syssi's third cousins, and the shared ancestress is their great-great-grandmother. She had two daughters. One was the grandmother of Syssi's mother, and the other was the grandmother of Eric and Gilbert's mother. We are meeting with Bridget later today to see if she can verify that they are actually related."

Toven crossed his arms over his chest. "What evidence do you have to support that relationship so far?"

"It's a long story, but the gist of it is that when we met them for dinner, Gilbert started talking about his quest to discover more relatives and the fruits of his research. He showed us a picture of his great-grandmother, and Syssi said that she looked exactly like her grandmother and showed us a picture of her as well. The resemblance is undeniable, and they are all originally from the same geographic area in Eastern Europe, but it still might be a coincidence."

Toven looked Kian in the eyes. "Where do I fit into the narrative?"

"Syssi's transition was difficult, and so was Andrew's, and they were both much younger than Gilbert and Eric. I expect both men will need a lot of help. Kaia's mother is also not young, and since Annani is not here at the moment, you are the only one who can help all of them. I need to know if you are willing to do that. If not, I will have to convince my mother to cut her trip short and come back to the village as soon as she can."

Toven chuckled. "I'm already giving transfusions to Mia's grandparents. If I need to help so many people to transition, I might become anemic. Perhaps you should ask Annani to come back to save me."

Kian wasn't sure whether the god was joking or serious. "I know how much blood is required, and it's not a lot. Even if you give each of them daily transfusions, it shouldn't have an adverse effect on you."

"I know." Toven laughed. "I was just joking. I don't like the idea of becoming a pin cushion, but since I don't expect scenarios like this to occur often, I can deal with it."

"Thank you. I appreciate your willingness to help."

Toven smiled. "I'm glad for the opportunity to pay back at least some of the debt of gratitude I owe you. You've been very generous with Mia and me. You took us in and even allowed her grandparents to live in your village."

"You are family, Toven. Your son is mated to my sister, your daughter is mated to my assistant, your grand-daughter is mated to my chief of Guardians, and your great-grandson and your grandnephews are part of our clan as well. Besides, my mother wouldn't have it any other way."

A smile brightened Toven's face. "I am truly blessed to have such a wonderful family. I thank the merciful Fates every day for the joy they've bestowed on me." His smile waned. "But I worry that I might lose it all because I don't deserve it. I didn't earn it. I failed in all my attempts to improve the lives of humans."

Kian leaned toward the god. "You did your best, and you sacrificed centuries to do so. It doesn't matter whether you succeeded or failed. Your failures are just as much a badge of honor as if they were successes—they attest to your tireless effort."

"Not tireless." Toven chuckled sadly. "I grew very tired of trying to do the impossible and allowed myself to sink into a state of ennui."

"You are immortal. You can embark on new adventures. You are already doing it with Perfect Match. Making it accessible to more people will enrich many lives."

"It's a small project, and all I'm offering humans is an escape from reality." Toven sighed. "Still, I hope it's successful. I can't stomach any more failures."

"There are no guarantees, and you might fail again, but you might also succeed. Those who do nothing, though, fail by default."

William
〰️

As William finished telling Morris and Marcel an abbreviated version of the discovery of Kaia's stepfather and his brother's connection to Syssi, Morris rubbed his hands. "I'm looking forward to comparing notes with a young pilot who's flown the latest fighter jet models."

William shot him an apologetic look. "Eric is no longer in Safe Haven. He and Darlene flew to the Bay Area on his executive jet, and from there, they will take a commercial flight to Los Angeles."

Morris didn't seem perturbed. "Then I'll catch him in the village when we return." He looked at Max. "You're coming back with us, aren't you?"

The Guardian nodded. "I am."

"Did Onegus assign you to William permanently?"

Max shrugged. "It depends." He turned to William. "You don't need me in the village, and you don't leave it often, but if you and Kaia plan to return to Safe Haven after her transition, I'll probably accompany you."

"Of course, we are coming back." William cast a silencing shroud around them to keep the bus driver from overhearing their conversation. "It might take time until Kaia transitions, though, and then it might take a week or two until she feels well enough to go back to work."

"Are you sure that Kaia is a Dormant?" Marcel asked. "Does she have a paranormal talent?"

She had memories of a past life, but William wasn't sure that counted as paranormal ability. He also wasn't sure that she was right about where those memories were coming from. Spencer had seen two auras around her, and that shouldn't be the case if the memories of a past life belonged to her. She was probably housing a spirit who was pretending to be her incarnation.

In either case, though, Kaia didn't like people to know about her male aspect, and he wasn't going to betray her trust and share it with Marcel.

"Kaia has an uncanny ability to solve complicated puzzles that even I can't," he said instead. "So perhaps that ability could be perceived as paranormal."

Marcel looked at their two companions. "I assume that it's okay for me to talk about the specifics of the special project you and Kaia have been working on in front of Max and Morris?"

William nodded. "They know."

Max had been with him in the Bay Area when he'd been recruiting bioinformaticians for the project, and Morris was a veteran on the force whose status was on par with that of the Guardians even though he hadn't gone through Guardian training. The pilot's time in the Air Force and military experience earned him a honorary spot.

"Who else knows?" Marcel asked.

Max spread his arms. "The head Guardians, the Guardians stationed here, the council members, Syssi and Andrew, and whoever else Kian decided to share this with, which probably includes Turner. Bottom line, too many people know about the journals and what's in them."

"There was no avoiding it." William reached with his hand intending to push his glasses up his nose, remembering at the last moment that he no longer wore them outside the lab. "The council had to be notified, the head Guardians are part of the council, and the Guardians stationed in Safe Haven had to know what information leaks to pay attention to."

"That's all true," Max conceded. "And I would trust everyone on that list with my life, but a secret is no longer a secret when so many people know about it." He leaned back and crossed his arms over his chest. "I'm glad to be out of Safe Haven, though. It's like living on a tiny island. It's too quiet, and the selection of ladies is too limited."

Morris eyed him with a raised brow. "I'm sure you didn't lack offers."

"I didn't." Max's lips lifted in a conceited smirk. "The community ladies are very generous with their affections, and most are willing to experiment, but I need more variety, and I need to hunt for my pleasure. It's not as much fun when it's offered to me on a silver platter."

William stifled an eyeroll.

Max never had to hunt for female affection.

Whenever the Guardian had managed to drag him to a nightclub, William had seen the ladies fight over him. All the guy had to do was strike an indifferent pose and hold a beer in his hand and a smirk on his face.

"The village is also like a tiny island." Morris waved a hand in dismissal. "And if you are tired of the selection, you can travel to one of the towns in the area." He turned to William. "You didn't use to have a Guardian assigned to you. Do you have one now because of the project and your knowledge of what's in the journals?"

"I don't think so." William sighed. "I think that Kian is just getting more and more paranoid. I don't leave the lab often, so assigning a Guardian to me would be a waste of a valuable resource. We don't have enough Guardians for all the rescue missions we could be running."

"You're a council member, and your knowledge is invaluable." Marcel cast him a rare smile. "We would be lost without you. Most of what I know I learned from you, not Caltech."

"Thank you." William turned sideways to stretch his legs into the aisle. "Still, when I dated a lady from Amanda's lab, I didn't have a Guardian following me around."

Max snorted. "That's what you think. Ever since the Doomer attack, there is always a team of Guardians sitting in a car outside the university when Amanda and Syssi are there. If something comes up on the security camera feed, they can be there in seconds."

"I know that. I installed the new security system after the attack. But those Guardians are there to protect Amanda and Syssi. When Hannah and I met outside the lab, no one was guarding me."

Max shrugged. "I wasn't on the force back then, but I bet Onegus sent someone to keep an eye on you as well. You are too valuable to the clan. We can't afford to lose you."

William sighed. "Enough about me and my security detail. We need to talk about the team." He turned to Marcel. "You need to remember that they are human and that they can't work eighteen-hour days. You need to adjust your expectations accordingly."

"I'm aware of that." Marcel popped the lid on his water bottle and took a sip. "Did you talk with them about the reason for your and Kaia's departure?"

"We didn't even tell them that we are leaving. I tasked Kaia with coming up with a convincing story, and I hope she'll have it ready by the time we get there."

Kaia

K aia straightened the throw blanket on the back of the couch, took a step back, and examined what she'd managed to do with William's bungalow.

It hadn't been overly messy before, just a few books lying around, a pair of shoes that had been left by the door, and several coffee mugs that had needed washing. But even when it was nice and tidy, the place lacked personality, and the pretty decor only made it look more like a hotel room.

She hadn't had much to work with, but the throw blanket added a splash of color to the gray couch, the books stacked artfully on the coffee table added interest, and the fluffed-up pillows added softness.

William was due to arrive at any moment with Marcel, Morris, and Max, and she wanted the living room to look inviting.

Kaia chuckled. She could call them the 3Ms for short or the MMM.

She'd come up with two possible explanations for why they were leaving in such a rush, and they needed to choose one and coordinate their stories before William introduced Marcel to the team. He also needed to scan Marcel's iris into the security system so the guy could open up the lab in the mornings and let the team out at the end of the day.

They didn't have enough time to do both before opening the lab this morning, so the eye scanning would have to wait for later. Work at the lab usually started at nine, but perhaps it would be a good idea for William to text the team members that there was a delay and that today they would start an hour later.

When the front door opened, she turned around and put a welcoming smile on her face.

"Good morning, gentlemen." She offered her hand to the one who wasn't smiling. "I'm Kaia."

From what William had told her about Marcel, the guy was a dry stick and rarely smiled, but what William had failed to mention was how handsome he was.

The guy was tall and slim, had great posture for a computer nerd, and he was meticulously groomed and dressed, also uncommon for people in his field.

That being said, his choice of clothing was strange. The black turtleneck was way too warm for summer, even in

Oregon, and Kaia suspected that he'd adopted a uniform of sorts, like Steve Jobs had done, and wore the same thing no matter the weather or the occasion. Perhaps the black turtleneck and the tailored gray slacks was a combination he'd gotten complimented on, so he'd decided to stick with it.

"It's a pleasure to meet you." He took her hand. "I'm Marcel."

"I'm Morris." The pilot offered his hand. "I'm the guy who will be flying you home."

"Hi." Kaia returned his smile. "William tells me that you flew fighter planes in WWI."

"I did." He held on to her hand and patted it with his other one. "I can't wait to meet your uncle and talk about fighter jets with him."

"I'm sure he would love to hear the perspective of an old timer like you."

It felt strange to call Morris an old timer. The immortal looked to be in his mid-thirties and had reddish blond hair like Marcel, just not as neatly styled.

"Are you and Marcel related?" She led them to the sitting area.

"Nearly all of us are." Max clapped Morris on the back. "Right, cousin?"

Morris chose an armchair to sit in. "Thank the merciful Fates for the influx of Dormants."

"Kalugal's men were supposed to infuse new blood into our clan." Marcel remained standing. "But things are not progressing as swiftly in that department as we hoped for."

"I'm sorry," Kaia said. "But I'm still sketchy on who is who, so I can't comment on that." She waved a hand at the couch. "Please, take a seat. Can I offer you coffee? We have a pod coffeemaker, so you can choose the type of coffee you like. I can make it strong, medium, or weak."

She doubted any of the immortals would want a decaf.

"The strongest you have, please." Morris steepled his fingers in a worshipful gesture. "I desperately need some java in my system."

Kaia chuckled. "Should I be worried about my pilot being sleepy?" She put a mug under the spout and popped the pod into the slot.

"Never. I can fly Betsy with my eyes closed."

"Betsy?" Marcel lifted one reddish-blond brow. "Since when do you call your plane Betsy?"

"It used to be Matilda, but I got tired of that name, so I changed it a couple of years ago."

When everyone had gotten their coffees, Kaia sat on the couch next to William. "I thought of two possible stories we can tell the team."

"Let's hear them," Marcel said.

"They all know that my family visited me over the weekend, but they don't know where they went from here. I can tell them that my mother has a medical emergency that requires an operation, and I need to be with her and also help my stepdad with my younger siblings. They also know that William is my boyfriend, so we can tell them that he's coming along to provide support for my family and me. The other alternative is to tell them that William is needed in the lab back home because of a problem only he can solve, and I'm accompanying him because we are so in love that we can't tolerate being apart. What do you think?" She looked at the men's expressions.

"I like the second one," Morris said. "It's more romantic."

"The first one makes more sense," Max said.

Marcel shook his head. "I vote for the second one as well. Humans believe that it's bad luck to lie about someone being sick because it might come true. It might be just a superstition, but just to be on the safe side, I wouldn't lie about my mother's well-being." He looked at Kaia. "Especially when said mother is about to attempt transition."

"You're right." Kaia gripped the end of her ponytail and wound it around her finger. "I didn't think of that." She looked at William. "Which version do you prefer?"

"I like the emergency problem that needs solving, but I suggest we modify it to include you. We are both needed to address the issue, and since it's top secret, we are not allowed to share any details with the team."

"Why just me, though? Everyone on the team is a bioinformatician."

William smiled. "Because you are the best, and they all know it."

Jade

"What are you searching for today?" Igor asked in his annoyingly calm voice.

The sound felt oily, and it slithered from Jade's ears to coat her organs on the inside and out.

She sat at the tiny desk at the far corner of his office with her back to him and, whenever she could, she searched the internet for news she could share with the others. It was her only window to the outside world, and if he took that away from her, it would be devastating. Especially now that she had a glimmer of hope of reaching out to someone.

Shaking the feeling off, Jade grunted. "I told you what I'm doing. I'm looking for human parables to convert into meaningful stories that I can tell the children. I'm tired of repeating the same fables over and over again."

"Wasn't that what you did a week ago?"

Letting out a breath, she turned around to face him. "I'm constantly searching for new material. Sometimes it's inspirational stories, other times it's motivational stories, and today I'm searching for transformative stories. That's my method of teaching. There are some paid sites that offer material to teachers. I could really use one of those if you'd allow it. They don't cost much."

She didn't really need any of those sites, but she was preparing the groundwork for contacting Veskar.

Igor bared his fangs. "Use whatever you can find for free."

"Yes, sir." She dipped her head in mock deference. "Some sites offer free subscriptions. Can you provide me with an email address I can use for that?" Her heart lodging in her throat, Jade waited for Igor's response.

He waved a dismissive hand. "You can create an email address for free."

"Isn't it dangerous, though?" She pretended not to know that all incoming and outgoing email was rerouted and checked by his men.

"It's not." He scribbled something on a piece of paper. "If they require a mobile phone number to create your email account, you can use this one."

She rose to her feet and walked over to his desk. "Thank you."

As she reached for the note, he held it back. "I heard you are telling the children tales of the just queen and her lover, the foreign king, the father of her twin children."

She could try to deny it or cower before him, but that wasn't what he expected from her, and it might make him suspicious.

Assuming her regular defiant expression, Jade put a hand on her hip. "You have a problem with that?"

"It doesn't matter what you tell them as long as you are not twisting their minds to turn them against me."

"I can't do that even if I wanted to."

Well, of course, she wanted to, but she couldn't say anything negative about him or even imply it.

Before allowing her to teach, Igor had compelled her to sing his praises, but she'd found a way around it. She simply never mentioned him, and since her lessons were always about the distant past, there was no reason to bring him up. What she attempted to do instead was to teach the children the Kra-ell way and let them make up their own minds about what was right and what was wrong.

"You are too smart for your own good, Jade. But if I catch you plotting against me, I'll make you pay."

She swallowed the lump of terror that formed in her throat.

Whipping and torture she could withstand, and even death didn't scare her, but Igor would never kill her. She was too valuable as a breeder, and he enjoyed tormenting her too much to give up his toy.

He would hurt people she cared about to teach her a lesson, and he wasn't above using his own daughter to punish her mother. Most likely, though, he would use Kagra.

"I'm not plotting anything. As you said, I'm smart, and I know what's good for me." She walked back to her desk and the laptop that he allowed her to use only in his office and only when he was there.

"But you should know all about plotting," she murmured under her breath.

"Look at me when you speak to me," he growled.

Goading him wasn't smart, but how else was she going to make him reveal anything?

Jade turned her chair around. "Did you have spies among the scouts? Did they report to you what they found, and that was why you sabotaged the ship?"

She'd tried so many times to get him to tell her something, anything, but so far, she'd failed every time.

"You have a vivid imagination, my dear Jade. How could the scouts report to me? I was born many cycles after they were deployed. They couldn't have known that I existed." He waved a dismissive hand at her. "Go back to the nonsense that you collect to teach the children. Your imagination will serve you better there."

Jade did as she was told.

He was right of course. Igor was more or less five hundred Earth years old, and the scouts had arrived thousands of years before. But he might have gained access to whoever the scouts had been reporting to, if they'd reported anything at all.

They must have known that the children fathered by Kra-ell males with human females could not bear long-lived Kra-ell offspring, and the promises the queen had made to the settlers had been lies.

If they had reported it to the queen and she'd still sent the ship with her children on it to establish a colony, the real agenda must have been different than what the rank and file had been told.

Maybe the queen had just needed to get the twins out of their home world. They hadn't been popular, to say the least, and she might have feared for their lives. She might have destroyed the reports she'd received from the scouting team and had lied by omission.

The queen had lured the male Kra-ell into joining the expedition by tales of the abundance of Earth females they would enjoy, but she hadn't mentioned their lack of compatibility. Jade and the other females had been recruited by promises of leadership positions over the new large tribes that would include many human slaves, both male and female.

Jade didn't regret her decision to join. The Mother had guided her to take part in this adventure, and despite the disaster and having no support, she'd managed to establish a thriving tribe and had enjoyed many good years until Igor had smashed her dreams and murdered most of her family.

At least he'd spared the humans, or so he claimed. She wasn't sure she believed him. There had been hybrid children among them who hadn't manifested Kra-ell features yet, so they might have been released along with their human mothers.

Jade prayed for that to be true.

Eric

⤬

"Okidu is not a man," Darlene whispered in Eric's ear.

They were in the back of the limousine with the partition up, so there was no need to whisper.

"What do you mean? Is he some other kind of immortal?"

She shook her head.

"Is he trans?"

Eric had wondered why Kian's butler looked older than the other immortals, thinking that he was a subspecies that aged faster, but he hadn't noticed anything feminine about the guy. He was small in stature, but there was nothing delicate about his facial features.

Darlene chuckled. "Funny that you should say that, because he can choose to look like either a female or a male but is neither," she said it in a barely audible whisper. "Okidu is a cyborg."

"No way." Eric looked through the clear glass partition at the butler's reflection in the rearview mirror. "Is he some kind of alien technology?"

During their flight to the Bay Area, Darlene had told him a lot about the clan, but there were many things she couldn't tell him because she was also new to the immortal world and still had a lot to learn.

They flew business class from the Bay Area to Los Angeles so they could have continued talking in relative privacy, but Darlene had fallen asleep, and Eric had followed her example and had napped as well.

"Shhh." She put a finger on his lips. "He has exceptionally good hearing. All the immortals do. They can hear even whispers, but with the partition up, I think we are safe."

"But he's not an immortal."

"He's not, but he's a product of the gods' technology, so he has the same abilities as the immortals and more." She scrunched her nose. "Well, also less in some areas. He's not very smart, and I think the gods did that on purpose. Artificial intelligence might be dangerous to organics."

He smiled. "Are you a science fiction fan?"

"No, but my son is." Her eyes widened. "I didn't tell Roni about you yet." She pulled out her phone. "I should text him."

Eric put a hand on hers to stop her. "Let's make it a surprise. Does he have a good relationship with his father?"

Darlene shook her head. "He doesn't. But it's a long story that I don't want to get into yet."

Every time Eric mentioned Darlene's ex, she clammed up and changed the subject. She'd given him some crumbs of information, so he knew that her ex was a piece of work, but whatever she chose to tell him was always on her terms, and he knew better than to ask.

Eric could understand that.

Her divorce was still like a fresh wound, and picking at it was painful. He'd been the same after his marriage had ended, and it had taken two years before he could talk about it without being consumed with rage.

In that regard, Kian's cyborg butler was a much safer topic.

"Is Okidu the only one the clan has?" Eric asked in a whisper.

Kian had sent his own butler to pick them up from the airport, which meant that the clan didn't have an abundance of cyborg servants.

Darlene shook her head.

"How many do they have?"

"Seven, and they weren't made by the clan. They were a present to the Clan Mother from her betrothed, and she doesn't allow William to tinker with them. She treats them like members of the family."

"Are they sentient?"

Darlene pursed her lips. "I don't know. To me, they look like they are, but I'm not an expert."

"What does William say?"

"He says that it's not a question for an engineer but for an ethicist. What does it mean to be sentient? How can we differentiate between real feelings and mimicry of them? William explained that the Odus learned human behavior by mimicking it."

"That's how children learn as well."

"Precisely." Darlene let out a breath. "The goddess is infinitely wise. She treats them as people, with kindness and respect as if they are sentient."

"What about your grandfather?"

Eric was looking forward to meeting the god, but he was also apprehensive. What if Toven didn't approve of him as a suitable partner for Darlene?

"Toven does the same." Darlene smiled. "In fact, he's quite fond of Okidu. Mia told me that when Okidu came to pick them up from their house, Toven greeted him like a long-lost relative and even hugged him, and he's not a hugger."

"Is he cold?"

She shook her head. "I wouldn't say that."

40

"So, how would you describe him?"

"Toven is aloof, and he seems condescending, but he doesn't do it on purpose. He's a god, so naturally he feels superior to everyone, including the immortals." She smiled. "That being said, he's changed a lot since he met Mia, and he worships the ground she rolls over."

Eric wasn't familiar with that expression, but maybe it was a new thing, and he didn't want Darlene to think that he wasn't keeping up with current trends and jargon.

"Is Mia your grandfather's mate?"

Darlene nodded. "She's very sweet. You're going to like her."

"What about your grandfather? Am I going to like him too? Or, more importantly, is he going to like me?"

Darlene leaned closer and kissed his cheek. "He's going to love you."

Darlene

s the windows of the limousine started to turn opaque, Eric watched the process with fascination. "They have this on Dreamliners, but I've never seen it done on car windows. Are the front ones also opaque?"

"I think so." Darlene leaned against his shoulder. "The Odus know where everything is, including Annani's sanctuary, so it's not necessary, but I never checked. We will enter the tunnel soon, and it will become a little darker and cooler in the car, but that's the only indication we will get. I'm dying to see how the entrance to the tunnels is hidden, but unless I somehow manage to become a head Guardian, that's not in the cards."

Eric regarded her with surprise in his eyes. "Do you want to become a Guardian?"

"No, but only the head Guardians are privy to that information. That's why I said it."

Darlene was babbling nonsense because she was nervous. She still hadn't told Eric that she didn't have a place of her own, and it annoyed her that she didn't have the guts to just say what needed to be said and be done with it.

Years with Leo had conditioned her to always choose safe topics for conversation and never mention anything that might be even a little bit upsetting or uncomfortable to him, which resulted in her often sounding like an airhead.

But Eric wasn't Leo, and she shouldn't repeat the mistakes of the past.

"I need to tell you something." She sighed. "I don't have a place of my own. Before coming to Safe Haven, I stayed with my mother and her partner. I would have asked William to help secure a house for us, but he had his hands full, and I didn't want to bother him."

Eric's hand squeezed her shoulder. "I don't mind staying with your mother and her mate if they don't mind hosting me. I assume that you have your own room?"

"I do, but it's time for me to assert myself and tell my mother that I'm too old to be babied by her. I stayed with her not because I had to or wanted to, but because it would have upset her if I said I didn't want to live with her."

It was a relief to finally tell Eric the truth and an even bigger relief that he hadn't made a big deal out of it.

As the limousine entered the tunnel, the temperature in the vehicle dropped by a few degrees, and it became dark.

"Why did she want you to move in with her in the first place?"

Darlene hadn't told Eric that story yet, and she wasn't in the mood to do it now. In fact, she didn't want to talk about the past at all.

This was a new start for her, and she didn't want to taint it with a history that was better forgotten.

"It's a long story. We haven't seen each other since I was a young girl, and when we found each other again, my mother became clingy and wanted to recapture all those lost years."

"Why were you separated?"

The limousine came to a stop and, a moment later, lurched up as the elevator platform started rising.

"Did you feel that? We are going up in an elevator for cars. Isn't that cool?"

Eric grimaced. "Every time I ask you something personal, you change the subject. I can understand you not wanting to talk about your ex so soon after the divorce, but why can't you talk about your mother?"

He was right, and there was no harm in telling him about her history with her mother. Especially not now when she no longer needed to come up with ways to tell the story without revealing that her mother was a demigoddess.

Darlene sighed. "That story is messed up as well. I thought she had died, and then nearly four decades later, she popped into my life together with my half-sister, and the two pretended to be my cousins, the daughters of my mother's nonexistent twin sister. I know that they meant well, and I know my mother didn't mean to disappear on me when I was twelve, but it still hurt no matter what the explanation was. I forgave her up here." She tapped her temple. "But the heart is not logical."

"Did she fake her own death because she wasn't aging?"

"She was in a nearly fatal boating accident and survived only because she was a god's daughter. Any other immortal would have died from an injury like that. She survived, but her memories didn't, and she didn't know that she had a daughter and a husband who were mourning her death."

As the limousine exited the elevator, the windows cleared, and Okidu lowered the partition. "Welcome to the village, Master Eric." He eased the limo into the designated parking spot and turned toward them. "Shall I bring the luggage to Mistress Geraldine and Master Shai's home?"

Darlene shook her head. "Can we leave it in the limo for now? I'm not sure where we will be staying yet."

Okidu affected a regretful expression. "I am afraid that it is not possible. I have another trip scheduled for later today to collect Masters William, Morris, Max, and Mistress Kaia from the clan airstrip. I need the trunk to be available for their luggage."

"Let's just take it to your mother's house." Eric opened the door. "We can leave our suitcases by the door and leave the unpacking for when we know where we will be staying."

Eric

∽

It seemed like Darlene was carrying even more emotional baggage than Eric had realized. It wasn't just her marriage that had left scars on her psyche, but also unresolved issues with her mother.

Evidently, even a demi-demigoddess's life wasn't charmed, and she had things to deal with like any other mortal.

Normally, he would have stayed away from a woman who needed to work through so much crap, but it was different with Darlene.

He wanted to be there for her, to help her heal from those soul wounds, and if he could, also to facilitate her transition.

He didn't want her to wait six months, though. If he could minimize the risk to her life even marginally by inviting an immortal male into their bed, he would do that with no hesitation.

Since his divorce, Eric had done some kinky shit and had thought nothing of it, so it shouldn't have been a problem, but the possessive way he felt about Darlene made it difficult. He didn't want to share her with another male or a female, but he would if he had to.

"So, what do you think?" Darlene asked.

She'd been showing him the village central square, but he'd been paying only cursory attention to what she'd been saying.

"It's very nice."

She tilted her head. "You don't seem impressed."

"I am. It's a nice little gem hidden from the world. I was just wondering whether you told your mother that you were coming back."

It was one thing for the daughter to come back unannounced, and another thing altogether for said daughter to show up on her mother's doorstep with a guy.

"Of course, I did. If I didn't call her every day while I was away and tell her in detail everything that was happening with me, she would have gone into a crying fit. Naturally, you were the star of my recent reports."

"Oh, yeah? What did you tell her about me?"

She smirked. "That you were a cad."

"Seriously?"

"I told her that you were a charming, good-looking player but that I found you irresistible nonetheless. She wasn't happy about that, but then I told her that you are a potential Dormant, and she said that once you become immortal, you would change your ways and leave your wild days behind."

As Darlene cast him a smile and resumed walking, he fell in step with her, pulling their suitcases behind him. "I wasn't always a player. I was loyal to my cheating wife. After the divorce, I didn't want to get attached to anyone, and I went a little wild."

Darlene gave him a pitying glance. "I'm sorry you had to go through that. Leo was a verbally abusive jerk, but as far as I know, he didn't cheat on me."

So that was the key to unlocking Darlene's tight lips. If he shared his pain with her, she would share hers with him.

"Well, my wife was both. She was disloyal and verbally abusive, sometimes physically as well."

Men didn't like to admit that they had been physically abused by their significant others, but Eric knew he wasn't the only one who had been subjected to that.

He didn't feel shamed by it, though.

The fact that he'd never raised his hand to a woman, not even in self-defense, didn't make him weak. It made him strong.

"What did she do?" Darlene asked softly.

"She threw things at me, slapped me, kicked me, but I never responded physically. I just walked out the door and came back hours later after she calmed down. My mistake was that I came back. After the first time it happened, I should have walked out and never come back. But she always apologized with tears in her eyes and real remorse in her voice, and then we made love, and it was great, so I forgave her time and again."

"You're a good man, Eric." Darlene put her hand on his arm.

"Am I? Or am I just a pushover?"

"You're not a pushover." She sighed. "It's not easy. I believed that people gave up on their marriages too easily, and I didn't want to be part of the depressing statistics. That was the lie I told myself to not feel like a failure. But the truth was that I was afraid of being alone, and I thought that if I left Leo, I would become a cat lady." She chuckled sadly. "And I don't even like cats."

"What gave you the push to leave?"

Darlene smiled. "Discovering that I was a demi-demigoddess. I realized that I should be worshiped, and Leo wasn't the worshiping type."

Darlene

Eric laughed. "You are absolutely right, and I'm honored and delighted to worship you."

"Thank you. I expect some worshiping tonight."

He stopped and turned to her with eyes that were molten with desire. "Come here." He let go of the suitcases and pulled her into his arms. "Let me give you a little aperitif to whet your appetite."

Darlene didn't care that they were less than fifty feet away from her mother's doorstep, and knowing Geraldine, she was standing at the living room window and watching them from behind the curtain.

Eric needed this after his confession, and so did she.

Melting into him, she kissed him with the same fervor he kissed her.

Poor guy.

She couldn't imagine this proud, charming, handsome man being treated so badly by his ex-wife. Hell, he'd been abused to the point of being traumatized.

Compared to Eric's ex, Leo hadn't been so bad. He'd been a cold bastard who'd thrived on putting her down, but at least he'd never hit her or thrown things at her.

Clearly, the woman had mental problems, and Darlene wondered why they had never been addressed. Perhaps she'd refused? Eric was an intelligent guy. She was sure he'd suggested therapy at some point.

When they came up for air, she chuckled. "My mother is probably watching us from behind the curtain, and we've just given her one hell of a show."

"Is she conservative? Will it upset her?"

Darlene laughed. "She's the opposite of that. My mother is unconventional in every way." She should warn him about Geraldine's flights of fancy. "Be prepared to hear some crazy stories." She resumed walking. "My mother still has memory issues, and she fills the gaps with fantastic tales, mostly about the fabulous lovers she had. Talk about being a player. Although in my mother's case, it wasn't really her fault."

Thankfully, Geraldine had enough sense not to talk about her former lovers in front of Shai.

"What do you mean? Were her memory issues so bad that she didn't remember her lovers? Then how could she tell stories about them? Besides, what's wrong with her being a player?"

"Nothing. It's perfectly okay for a single woman to enjoy herself with as many men as she pleases, but she was still married to my father. She just didn't know that she was."

The curious thing, though, was that Orion had tried to bring back the memories of her past boyfriends that he'd confused and muddled, but it hadn't worked. Her mother's head was either too messed up for him to make sense of what was going on inside of it, or maybe Geraldine just enjoyed telling those stories too much to let go of them.

"Was it because of the accident?" Eric asked.

"Yeah." Darlene smiled apologetically. "There is more to the story, but I'll save it for another time."

As they climbed the steps to Geraldine's front porch, the door opened, and her mother flew out, looking like a butterfly in her yellow voluminous skirt and white, form-fitting blouse.

"Darlene!" She pulled her into her arms. "I missed you so much." She squeezed her tight.

"I missed you too," Darlene lied as she untangled herself from her mother's arms. "Let me introduce you to Eric."

The truth was that she hadn't had the chance to miss Geraldine since they'd talked every day.

"Hello." Geraldine wiped the tears from under her eyes.

"It's a pleasure to meet you." Eric offered her his hand.

Her mother took it and then pulled him in for a quick hug. "You are even more handsome than my daughter let on."

"Thank you." He smiled, and one adorable dimple appeared on his left cheek.

"Please, come in." Geraldine ushered them inside. "You must be hungry after so many hours of travel."

"We flew business class," Darlene said. "The food wasn't bad."

"Good. I made dinner early today, but if you're not hungry, we can wait for Shai to get here." Geraldine waved them toward the couch. "Please, sit down and tell me everything."

Eric left the suitcases by the door, took Darlene's hand, and walked with her to the couch.

Geraldine sat in the armchair facing both of them. "Shai wants to meet the man who finally convinced Darlene to end her self-imposed celibacy."

Darlene rolled her eyes. "Really? That's the first thing you say to my new boyfriend?"

Geraldine laughed. "Isn't that funny how mothers and daughters interact the same way no matter what age they are?"

Eric chuckled. "I can't think of you as mother and daughter. Sisters, maybe."

Geraldine's eyes widened. "Speaking of sisters, I almost forgot. Cassandra and Onegus are joining us for coffee and dessert. Cassy is cutting her day short and coming home early so she can see you."

Eric looked at Darlene. "I don't think we can stay that long. My brother and Karen are scheduled to meet the doctor later today, and we are supposed to take part in that meeting."

"I see." Geraldine's happy smile wilted. "That takes precedence, of course. We will work around your schedule." She rose to her feet. "Can I offer you something to drink while we wait for Shai?"

"I'll get it." Darlene followed her up. "I'm in the mood for beer." She turned to Eric. "Do you want one too?"

"Yes, please."

In the kitchen, she pulled her mother aside. "I didn't want the waterworks to start in front of Eric, but I hope you don't expect us to stay with you and Shai. I want us to get a place of our own."

Surprisingly, Geraldine didn't start crying. Instead, she smiled. "Of course. I only want what's best for you, and right now, that's playing house with Eric." She leaned closer to whisper in her ear. "He's adorable. I felt the affinity as soon as I saw him. He's a Dormant for sure."

"I certainly hope so."

William

"It's amazing here." Kaia turned in a circle. "I love it." She waved her hand at the café. "Is that the only place to eat in the village?"

"For now," William said. "Callie's restaurant is about to be opened. Everyone is looking forward to the day it does."

"Callie is mated to the blond Guardian, right?"

"She is." Max stopped at a fork in the pathway. "I'm heading home. If you need me, give me a call."

Kaia lifted on her toes and kissed the Guardian's cheek. "Don't be a stranger. As soon as I get settled in William's place, you're invited for dinner."

He lifted a brow. "You cook?"

"I do, and I do it well."

He shook his head. "That's not fair. You're smart and beautiful, and you can cook. Couldn't you have an older sister instead of a younger one?"

Kaia laughed. "Cheryl might be the one for you. You'll just have to wait a few years."

He grimaced. "She's a kid. I can't even think of her that way."

William echoed his expression. "I thought the same about Kaia, and here we are."

"Kaia is at least of legal age." The Guardian clapped him on the back. "Good luck to both of you."

"Thanks," Kaia said.

When they were alone on the path, she looked over her shoulder. "Where is Okidu? He was supposed to bring our luggage to your house."

"He's probably taken a shortcut and is already there, but we are not going to our house. We are going to see your family first."

"Why? I want to see your place and then go to theirs."

He smiled sheepishly. "I asked Okidu to clean up before we got there. I left the place a little messy." That was an understatement, but he didn't want Kaia to think that he was a slob.

"Don't you have a roommate?"

He shook his head. "I used to have one, but once the latest phase of the village was completed, Kian moved the council members, the head Guardians, and most of the Guardian force to the new houses. My roommate decided to stay in the old one."

She threaded her arm through his. "Did you get lonely?"

William chuckled. "I work such long hours that when I come home, it's to shower and sleep. My life is in the lab."

"Not anymore." Kaia leaned her head on his arm. "Things are going to change now that I'm here. I'm going to cook dinners and invite people over. I want us to have a life outside of work."

William swallowed. "I would love that, but I don't know if I can. I have so much work to do, and I'm always behind. I wish I could find a solution for that, but there isn't one. I've already hired everyone that I could hire, and we are maxed out. It stresses me just to think about all the projects that I put on hold so I can work on the journals."

"I have a solution." Kaia smiled conspiratorially. "We will build a team of Odus to help in the lab."

He narrowed his eyes at her. "That's the least suitable work for cyborgs. I want to build gardeners, house cleaners, and maybe construction workers. That's what we need most in the village."

"I was just joking." She tilted her head. "I know that the village needs to remain a secret and all that, but you can bring Emmett and Eleanor here to compel the humans you hire to keep quiet about it. There are many talented people out there who can ease your workload in the lab.

We will also need a geneticist and an ethicist, and I don't want to wait for your immortals to get their PhDs in those fields."

"When we get to that stage, we will be back at Safe Haven, and I can hire whoever you want out there."

"Good point. You could also build a proper DNA testing facility out there. You need one."

He stopped and turned to her. "That's a brilliant idea. After we are done with our research, we can convert the lab in Safe Haven into a genetics lab."

"I don't think it's big enough. Some of the equipment is bulky, and you need a whole crew of people to operate it."

"That's solvable." William resumed walking. "What's not feasible is moving Bridget to Safe Haven, and she's the only one who has any knowledge in the field. She's not a geneticist, but she's been doing research on the side for years."

"Why can't she move to Safe Haven? You said that there are three doctors in the village, which doesn't really make sense because no one gets sick."

"We still need to take care of transitioning Dormants, births, injuries, and so on. Bridget is our most experienced doctor, but medicine is not the only thing she does. She's also in charge of running the rescue missions."

"Can't you assign that task to someone else? It's not like a doctor needs to be in charge of raids. One of the head Guardians can do that."

"She's also a council member, and she's mated to a guy who has an office in Los Angeles. She wouldn't want to move, and even if she did, Kian would not allow it."

Kaia

After Kaia was done hugging everyone as if they hadn't seen each other for at least a month, her mother offered to take her on a tour of the house.

It started with the kitchen, continued in the two kids' bedrooms, and culminated in the primary bedroom, which had an awesome bathroom with a jacuzzi tub big enough for two.

"The bathroom is almost as nice as the one in our house."

Her mother nodded. "As I said, this house is very nice but small."

"It's small only when compared to ours." Kaia followed her mother back to the living room. "It's more than sufficient for most families."

"It's smaller than the homes I build," Gilbert said. "And my gated communities are meant for ordinary people, not rich folks."

Kaia shrugged. "I can see myself raising a family in a house like this. It's big enough for a couple with three kids."

"I guess so." Her mother sat on the couch and glanced at her watch. "They should be here already."

"They'll be here soon," William said.

Her mother turned to Cheryl. "Do you mind taking the little ones to our bedroom? You can put on one of the shows they like to watch."

Since the conversation would no doubt include adult themes, Kaia could understand her mother's wish to have just the adults in the living room. But in her opinion, Cheryl was old enough to hear whatever the doctor had to say, and since it involved her future as well, she should. Then again, they needed someone to watch the little ones, and Cheryl had plenty of time until the information became relevant to her.

"Fine," Cheryl agreed grudgingly. "Come on, Idina. Let's go." She picked up the boys and carried them to the bedroom.

For a long moment, a tense silence stretched over the living room as they waited for Syssi and Kian to arrive with the famed physician.

"What are your plans for dinner?" Kaia asked her mother to break the silence. "Do you want me to quickly whip something up?"

Her mother smiled. "I have a fridge full of casseroles, stews, and pasta that were left on our doorstep. I assume that when people heard about a family of humans with four kids staying in the village, they assumed that we would need food, but they didn't want to come in and say hello in case we don't transition."

Kaia cast William a sidelong glance. "Is that so?"

He nodded. "Makes sense."

"One of the casseroles is from my mother," Darlene said. "She didn't knock on your door to say hello because she knows how overwhelmed you must feel." She turned to Karen. "She asked me to get your phone number so she could invite you for dinner at her house once you get settled in."

"Darlene's mother is very nice," Eric said. "She's a beautiful woman like her daughter, and she's a great cook as well."

"When did you have time to eat?" Kaia asked.

"Geraldine planned for us to stay for dinner, and when she found out that we couldn't, she insisted we eat earlier. We had to leave before Darlene's sister and her mate arrived, but we got to meet Shai, who is Kian's assistant. A very pleasant fellow as well."

Was Eric putting Shai and Kian in the same category of pleasant fellows? Or had he meant that Geraldine and her mate were both pleasant people?

Kian was many things, but pleasant wasn't one of them. He was intense, intimidating, and too handsome. It wasn't that she was attracted to him, but her eyes were drawn to him like to a beautiful work of art.

Perfect and unapproachable.

The only times the guy seemed remotely human was when he interacted with his daughter.

When the doorbell chimed, Gilbert jumped to his feet and rushed to open the door.

"Good afternoon." Kian strode into the room with Syssi on one side and a petite redhead on the other. "Let me introduce our prestigious physician, Doctor Bridget."

The woman wasn't wearing a white coat or the sensible shoes most doctors wore. She wore loose slacks, a fitted blouse, and a pair of high heels. And yet, it wasn't difficult to guess who she was, and it wasn't just the old-fashioned black doctor's bag that gave her away. It was the air of authority and confidence.

Kaia was willing to bet that even Kian couldn't intimidate her.

"Hello." The doctor smiled brightly.

A round of introductions ensued, and when it was done, and everyone was seated around the dining table with a cup of tea or coffee in hand, Kian turned to Bridget. "The stage is yours, doctor."

She nodded. "I'm sure you have many questions, and I'm here to answer them to the best of my ability. I also brought swabs, syringes, and test tubes with me, so once we are done, I'll take samples from Gilbert and Eric. I already have Syssi's results, so I don't need to take hers."

"Well, that answers half of my first question," Kaia said. "It was whether you could perform the tests and evaluate the results in-house."

"I'll have the results ready by tomorrow. I understand that you are not related to Gilbert and Eric, but I still need a sample from you as well. I like to take a sample before the transition starts. It helps me evaluate your progress during the process and then post-transition. I will also keep your mitochondrial DNA results on file for future reference."

"Do you test the mitochondrial DNA of every newcomer?" Karen asked.

"I do. We have a strong taboo against matings between people of the same matrilineal descent, no matter how far back it goes. Our clan used to be comprised solely of Annani's descendants, so we always treated each other as if we were first cousins, but since the influx of new members in the last several years, it's become important to keep track of who was the descendant of which line. That's why I collect that information from new arrivals. We will need it when the next generation comes of age." She smiled. "As I said, I like to take samples before and after the transition, but many times I don't have access to the before and have to make do with just the after. I'm glad that this time I get to take them from all of you."

No one was getting near her baby brothers and Idina with needles for no good reason.

"You don't need samples from the little ones." Kaia cast Bridget a hard look. "You can take samples from my mother and me. The others are not about to attempt transition anytime soon, so there is no rush."

The doctor returned a hard look of her own, but she softened it with a smile. "I didn't intend to. I'm only interested in samples from those who are about to get induced in the very near future."

Kian

Kian hadn't talked with Bridget about her research in a long time, and he was curious about whether she'd found connections between the Dormants. Jacki and Turner had similar coloring and were both immune to thralling and compulsion, which made him suspect that they had a shared ancestor. Although it could be that they were the descendants of the same male god and not the same goddess or an immortal female.

Kalugal and Lokan had inherited their compulsion ability from Navuh, not Areana, and Orion inherited his ability from Toven. The source was no doubt Ekin, Mortdh and Toven's father, but curiously, Annani had never mentioned that about her uncle. Perhaps he hadn't used it, or maybe he'd inherited it from his father or mother but hadn't manifested the ability and only gave it to his sons.

"What kind of equipment do you have in your lab?" Kaia asked.

Bridget lifted a red brow. "I can give you a tour if you like. What are you interested in?"

"You can obviously perform mitochondrial DNA analysis, but can you do a full gene sequencing?"

Bridget shook her head. "I can't. Now that the prices of the equipment have dropped and the machines themselves have shrunk in size, I've been contemplating equipping my lab with everything needed for full sequencing and playing around with it, but the truth is that I don't have time. I would love for one of our clan members to study genetics and take over the research." She smiled at Kaia. "Are you interested?"

"I'm a bioinformatician. I analyze the data geneticists collect."

"And I am a physician who also heads the clan's rescue operations. I can't wear one more hat."

Kian lifted his hand to stop their oddly combative conversation. He liked both of them, but maybe they just rubbed each other the wrong way.

He turned to Bridget. "Can you please explain to me in layperson's terms what you can find out about people's genetics with what you have, and what more can be learned with better equipment?"

"Yeah," Gilbert said. "I didn't even know that there were different types of DNA. What is mitochondria, and does it have anything to do with hypochondria?"

Kaia chuckled. "Don't take him seriously. He just likes to make silly comments like that to get a rise out of people."

Bridget smiled one of her indulgent smiles. "The mitochondrial DNA is a small portion of the total DNA, containing only 37 of the many thousands of protein-coding genes in our bodies. The chromosomal DNA is encoded in the nucleus of the cells and is contributed by both parents. The mitochondrial DNA is encoded in the mitochondria of the cell and is contributed only by the mother."

"Forgive my ignorance," Eric said. "But what is mitochondria? I'm afraid I wasn't a good biology student." He smirked. "Probably because the teacher was a hottie, and I kept fantasizing about her seducing me instead of paying attention to what she was trying to teach us."

Laughing, Darlene slapped his arm. "I was right to tell my mother that you were a cad. You were bad even as a boy."

Gilbert snorted. "There are no worse pervs than teenage boys. I remember those days, and not fondly."

Bridget waited patiently until everyone quieted again. "Mitochondria are organelles inside the cell that are membrane-bound. They generate most of the chemical energy needed to power the cell's biochemical reactions. But the mitochondrial function is helped by about fifteen hundred genes, so it's not like we can learn the secret to immortality just from looking at the mitochondria." She sighed. "I hoped that would be the case, but it wasn't."

"Why would the secret be limited to the mitochondria?" Karen asked. "If it's made from just 37 genes, it would have been easy to identify an extra one or find one that was different from the others."

Bridget nodded. "That's what I checked for and regrettably didn't find. What led me to research the mitochondria was that the immortal genes are passed through the maternal line and follow the same rules as a mitochondrial inheritance in humans."

"What do you mean?" Eric asked. "How does it work in humans?"

"Females inherit mitochondrial DNA from their mothers and pass it on to both their sons and daughters. Males inherit the mitochondrial DNA from their mothers but do not pass it on to their children. They inherit the Y-DNA from their fathers and pass it on to their sons but not their daughters."

That could explain why Orion had inherited Toven's compulsion ability, but Geraldine hadn't. But it didn't explain how male gods could produce immortal children with human females. According to Bridget's explanation, they shouldn't be able to. Also, unless his maternal grandmother was also a compeller, Annani had inherited her compulsion ability from Ahn, and supposedly, he couldn't have passed it to his daughters.

Perhaps the gods were built differently, and when they mated with humans, they passed their complete DNA to their children, but the offspring's DNA followed the split human structure.

"Now I get it." Eric leaned back in his chair. "That's why only the children of immortal females carry the immortal genes. The immortal males can't pass them to their children."

"Precisely." Bridget gave him a bright smile. "The nuclear DNA is worth investigating, but the secret of immortality is obviously hiding in the mitochondria, which is why I focused my research just on that. When we get a geneticist in the clan, we might consider building a proper lab. But until then, it would be a waste. The equipment is getting better and better, and if we buy it now, it will become obsolete by the time someone from the clan becomes a geneticist."

"We can build a genetic testing lab in Safe Haven," William said. "Over there, we can have humans operate it and just compel them to take the secrets they discover to their graves."

Kian shook his head. "It's too dangerous. Compulsion is not foolproof. But that's a discussion for a different time. Let's focus on Gilbert and Eric's relationship to Syssi."

Bridget nodded. "Are there any more questions?"

"How far back can the mitochondrial DNA be traced?" Karen asked.

"That's an excellent question," the doctor said. "Mitochondrial DNA tests are effective for tracing your maternal lineage up to 52 generations, but they are not accurate. That far back, the test can only tell us the direct-line maternal haplogroup, which can tell us which region of the world the mother's maternal line came from. But since we need only three generations, we are good."

Gilbert let out a breath. "Perfect. We only need to confirm that we share a great-great-grandmother with Syssi."

"What about finding other maternal lineage relatives?" Kaia asked. "You might find many more Dormants that way."

Bridget shook her head. "I don't have access to a large database like 23andMe and others like it to find people who might be related to the Dormants we've found so far."

"I tried it." Gilbert waved a dismissive hand. "It confirmed what I already knew about my heritage, but it didn't find any new relatives that I didn't know about before. If there are any, they didn't submit their samples for testing."

"We can hack into the database." William looked at Kian. "If that's okay with you. Maybe Bridget can find maternal relatives of the other Dormants."

"Do it. If we can find even one more Dormant through the information those labs keep on file, it's worth the effort."

Next to him, Syssi shook her head. "It won't work. Every scientific method we have tried so far has failed. All the Dormants were found seemingly by chance, but when it happened time and again, we had to concede that it must be orchestrated by the Fates."

"The Fates?" Eric asked.

Darlene put a hand on his arm. "Syssi is right. I'll tell you later how Cassandra met Onegus and how Orion was found, and you'll see what she meant by that."

He nodded.

"I have a question," Kian said. "How far back can the Y-DNA test go?"

"Y-DNA testing can tell us some information about our ancient direct-line paternal ancestors going back a hundred thousand years." Bridget reached for her doctor's bag and lifted it onto her lap. "All men living today inherited their Y-chromosome from a single direct-line male ancestor. But like mitochondrial testing, it covers only about one percent of our ancestors. We can learn much more about recent direct-line paternal ancestors going back no more than a thousand years."

"So we can't trace lineage to the original male gods." Kian crossed his arms over his chest.

"That's correct."

That was interesting.

The Sumerian myths talked about the essence of one male god being used to impregnate local creatures and create humanity. Perhaps that god had been the singular male ancestor all Y-DNA could be traced to.

Eric

After the swabs had been taken and the doctor had left with Syssi and Kian, Eric and Darlene got ready to leave as well.

Shai had arranged a meeting for them with the interior designer who was in charge of housing in the village, so she could show them what was available.

"Stay for dinner," Karen urged. "You can call Ingrid and ask to meet her later."

Eric gave her a one-armed hug. "It's getting late, and I'm sure she wants to end her workday. When Darlene chooses the house she wants, we will come back for a cup of coffee." He kissed her cheek. "Save us some leftovers."

"I will."

"There is no shortage of vacant houses in the village," William said. "You can have your pick."

"I know." Darlene took Eric's hand. "I want to find out what's available, which is why we are meeting Ingrid at the café to go over the options. It's a big day for me." She sighed. "It will be the first house that I'm not sharing with Leo."

"Good luck." Kaia waved at them before ducking into the kitchen.

Opening the door, Eric leaned down to whisper in Darlene's ear, "I hope you'll be sharing it with me."

"Of course." She beamed at him. "That's why we are meeting Ingrid together."

"Good save." He gave her hand a light squeeze.

Their relationship was progressing at warp speed, which usually wasn't a good thing, but from what he'd heard from the immortals, that wasn't uncommon for them. Dormants and immortals felt an affinity for each other, and those who found their truelove mate fell in love fast and hard.

Was Darlene his one and only, though?

He wasn't a great believer in mystical connections, but he wasn't a disbeliever either. He was a maybe kind of guy, and he was willing to suspend disbelief and embrace the immortals' explanation. It made life easier, and it reduced self-doubt to manageable proportions.

"My head is spinning from all we've learned today." Darlene put a hand on her temple. "The field of genetics is fascinating, but it's so complicated. There are so many terms I'm unfamiliar with that even though Bridget tried to dumb it down for us, I had a hard time following her."

"Same here." He looked at the path forking ahead of them. "To get to the café, we need to take the left turn, right?"

Darlene chuckled. "Left or right?" She pointed to the left. "It's that way. Do you know that the immortals can smell it even from here? Their senses are incredible."

"We are about to become them, so you should start thinking in terms of we, not them."

Darlene looked at him with fearful eyes. "I don't think I'll be able to get any sleep tonight. I'm so anxious to hear back from Bridget."

He stopped and wrapped his arms around her. "I'm going to attempt transition regardless of Bridget's findings. I'm sure that I'm a Dormant even if I'm not related to Syssi. How else would you explain us? We are going to choose a house together, and it feels as natural as if we had been dating for months."

"You are right." She lifted on her toes and kissed him lightly on the lips. "Being with you is so easy. I don't have to work hard to please you. I can be myself, and you seem happy with me the way I am."

He pressed a soft kiss to her forehead. "I don't want to change a single thing about you other than your longevity. I want you to live forever." He leaned away and looked into her eyes. "I want you to go for it right away and not wait until I can induce you."

Darlene shook her head. "How can you say that given what's required for that to happen? Can you tolerate knowing that I'm having sex with another man? Especially after what you've been through with your ex?"

"As long as it's not behind my back, and I'm there with you, I think I can." He sighed. "After the divorce, I experimented a lot. I've done threesomes, some with two women, others with a woman and a man. It was exciting, and I enjoyed myself, but those were people I didn't have an emotional connection with. I know it's going to be difficult to share you with another man, but my difficulty is immaterial. If we find someone who we both like and who is open-minded about sex, I think we can pull it off without it destroying what we have."

Darlene

The image that Eric's words evoked was Max's smiling face. Darlene remembered vividly how he had looked when he'd flirted with her on the bus, and it wasn't a bad memory. Max had been a little pushy but never obnoxious, and she'd enjoyed flirting with him, but she couldn't see herself with him and Eric in bed.

It was just too scandalous.

After it had become known that Eric was a potential Dormant, Max had backed off, and she'd thought that was the end of it. But when Kaia had told her that Max had requested to be transferred back to the village and had returned with them, Darlene suspected that it had something to do with her.

"We can worry about me later." She took Eric's hand and led him toward the café. "First, we need to find you an inducer, and you need to transition."

"I thought that William would induce me."

She chuckled. "He's not the best candidate for that. William abhors anything that has to do with sports, and he doesn't know the first thing about wrestling. You need to choose someone who is a capable fighter, like a Guardian, and he should be someone you like."

"Why? All I need to do is provoke his aggression. I don't need to be friends with him."

"Wrong. The inducer and the inductee promise eternal friendship to each other."

Eric shrugged. "I can be friends with William. I don't know any other immortal males."

"What about Anandur or Brundar? They are both head Guardians, and they are among the best, if not the best. After all, Kian wouldn't choose inferior warriors as his bodyguards."

Eric frowned. "Brundar is a killer, and he scares the hell out of me. Anandur is just too big. I need someone who I stand a chance against for at least a few minutes. If I'm flat on my back in seconds, it would be devastating to my ego."

Darlene wasn't sure whether he was being serious or not, and she didn't want to make a choice for him. "Choose whomever you like." She waved a hand at the café. "I can introduce you to some of the males. That's Richard." She pointed. "He's a newly transitioned immortal, but it has been more than six months since his transition. He would be honored to be chosen." She scrunched her nose. "But maybe he's not your best candidate. I heard that he had a really hard time entering his transition and required multiple attempts by different immortals. That means that his genes are highly diluted."

"Who ended up inducing him?"

"I think it was Kian, or maybe it was Kalugal? I'm not sure. Anyway, Kian induced Roni after several others failed to initiate him." She snorted. "My Roni is no fighter either. He spurred Kian's aggression by reciting particularly vile slam poetry."

She still had to introduce Eric and Roni, but she wanted a word with her son first. Roni could be very rude without meaning to be, and she didn't want him and Eric to start their relationship on the wrong foot.

After they'd ordered coffees and pastries, they took their order to a table next to Richard's.

He got to his feet and offered his hand to Eric. "I heard that an entire family of potential Dormants is staying in the village. You must be the younger brother who snagged our Darlene."

"That's me." Eric grinned. "Eric Emerson."

"Richard." The men shook hands.

"Can I join?" a familiar voice said from behind her.

Darlene turned around. "Max. What a nice surprise." She felt her cheeks heating up. "I didn't expect to see you here. Of course, you can join us."

She hadn't seen the Guardian standing in line, and given the paper cup he was holding, she knew why. He'd used the vending machines.

"I'm heading home," Richard said. "Good luck to you and your family." He turned to Darlene. "If you need anything, let me know."

"Thank you." She sat down.

Max watched the guy walk away and snorted. "What can he do for you? Are you remodeling a house?"

Was that what Richard did for a living?

As far as she knew, he worked as a supervisor on Kian's building projects. He wasn't a handyman. But who knew? Maybe it was his side gig.

"I might. We are meeting Ingrid to go over housing options."

Max pulled out a chair and sat down. "Together? Isn't that too early?" He turned to look at Eric. "You didn't transition yet, and there is no guarantee that you will. Or did Bridget already confirm that you and Gilbert are related to Syssi?"

"She took swabs from us and said that she would have the results by tomorrow, but I'm sure that I'm a Dormant."

Max lifted a brow. "Based on what?"

Eric cast Darlene a charming smile. "The affinity I feel for all of you and how fast Darlene and I fell for each other."

She swallowed.

He hadn't told her that he loved her, and she hadn't told him that either. It was too early even for Dormants and immortals. They barely knew each other, and the crazy attraction could be all about sex.

Max nodded. "I felt it too." He leaned over and put his hand on Eric's shoulder. "If you didn't select your inducer yet, I'll be honored if you choose me. But you will have to buy me dinner first." He batted his eyelashes. "I'm not going to put my mouth on your neck unless we go out on a date first."

Eric laughed, but Darlene didn't.

What were Max's motives?

Why did he offer himself?

Wasn't he jealous of Eric?

What if he planned to sabotage Eric's induction?

If Max was still interested in her, it would benefit him if Eric didn't transition, but on the other hand, it would be a blow to his ego, which was substantial.

Then again, Max wasn't responsible for the blood pumping in his veins, so if his venom didn't do the job, he would have nothing to be embarrassed about.

Eric

⌒∽⌒

Eric followed Ingrid and Darlene around the third house on their tour, focusing on the sound of the interior designer's high heels clicking on the hardwood floor and trying to match a tune to the staccato. The houses differed slightly in their decor scheme, but otherwise they were nearly identical, and he was bored.

Hopefully three times was the charm, and Darlene would settle on the one they were touring now, and they could go back to Gilbert and Karen's place for coffee.

"What do you think?" Ingrid asked.

"It's perfect." Darlene sat on the couch and patted the spot next to her for Eric to join her. "We are not too close to Geraldine or Orion, but not too far away either. If my mother decides to visit me, it will take her five minutes to get here, which will give me enough time to get dressed if I need to or to straighten up things." She turned to Eric. "What about you? Which one do you like best?"

"Frankly? All these little houses look the same to me." He smiled apologetically at Ingrid. "No offense to the decor. I think you've done an amazing job. They are cozy and yet stylish, which is not an easy combination to pull off."

"Thank you." Ingrid sat on one of the armchairs. "That's exactly what I was going for, but with Kian wanting everything done yesterday, I had very little time to plan. That's why there is not much variation in the decor. If I had more time, I would have made each house unique."

"Is Kian always rushing things?" Eric asked.

She nodded. "I'm also designing the decor for the boutique hotels the clan is building, and his instructions are always the same." She squared her shoulders and assumed a hard expression. "Don't reinvent the wheel, Ingrid. Do what you've done before, that worked," she said in a gruff voice. "Time is money."

Darlene laughed. "That was good. I can imagine Kian saying that."

Ingrid rose to her feet. "I'm no longer giving out keys because there is no need to lock the door, but if you want, you can add a deadbolt. I'll mark the house as yours on the village map, so everyone will know where to find you."

"Thank you." Darlene got up. "I appreciate the time you took to show us the homes."

"No problem. I always enjoy showing houses to new members." She turned to Eric. "Good luck with your transition. When should I expect the induction ceremony?"

While touring the homes, Darlene had told the designer about Gilbert and Eric's possible relation to Syssi, and Eric's wish to be induced as soon as possible.

"Tomorrow." He offered her his hand. "Max volunteered to be my inducer, and he's taking care of the preparations."

"Wonderful." Ingrid shook his hand. "I'll be there to cheer you on."

"Thanks." He winced. "Although I'm not sure I want witnesses to my humiliation. Max is a Guardian, and he's immortal. I was told that I have no chance against him."

"No one expects you to last long." Ingrid patted his arm. "It's considered an achievement if you manage to stay on your feet for a whole minute. I'm sure that you could last that long against Max." She gave him an appreciative once-over. "You look like you work out."

Eric could practically feel the glare Darlene was aiming at the designer, and he tried hard not to show his satisfaction.

"Thank you for the compliment." He smiled.

"You're welcome. I'll see you both tomorrow." Ingrid turned on her high heel and walked out.

As soon as the door closed behind her, Darlene turned to him. "I didn't have a chance to say anything before, but I don't think that Max should be your inducer."

"Why not? I like him."

"Because he might botch it on purpose. Max hoped that I would choose him, and when he found out that you are a potential Dormant, he backed off. But he still sees you as a rival. Those immortal males are predators, and they don't give up easily."

"Did you encourage him? I mean before I showed up."

Darlene shook her head. "I was friendly." She blushed. "When I still thought of you as just a weekend fling, I considered Max as my next step. He is attractive, and he has a rough kind of charm, but he's not you." She wrapped her arms around his neck. "The Fates sent you to me, and I knew right away that we would be great together. But I thought that I couldn't have you because I was supposed to find an immortal male to induce me."

Darlene had sounded apologetic, probably attributing his frown to jealousy, and she was right. She just didn't know what was really going through his head.

Max was the perfect solution Eric had been searching for, the ideal third partner in the threesome he had envisioned, but he couldn't get the words out and actually suggest it.

"What's the matter?" She cupped his cheek. "Are you jealous?"

He nodded but then shook his head.

"Then what?"

Eric swallowed the lump in his throat. "Perhaps Max can induce us both."

Darlene's eyes widened. "You want us to have a three-some with him?"

"I don't, but he's the perfect choice. We both like him, he's into you, and I have a feeling he is a little into me as well. He might be bisexual."

"He's not. He was just teasing. Max is as heterosexual as they come."

"How do you know?"

She shrugged. "The way he was devouring me with his eyes when he was flirting with me. He didn't look at you like that."

As a growl rose from somewhere deep in his throat, Eric slapped a hand over his mouth. "Forgive me. I don't know where that came from."

Darlene grinned. "That's just more proof that you are a Dormant. Your possessive nature is rearing its head."

"It's never happened to me before, and I had plenty of reasons to be jealous about my ex."

"She wasn't your fated mate." Darlene smirked. "Some-how, I don't foresee a threesome in our future. You won't be able to handle it, and neither will I. I'm just a simple girl at heart, and I can't see myself doing something so scandalous."

She'd hoped that would make Eric smile, but his expression remained serious.

"We have to." He cupped her cheek. "You are precious to me, and I won't put your life in danger just because the thought of sharing you with another male makes me feel physically ill."

Kaia

W illiam's house was in the new section of the village that was separated from the rest of the homes by a bridge.

There was another section a little farther away that was also accessible only by a bridge, and William had promised Kaia to take her on a tour the next day and tell her the story of its inhabitants.

As they stepped onto the bridge, Kaia looked up and around, searching for security cameras, but she couldn't see any. It was dark though, so she might have missed them with her human eyes.

"What are you looking for?" William asked.

"I expected a gate and at least some surveillance. You said that this was the secure section where Kian lived."

"They are there," William said. "But they are very well hidden."

"Security cameras?"

"That's what you were looking for, right?"

"Yeah. All the important people live here, so I expected the security to be more robust. Where are they?"

"Some are embedded in the railing. They look like decorative elements."

"Show me."

"I'd better not. I'm not supposed to tell you where they are, and if you are seen staring at them, the guys in security will know that I showed them to you."

"What about sound?" she whispered. "Can they hear us talk?"

"It's turned down. They only turn it up when they suspect something is going on, but thankfully, nothing ever is."

"What do you expect to happen?"

He shrugged. "Nothing, really. Kian needed a bigger place, and he wanted a super secure location for his mother if she ever decided to move into the village, so we amped up the security around this section."

The village was extremely well hidden and inaccessible to anyone who wasn't supposed to be there. The whole place was like a fortress, and making a secure inner zone only made sense if Kian and his mother suspected that they had enemies from within, which was possible even though most of them were related to each other. Not all families were supportive, and some were damn deadly. Brothers killing brothers for power and money.

As a shiver ran down Kaia's spine, she clung closer to William.

There were no streetlights to illuminate the way, and she could barely see a few feet ahead of her, but from what she could glean, the homes were bigger than the one her family was staying in.

"I'm glad that the houses are small. My mother couldn't insist on me staying with them because there was no room."

"I think Karen and Gilbert have made peace with us being together. They have more pressing things on their minds now."

"I know." Kaia let out a breath. "We all feel as if we are sitting on a ticking bomb. I'm waiting for my transition to start, my mother and Gilbert are waiting for Bridget to give them the results of the genetic testing, and Eric and Darlene are getting ready for his initiation ceremony. He's so convinced that he's a Dormant that he doesn't even want to wait for the results."

"He might be right." William turned into the walkway of the fifth house from the bridge. "This is us." He led her up the two stairs to the front door. "There are no front porches in this section, and I miss the one I had in my old house, which is funny since I never used it." He pushed the door open and switched the light on.

"Oh, wow. That's much fancier than the one my family is staying in." She walked up to the marble fireplace. "Did you have a chance to use it?"

"Not yet. I only moved here a week before leaving for Safe Haven. Do you want to see the bedrooms?"

Kaia smiled. "Someone is impatient."

A slight blush colored William's pale cheeks. "I've been thinking about getting you in bed all day long, and it has been a long day."

"It's not over yet." She cupped his cheek and pressed a kiss to his soft lips. "Show me your bedroom."

She wanted to take a peek at the kitchen, but that could wait for tomorrow.

William took her hand and led her down the hallway. "There are three bedrooms." He opened the door to what looked like a home office and a library combined. "Ingrid thought that I would like to work from home, so she organized this space for me, but I do all my work in the lab."

Kaia eyed the executive chair and the large desk. "I can use this space if you don't." She walked up to one of the bookcases. "Are those yours? Or did Ingrid fill the shelves with nice-looking books to make your office look good?"

He chuckled. "Those are mine, but they were sitting in cardboard boxes in my lab until now. Ingrid brought them here, cleaned them up, and organized them on the shelves."

"She must be a superwoman to find time for all the things she does."

"Ingrid has help. She doesn't do everything by herself." He tugged on her hand. "Let's continue the tour."

William was obviously eager to get her to the bedroom, and Kaia was eager for that as well, but his office was just too cool for a casual inspection.

"I'll give it a more thorough look tomorrow." She let him pull her out of the room.

"This is the guest room." He opened the door. "Nothing special to see here." He tugged her hand toward the last door. "This is my bedroom." He opened the door to a large room with a massive four-poster bed.

"Did you pick out that monstrosity?"

William was so low-key that she knew he would never have chosen an ostentatious bed like that. What had Ingrid been thinking?

He frowned. "I didn't pick anything in the house. Ingrid chose everything. If you don't like it, we can get a different bed."

Kaia turned toward William and wrapped her arms around his neck. "It can stay. Those carved posts give me ideas."

"Oh yeah? What kind of ideas?" Given the blush coloring his cheeks, he knew precisely what she was thinking about.

Kaia laughed. "The kinky kind, my prince."

William

$\qquad$❦$\qquad$

Even though William didn't know what those kinky things were and whether Kaia wanted to tie him up or to be tied by him, both options equally excited him, and he got so hard that the integrity of his zipper was threatened.

Lifting her up, he intended to carry her to the bed, but she tapped on his shoulders, demanding to be put back down.

"We need to shower. I'm not getting into this lovely bed with the clothes I've been wearing all day, and neither are you."

That was not a problem. He could think of a few interesting things that they could do in the shower, or the bathtub, or on top of the counter, or inside the closet. Now that Kaia had opened that Pandora's box, all kinds of things floated to the surface that William had never given much thought to before.

He was a simple guy with simple needs, but he was ready and able to fulfill any fantasy Kaia might have, and it excited him to no end to imagine what her brilliant mind could come up with.

"May I carry you to the bathroom?"

She laughed. "Yes, you may."

Shifting her in his arms so he could carry her like a princess, he walked into the bathroom and flicked the lights on with his elbow. "Take your pick. The shower, the tub, or the counter."

"Tsk, tsk. Bossy, bossy." She glanced around the bathroom. "The tub looks super inviting, and it's big enough for two."

"As you wish, your highness." He set her down on the counter and walked over to the tub. "How do you like your water? Hot, warm, or something in between?" He turned the faucet on.

"The third option." Kaia hopped down from the counter. "I need to pee."

"The toilet is over there." He pointed. "And there is also a bidet if you fancy those."

A smile bloomed on her face. "I do. Gilbert put bidets in all of our bedrooms, and I got so used to having one that I can't live without it."

She'd never mentioned that or complained about not having one.

"There were no bidets in the bungalows."

"Tell me about it." She walked into the powder room but didn't close the door behind her. "It was a drag to shower after every poop. And given the goop they fed us in the dining hall, there were a lot of those."

William stifled a snort.

Kaia was so unabashed about everything, and it was just one more thing among many that he adored about her. Even now, she was using the toilet with the door open as if they were a couple who'd been together for years and didn't feel shy about anything...

Or like a couple of guys sharing a dorm room.

That was a sobering thought.

Did she even realize that most women wouldn't talk about pooping with their boyfriends or use the toilet without closing the door?

Did it bother him, though?

As long as it didn't bother her, he couldn't care less. Kaia was Kaia no matter what parts made the whole, and he loved her just the way she was.

After washing her hands, she sauntered over, sat on the lip of the tub, and put her fingers in the water. "It's a little too hot for me. Can you add some cold water?"

"Of course."

He wondered what she would do next. Would she start undressing or wait for him to do it for her?

Her flip-flops were the first to go. She just flung them off and stretched her toes. "Do you know what I miss?"

"What?"

"Cheryl and I used to paint our toenails for each other."

"You can do that tomorrow. You are officially on a semi-vacation."

"I want to see your lab, and I want to meet Roni and everyone else you told me about. Does Roni know about his mom hooking up with Eric?"

The last thing William wanted to do was talk about Darlene or Roni, or Eric. But that was just one more thing about Kaia that was so different from any woman he'd ever met. She didn't need a long buildup. She was on or off in an instant, one moment being all business and talking about their research, or her family, or anything else under the sun, and the next, she could be all over him.

That was also a male trait.

William shook his head. He should stop analyzing every-thing Kaia did and said through that prism. Every person had feminine and masculine traits combined, and Kaia's were just tilted in favor of the masculine a little more than the average female's.

"I guess we will find out tomorrow." He turned the faucet off and knelt in front of his princess. "Let's not talk about it now." He reached for her jeans button and popped it open. "Tonight is all about us."

Kaia leaned to plant a kiss on the top of his head. "I have a strange feeling in the pit of my stomach," she said quietly. "It's excitement mixed with anticipation and anxiety. Maybe my transition will start tonight."

Kaia

Kaia had been looking forward to tonight. It would be their first time with no barriers between them, but it could also be the start of her transition, and it scared her more than she was willing to admit.

William claimed that it was unlikely it would start right away, but Kaia had a feeling that it would.

She should be excited, but the truth was that she envied all the Dormants who hadn't known what was coming and just enjoyed fabulous sex with an immortal male, ignorant of the consequences.

For some, fear might enhance excitement, but for her it was a mood dampener.

Maybe she was just tired?

William paused with his fingers on her zipper. "What's going on?"

"Nothing." She forced a smile.

Lifting up, he sat on the lip of the tub beside her. "You forget that I can sense changes in your mood. You're anxious."

Kaia let out a breath. "I'm scared," she admitted. "It's hard to feel sexy when I have this sinking feeling in my stomach." She put a hand over her tummy.

He took her hand and lifted it to his lips. "We don't have to do anything tonight, or we can just fool around, or we can use a condom. You've had enough excitement for one day."

William was so sweet, so patient and understanding, but Kaia didn't want to wait.

"We are in the village because of my impending transition, and we have a team idling in Safe Haven awaiting our return. We don't have the luxury of waiting for me to get over my irrational fears."

"They are not irrational, and I don't want you to feel rushed." He wrapped his arm around her and pulled her onto his lap. "Tonight, just let me pamper you. I'll wash your hair, massage your scalp, and soap you all over, and if you manage to relax and get in the mood, we will take it from there. If not, I'll carry you to bed and tuck you in."

"I love you so much," she whispered. "You are so perfect for me that I can't imagine anything tearing us apart. But life is often unfair, and I'm afraid that this fairytale is going to end badly."

"It won't." He tightened his arms around her. "I won't let it happen. We will wait until Annani returns to the village before we attempt your transition. I'll call Kian tomorrow morning and plead with him to ask her to come back earlier than planned."

Kaia lifted her eyes to him. "What can she do to help?"

"She gives her blessing to Dormants who have trouble transitioning. I used to dismiss it as her way to give hope to their mates, but then I realized that being a goddess is not just about being more powerful than her immortal descendants. Annani must exude some kind of energy that we can't detect yet. That's why the little girl Dormants transition just from being around her, and that's how she helps adult Dormants transition when they are having difficulties."

That made sense, and it gave Kaia a boost of confidence. "When is she supposed to come back?"

"She didn't give us exact dates, but I guess two or three weeks. If she's not willing to cut her trip short, we can just wait. We will go back to Safe Haven, continue working on Okidu's journals, and come back here when she returns."

Kaia shook her head. "I can't do that, not after I dragged my family here. What am I going to tell them?"

"The truth. Besides, you didn't drag them. They informed you that they were coming."

"Still, they are here. What about Darlene's grandfather? He's a god. Can't he give me his blessing?"

William grimaced. "I don't know. Toven is supposed to be a powerful god, but something happened to him along the way, and he lost his glow. The popular theory is that he suffered from depression and that it depleted his energy reserves. I don't know if Annani's energy manifests in part in her luminescence, and the fact that Toven doesn't have it makes me doubt his ability to help you. I'd rather wait for Annani, who has a proven record of helping transitioning Dormants, than risk your life because we felt rushed."

Kaia was still stuck on the luminescence. "You didn't tell me that the goddess glows."

"She does, but she can suppress the glow when she wants to appear human, although with her otherworldly beauty, that's not enough. She usually uses a shroud to make herself look plainer."

For some reason, hearing William talk about the goddess helped ease Kaia's anxiety.

"Tell me more about Annani. You said that she's tiny. How tall is she?"

He chuckled. "She's about five feet tall, maybe half an inch over that, has a mane of flaming red hair that cascades all the way down to her hips, and she emits power like a mini nuclear reactor. When you meet her, you'll get what I mean. If she doesn't suppress her power and shroud her beauty, no one could mistake her for a human, but when she does, she can pass for a seventeen-year-old high school girl. The one thing that gives her away, though, is her eyes. The wisdom of the ages is reflected in them."

William

At some point during William's pampering, Kaia's expression had turned from stressed to relaxed. She lay sprawled in the tub, her limbs floating loose, her eyes closed, and a small smile lifting the corners of her lips.

He'd put a lot of effort into achieving that change in mood, treating her to a long scalp massage and then giving her feet the same attention, one little toe at a time.

William's clothes were wet, he was so hard that it was painful to bend over, his fangs were demanding their due, and his venom glands were full to bursting, but if that was what it took to get that angelic expression on her face, he would keep tending to her beautiful, nude body until she fell asleep.

Kaia's well-being came before his needs, and her survival came before any other consideration.

He should have thought about waiting for Annani's return before attempting her transition, but he'd been so sure that her youth would make it easy for her that it hadn't even occurred to him. But what if Kaia was the exception? What if she lost consciousness and Bridget couldn't keep her alive?

Kian wouldn't like the change of plans, especially if Kaia's family decided to wait with their transitions as well, but William could handle the grumpy regent.

In his heart, Kian was a romantic, and he would understand William's fear.

The same was true for Annani.

If he asked her to come back to bless Kaia, she would.

Letting out a contented sigh, Kaia turned her head to look at him with hooded eyes. "Take off your clothes, William, and get in here with me. This tub is big enough for both of us."

He hesitated. "It's incredibly difficult to keep it platonic while I'm dressed. It will be excruciating to be naked with you and not take it any further than caresses."

She smiled. "I want much more than caresses from you."

William shook his head. "We didn't bring condoms with us."

"That's okay." Kaia reached for his cheek with a soapy hand. "While you were doing all those wonderful things to me, I was thinking about my transition and decided that we shouldn't wait."

When he opened his mouth to protest, she put a finger on his lips. "The transition is not going to start right away, and when it does, it might go smoothly. Tomorrow, you should talk with Kian and ask him if his mother is willing to be on standby in case of an emergency. If it looks like I'm having a hard time, Toven can give me his blessing, and if that doesn't work, the goddess could get on the clan jet and be here in a matter of hours."

"Annani is in Scotland. It will take her more than a few hours to get here."

"I'm willing to take the risk. I don't want to wait any longer."

William shook his head. "But I'm not."

Kaia frowned. "You were all for it until I opened my mouth. Did I scare you?"

"You did," he admitted. "You told me that sometimes you get premonitions, and you've been hesitant to start working on your transition for a couple of days now. I don't take premonitions lightly."

"It wasn't a premonition." Kaia rose to her feet, the soap bubbles clinging to her gorgeous body and her long, wet hair flirting with her bottom. "Can you hand me the small towel for my hair, please?"

When he handed it to her, Kaia flipped her hair forward, covered it with the towel, twisted both together, and tucked the corners under the sides, making a turban out of it.

He was so mesmerized watching her that he hadn't thought to ready a bath sheet for her.

"Can you reach the big towel?"

"Of course." He turned around, reached for the bath sheet, and unfurled it. "Can I pat you dry?"

She smirked. "Given how long your fangs are, are you sure that it's a good idea? Not that I mind, but you seem to be against making love to me tonight."

He wrapped the towel around her and lifted her into his arms. "There are ways to make love that will keep you safe."

Shifting to circle her arms around his neck, Kaia let the towel slide down and expose her breasts. "I don't want those other ways tonight. It's either all or nothing."

He arched a brow. "Is that blackmail?" He put her down on the bed.

Letting the rest of the towel drop away from her, Kaia batted her eyelashes in mock innocence. "I'm just not in the mood for oral tonight." She cupped her breasts. "I want that magnificent length of yours thrusting in and out of me, and I want your fangs at my neck."

She was killing him.

William groaned. "You're playing dirty, you shameless flirt."

Kaia pouted and turned to lie on her stomach. "Do you want to spank me for being so naughty?" She lifted her gorgeous ass and wiggled it.

William's defenses were crumbling.

Maybe Kaia was right?

He could call Kian tomorrow and ask him to convince Annani to come back right away. Hell, he could call her himself and beg her to return. The goddess liked him, and he was a valuable member of the clan. She wouldn't deny him.

Besides, Annani was the ultimate romantic.

She would do that for love.

Kaia

"Ouch!" The hard smack landing on her ass took Kaia by surprise.

She hadn't thought that William had it in him.

Her taunting had been meant to get him so aroused that he would forget about her mini-panic attack and succumb to her seduction. Kaia had never expected him to actually accept her invitation and spank her.

"That was for driving me crazy." He massaged the small hurt away.

Would he spank her again?

Did she want him to?

It had hurt a little, but it was also oddly arousing.

Looking at him over her shoulder, she wiggled her bottom again. "I don't think one spank counts as spanking."

His eyes widened. "You want more?"

"How crazy did I get you?"

The next smack was followed by three more in quick succession. "That crazy." William caressed her heated bottom.

Turning around, she made it clear that the game was over. "Take off your clothes."

"Yes, ma'am." William popped a couple of buttons open, pulled the shirt over his head, and tossed it on the armchair that stood in a corner.

Apparently, he had no problem switching roles on a dime.

Kaia loved him when he was bossy, and she loved him when he was obedient, but bossy was just a tad sexier. Nevertheless, she wasn't going to say anything until he stripped for her and she got her fill of ogling him.

When he dropped his pants along with his boxers, freeing his impressive shaft, Kaia licked her lips.

"Do you like what you see?" He stroked the hard length lazily.

"You know that I do." She beckoned him to her. "I can't wait to feel it inside me with no barriers."

Before her eyes, his erection lost some of its volume. "Are you sure about that? I'll be very happy with oral."

"But I won't be." She spread her legs a little, letting him see the moisture that had pooled there just from their little game.

His nostrils flaring, William sucked in a breath. "You're playing dirty again."

She kept forgetting about his immortal sense of smell. He could not only see her arousal, but scent it too, so the effect was doubled.

"Are you going to spank me some more?" she taunted.

"Maybe later." He smiled evilly. "You wanted us both to take a shower, and I haven't yet. I'll do it now." He walked away from her.

Who was playing dirty now? He couldn't get her all hot and bothered and then leave her hanging.

"No, you won't. Come back here."

Looking at her over his shoulder, William smirked. "You'll have to wait patiently, my princess." He walked into the bathroom and closed the door behind him.

"Ugh. Frustrating man."

But if he thought that she would cool off while he was gone, he was mistaken.

Five minutes later, when William emerged from the bathroom with a towel draped over his hips, she was even readier for him than before.

"Did you have a nice shower?" She spread her legs, and the full impact of what she'd been doing hit him hard.

His nostrils flared. "You've been a naughty girl again."

She reached with her hand between her legs and stroked herself. "What are you going to do about it?"

Dropping the towel, he prowled over her and settled between her spread legs. "I need to feast." He looked into her eyes. "You're not going to deny me a taste, are you?"

She'd said that she wasn't interested in oral, but that was when he'd offered it as a substitute for intercourse. She had no problem with oral as foreplay.

It was on the tip of her tongue to tell him to turn around so they could pleasure each other simultaneously, but then she realized that once William's immediate need was fulfilled, he might decide not to penetrate her tonight and wait for the goddess to return.

She smiled up at him. "As long as it's just foreplay, I'm more than happy to be on the receiving end. But I'm not going to reciprocate tonight. You are coming inside of me or not at all."

Chuckling, he shook his head. "You just added to the spanking I'm going to give you later."

Kaia's bottom tingled, and not unpleasantly. "Promises, promises." She lifted her head and smashed her mouth over his.

William

Kaia never ceased to amaze William. She was so assertive that discovering she had a playfully submissive side to her was a complete surprise.

He had a feeling that there were many more surprises in store for him, and he was looking forward to a lifetime of them.

When Kaia let go of his mouth, his lips were tingling, and his fangs were pulsing with the need to bite her, but he needed a taste first.

Sliding down her supple body, he paid a short homage to her breasts, just a few swipes of his tongue on each nipple and a couple of kisses, and then he kept going until his face was buried between her legs.

He closed his eyes to enjoy the full impact of her sweet feminine scent, and as he swiped his tongue over her slit, the taste of her had him groan like a beast.

They were both close to the edge, so he couldn't spend as much time feasting on her as he normally would, but he needed to bring her to a quick climax before penetrating her.

He couldn't tolerate the thought of giving her anything but pleasure, but it seemed like she included a little spanking play in that definition, and he had no problem with that.

Whatever Kaia wanted, Kaia got.

In moments, he had her writhing around his tongue, and as he added two fingers to the play, she detonated with a scream that nearly had him spill on the bedsheet.

Only fear of Kaia's retaliation stopped William from biting her inner thigh and releasing onto the bed. She wanted him to come inside her while he bit her neck, and if he disobeyed, he would incur her wrath.

Lifting over her, he gripped his aching shaft and positioned it at her entrance, coating it in her copious juices before pushing in.

She was so slick that he didn't stop and pushed all the way inside her with one thrust.

"William," she gasped his name, and for a moment, he feared that he'd hurt her, but then she added, "It feels so good, so right." Her fingers dug into his buttocks, and she arched up, signaling that she wanted him to move.

He wanted to stay connected like that for a moment longer and savor it a little. The moment he started moving, he would be overtaken by the frenzy of coupling, and their joining would be over too soon. Kaia would black out, and he would lie beside her in agony, waiting for her to wake up so they could go for another round.

When she turned immortal, he could keep making love to her throughout the night, but for now, he had to live with her human limitations.

"William." Kaia bucked up again.

"Give me a few more seconds." He cupped her cheeks and pressed a loving kiss to her lips. "Where are you rushing to?"

She smirked. "Another orgasm or two or three from my beautiful monster."

It was silly of him to love her calling him that whenever his fangs were out, but he did. Kaia was his beauty, and he was her beast, and yet she thought that he was as beautiful in his beast form as he was as a man, when in reality he wasn't a great looker in either.

He didn't doubt her sincerity, though. She saw him through lenses tinted by love.

When he started moving, Kaia's fingers dug even deeper into his butt muscles, and when he swelled inside her and hissed through his fangs, she turned her head and offered him her neck.

He still had enough presence of mind to swipe his tongue over the spot before sinking his fangs into her.

Kaia climaxed, her sheath fluttering around his shaft, and as he erupted inside of her, it kept squeezing until there was nothing left.

Nevertheless, he kept pumping his hips until Kaia's string of orgasms ended, and her body went lax under his.

She was out, a satisfied smirk painted on her gorgeous face, and as William braced on his forearms and looked at her, he hoped they hadn't made a grave mistake.

Premonitions were nothing to sneer at, and the rock sitting in his gut hadn't gone anywhere just because he and Kaia had found a way to rationalize their haste.

The problem with logic was that it wasn't objective, and it was based on what was known. But since the unknown was far greater than the known, trusting in one's logic wasn't logical.

Kian

"Good morning." William walked into Kian's office and sat on one of the chairs in front of his desk. "Thank you for agreeing to see me on such short notice."

"My door is always open to you. You don't even have to make an appointment." Kian leaned back in his executive chair and crossed his arms over his chest. "Now that the pleasantries are out of the way, you can tell me what's bothering you."

William pushed his glasses up his nose. "Is it that obvious?"

"Yesterday, you didn't wear your glasses, and you spoke at a nearly normal speed. Today, you're hiding behind your spectacles again, and you are talking at machine-gun speed, so I assume something happened."

Kian was proud of himself for noticing, and Syssi would be even prouder of him when he told her about it.

William closed his eyes for a brief moment and let out a slow breath. "Kaia and I started the initiation process."

That was what they were in the village for, so it wasn't a great revelation. "Congratulations."

"Well, I'm not sure. Kaia was all gung ho to start up until two days ago, and then she started to feel fearful. To be frank, it scared me. I wanted to stop everything and wait for Annani to return to the village so she could bless Kaia in case she needed it, but then Kaia had a change of heart and seduced me last night."

Except for the first sentence and the slight pause after it, the entire speech was delivered in William's regular manner of a thousand words per minute.

"Good for her. I knew I liked the girl. She has spunk."

"Yeah." William's cheeks reddened. "That she does in spades. But I'm terrified that she might start transitioning before the Clan Mother returns, and there would be no one to bless her. Is there any way you can get Annani to come back earlier?"

So that was the reason for William's urgent request to see him first thing in the morning.

Uncrossing his arms, Kian leaned forward. "I know that the prospect of your mate facing any kind of danger is terrifying, but Kaia is very young and seems to be in perfect health. Her odds of transitioning easily are great."

"That's what I thought as well until she started having those foreboding feelings, and I can't dismiss them as irrational fears. I have to take them seriously. Too much is at stake. I can't lose her."

"You won't." Kian put his hands on the table. "I'm just surprised that you, of all people, put so much faith in Annani's blessings. You are an engineer and a scientist, not a spiritualist."

Perhaps he shouldn't have said that.

Kian was surprised that William hadn't figured out the truth behind the so-called blessings yet, and it was good that he hadn't. Reminding him that he was a scientist and should look for a logical explanation was a mistake.

The guy was very good at solving puzzles, and now that he was working with Kaia, who was just as bright as he was, if not more so, and seemed to be an extremely talented puzzle solver in her own right, they could easily figure it out.

"It helped others." William took his glasses off, folded them carefully, and put them on the table. "Our little girls transition just from being around Annani, so I assume that her glow and the palpable energy she emits facilitates transition. I'm the last person to tell you that science has everything figured out. What we know covers an infinitesimally tiny portion of what there is to know."

Kian stifled a relieved breath. William had looked for a scientific explanation for why the blessing worked, but he'd looked in the wrong direction.

"We are in agreement on that." Kian cast him an encouraging smile. "We have another god amongst us, though, and Toven can do everything Annani can. If Kaia encounters trouble transitioning, I will ask him to give her his blessing."

Kian had already secured the god's promise to donate his blood to the older members of Kaia's family, and he didn't anticipate Toven refusing to add her to the list of recipients.

William grimaced. "Toven doesn't glow, and being next to him doesn't feel the same as being next to Annani. She radiates power. He doesn't."

"That's because he's gotten so used to suppressing his glow and his power that his body does it on autopilot. It doesn't mean that he's less powerful or that his blessing is less effective."

William didn't look convinced. "We don't know that. When Mia was transitioning, it was Annani who gave her the blessing, not Toven."

Damn. How was he going to explain that one?

"Mia was in very poor health, and she needed double blessings. Toven had been blessing her ahead of her transition to strengthen her so she could even enter it, and once she got strong enough and the process started, he asked Annani to reinforce his blessings."

Thankfully, William wasn't particularly talented at detecting lies, or he would have sensed the half-truths Kian had been spouting. He was also distraught, so that might have affected his bullshit radar as well.

"Annani has more experience." William cast him a pleading look. "I trust her. Can you please ask her to come back? She's been gone a long time already."

"Fine," Kian relented. "I'll call my mother. She's probably heard already about the family of Dormants visiting the village and is curious to meet them. It might incentivize her to shorten her stay in Scotland. But if Sari calls to yell at me for luring our mother and sister away from her, I'm telling her to direct her complaints to you."

"No problem." William took a deep breath. "For Kaia, I'd fight dragons and angry sisters."

Kian laughed. "I don't know which one is more terrifying."

Jade

J ade spun her staff in her hands, giving Drova a short reprieve before leaping into the air and swiping it at her daughter.

Drova offered a clumsy defense, catching the stick with her own but then losing her balance and falling on her ass.

It was pathetic that Drova was the best fighter in her age group, but she was still inferior to the weakest female of Jade's former tribe.

Perhaps that would be the downfall of Igor's legacy.

The generation of pure-bloods he was raising in his compound was so inferior that they were nearly as ineffective as humans. When Igor and Jade's generation died out, humans would find these weaklings and eliminate them because there would be no one capable of leading them.

But that wasn't what Jade wanted. If she had her way, Igor would die, preferably a horribly painful death, and she would take over, turning these weaklings into tough warriors worthy of the Kra-ell name.

She could only dream, though. With Igor's compulsion rendering her helpless to affect any meaningful changes, all she could do was pray for his premature death and hope that it happened before he got old and one of his many sons took over.

Drova would never become the next leader of the compound because her father believed in and practiced patriarchy, which was an abomination to the Mother of All Life. She would be given to one of his trusted lieutenants and become a breeder like all the other females.

As long as her father lived, she would be treated well, but once he was gone, all bets were off.

Jade's only satisfaction would be watching Igor's empire deteriorate and crumble.

"You are lucky that no other female here will challenge you." Jade threw down her staff with disgust. "If you were in my tribe, you would have been at the lowest position."

"Then I'm lucky that I'm not in your tribe." Drova jumped back to her feet, picked up Jade's stick, and tossed it at her. "Let's go another round."

Leaning against the fence, Kagra chuckled. "Are you up for more humiliation, girl?"

Drova bared her fangs at Kagra. "One of these days, I'll wipe that smirk off your face. You might have been a beta to my mother's alpha back in your glory days, but you are no one here. I suggest that you either shut up or leave."

"Or what? Are you going to tattle on me to Daddy?"

Uttering a battle cry, Drova launched an attack on Kagra, who hadn't been armed with a staff to defend herself, but she still danced out of the way with ease.

"Here." Jade tossed Kagra hers.

"Thank you, my alpha." She sneered at Drova.

Alpha and beta were human terms, but even though the Kra-ell didn't use those designations, they were fitting.

Except, Kagra had served as a beta only because she was younger and less experienced, not because she lacked leadership.

The three of them were all natural alphas, but being born with an innate ability was worthless without putting in the effort to hone it, master it, and own it.

As her daughter and her second charged at each other, Jade dusted off her pants and walked over to stand by the fence and watch.

"You are telegraphing your intentions, Drova."

Her daughter growled in response.

The girl was physically strong, and she wasn't stupid, but she was lazy and thought that everything would always be handed to her on a silver platter because she was Igor's only daughter and everyone in the compound treated her like a princess.

How wrong she was.

Her father cared about one thing and one thing only, and that was power. He wouldn't hesitate to sacrifice his only daughter and his fifteen sons for more of it.

"Let's go for one last round," Kagra said after disarming Drova for the second time.

"I'm done." Drova picked up her staff and started toward the main building.

"The girl has no respect." Kagra walked over to Jade. "I don't know why you bother training her."

"She has potential, and I haven't given up on her yet."

Kagra cast a quick glance around before leaning closer to Jade. "How is it going with the parable?"

Jade winced. "It was ready, but then it occurred to me that I needed to add a warning about the children," she whispered. "I don't expect anything to come out of it, but on the remote chance that Veskar assembles a force and comes to our rescue, I need to let him know that there are children here."

Kagra let out a breath. "I thought a lot about it last night, and maybe you shouldn't send it at all. If Veskar has allies, they might not come here to rescue us. They might come to eliminate the threat of Igor, and they will kill everyone here, including the females and the children. And if they want more females the way Igor does, they will kill all the males, including the young ones and those who are not evil."

Her second had two sons, and she'd raised them as best she could so they weren't as bad as the others, but that didn't make them good either. They treated the captive females only slightly better than the rest of their brethren.

"It's a risk that I'm willing to take. If we do nothing, we will die in captivity. I'd rather die fighting."

Darlene

arlene crumbled her coffee cake, picking at it with her fork and making a mess on her plate. "Don't be offended if Roni says something rude." She lifted her gaze to Eric. "It's his style, and he usually doesn't mean anything by it."

They were meeting for breakfast, and Roni was predictably late. Her son wasn't a morning person, and since he didn't have a timecard to punch in, he showed up at the lab whenever he wanted. That didn't mean he was slacking, though.

Fates knew that he worked his skinny bottom off in that place.

Eric put his hand over hers, stopping the cake's destruction. "Why are you so nervous? You said that Roni hated his father. He should have no problem with me."

"It's important to me that the two of you get along, but you are very different people. I don't want your relationship to start off on the wrong foot."

"Don't worry about it." Eric leaned and kissed her cheek. "I'll be my charming self no matter how crusty your son gets."

"Thank you." She lifted her coffee cup and took a sip.

Last night she'd called Roni and had a long talk with him about Eric, the possibility that he was a Dormant, and whether she should wait for him to transition first and induce her or find another solution.

Thankfully, Roni had assumed that she'd meant finding a substitute, not a threesome with an immortal as Eric was pushing for.

Gosh, that was such a scandalous proposition that it made her blush just thinking about it. Well, blushing wasn't her only physical response to the idea, but she wasn't going to admit that the prospect aroused her.

Darlene wasn't a prude, and she'd read her fair share of ménage romances back in the day, but there was a big difference between reading about other people doing it and actually participating in a threesome herself.

How would it even work?

She shook her head.

Now was not the time to be thinking naughty thoughts. Eric might still be a human with a human's limited sense of smell, but Roni was joining them shortly, and she would die from embarrassment if her son smelled her arousal.

"Tell me a sad story," she blurted. "Something really bad."

Eric arched a brow. "Why?"

"Just do it. I need something to distract me."

He looked puzzled. "Wouldn't it be better if I tell you a happy story?"

"No."

A happy tale wouldn't kill her arousal.

"I was Kaia's age when I lost my mother. Our father died less than a year earlier, and she never recovered from his death. She lost her will to live."

Darlene frowned. "Did she die from a broken heart?"

She'd read that it was an actual thing and not just a phrase. It was called broken heart syndrome, and it was life-threatening. It could develop after a stressful event like a breakup or a loss of a loved one, and women in their fifties were the most affected group.

Eric nodded. "Her heart gave up. Gilbert, Gabi, and I had barely recovered from our father's death, and then she was taken from us as well. It was tough, and Gilbert took it upon himself to take care of Gabi and me."

"How old is your sister?"

"She's thirty-eight. I'm the middle child."

"Does she have kids?"

He shook his head. "She got divorced after five years of marriage and hasn't remarried. She's a dietitian and has a successful practice."

"You should bring her here. She might be younger than you, but she shouldn't wait too long either."

"I know." Eric sighed. "Let's see how my induction goes tonight."

"Are you nervous?"

He laughed. "Yeah. Max is a big guy, and he has his eye on you. He won't go easy on me."

That was what she was afraid of.

Thankfully, the ceremony would have many witnesses, so Max couldn't cause Eric excessive damage without someone stepping in to stop him.

"Don't provoke him too much. Just enough to make his fangs elongate."

"I'll be fine." He gave her one of his charming smiles. "I'm not afraid of getting knocked around a bit. Besides, Max is a good guy. He barely knew me, and he volunteered to induce me and to make all the arrangements for the ceremony. We are going to be best buddies forever." He winked.

Was he naive? Or was he just joking?

It was sometimes hard to tell with Eric. He smiled a lot, which she loved, and he didn't take himself or anyone else too seriously, which was great as well.

"Just be careful. Don't trust Max blindly."

Eric

❦

"Sorry I'm late." A gangly young man leaned over Darlene and kissed her cheek.

He didn't look anything like his mother. Did he look like his father?

"Hello, Roni." Eric offered the guy his hand. "I'm Eric."

"Hi." Darlene's son shook his hand. "My mother told me that you are having an induction ceremony tonight." He pulled out a chair and sat down. "Who is your inducer?"

"Max. Do you know him?"

"Yeah. He's cool. He usually accompanies William when he has to leave the village." Roni gave Eric a once-over. "You seem to be in good shape, but I hope you know that wrestling an immortal is like wrestling a gorilla. They are freakishly strong and aggressive as hell."

"A gorilla, eh? Is that an exaggeration, or are they really that strong?"

"They are that strong." Roni let out a breath. "I had to go through that crap four times, and each time I nearly shat my pants from fear. It wasn't fun."

It hadn't occurred to Eric that he might need to repeat the ceremony. "Why so many times?"

"I wasn't well." Roni took Darlene's plate, picked up several of the larger crumbs of the demolished cake, and stuffed them in his mouth. "I had pneumonia, which we mistook for transition at first. Then I recovered, but I was still weak. I couldn't enter transition until my body was back to normal. We didn't know that back then. Anyway, the last one to try was Kian, and I knew that if he couldn't induce me, no one could. Luckily, it worked."

Eric pieced together the bits of information he'd collected so far, trying to figure out how Roni had gotten to the clan before Darlene, but he just didn't have enough information.

"How did you find the clan? Or how did they find you?"

"It's a long story." Roni collected a few more crumbs and licked them off his fingers.

Eric rolled his eyes. "That's the answer everyone gives me. I need more information."

Roni leaned forward and looked him in the eyes. "It's not relevant to you, so it would be a waste of time telling you a story that someone might have to erase from your memories later. If you transition, you can come over to my house on the weekend, I'll grill some steaks for us, and I'll tell you my story over a couple of beers."

That was direct and only borderline rude, not nearly as bad as Darlene had warned him. Was Roni making an effort to be cordial?

"Thanks for the invitation. I would love to eat your steaks and drink your beer."

Roni grinned. "Have you been treated to Snake's Venom yet?"

Eric's mouth twisted in distaste. "That's one of the worst beers I ever had the displeasure of tasting. Is that what you drink?"

Roni laughed. "You are correct about it being horrible, but immortals metabolize alcohol so fast that any beer that is less potent than that tastes like piss water to us."

That was another factoid to add to Eric's small cache of knowledge about immortals. He knew now not to challenge any of them to a drinking competition.

"So, Eric." Roni leaned back in his chair. "What are you planning to do when you turn immortal? Are you going to sell off your planes?"

Eric shook his head. "I can lease them to a buddy of mine who runs a similar business, or I can offer my services to the clan. I was told that there is plenty of work for an experienced pilot."

That wasn't exactly what Max had told him, but it would do for now.

The answer seemed to satisfy Roni. "So you plan to stay in the village?"

"Of course." Eric wrapped his arm around Darlene's shoulders. "I can't leave my fated mate."

Roni's smile was the first genuine one Eric had seen so far. "That's the right answer. My mother deserves a man who adores her. I hope you erase the memory of damn Leo from her psyche forever."

The vehemence in Roni's voice surprised Eric.

According to Darlene, her ex hadn't been physically abusive, and verbal abuse usually didn't trigger such an angry response. It seemed that Roni had unresolved issues with his father.

"It's not good to hold on to such anger. Maybe you should meet up with your father and talk it out of your system."

The therapy sessions Eric had been through with his ex were good for something, after all. He could spout things and sound like he knew what he was talking about.

"Leo is not my father."

"I understand that you feel resentful toward him, but it might benefit to share with him what you feel. The fact that your parents are divorced does not mean that you can't have a relationship with your father."

Frowning, Roni turned to his mother. "You didn't tell him."

"I did not."

"Then maybe you should."

Darlene

Darlene's throat suddenly dried out, and a hundred excuses rushed into her mind.

There hadn't been enough time.

They hadn't known each other long enough.

It wasn't relevant to their relationship.

But the truth was that subconsciously she didn't want to tell Eric that her son hadn't been fathered by her ex-husband and that the affair he was the product of had taken place while she had still been married to Leo.

With what Eric had gone through with his ex-wife, he might not believe her that she and Leo had been separated at the time, and that she was not the kind of woman who cheated on her husband even though she hadn't been happy in her marriage.

"What didn't you tell me?" Eric asked.

She let out a breath. "Roni is not my ex's son, but Leo is listed on Roni's birth certificate as his father, and he raised him as his."

Eric lifted a brow. "So?" He turned to Roni. "What's the big deal? You should be glad that the abusive jerk didn't contribute his genetic material to you."

"Oh, I am." Roni smiled. "But since you are serious about my mother, you should know stuff like that. I don't want you looking at me with suspicious eyes and waiting for my asshole qualities to surface."

Eric chuckled. "From what your mother told me about you, you are far from cherubic. Apparently, nurture is as influential as nature, and you absorbed your adoptive father's behaviors."

Roni tilted his head and eyed Eric from under his thick, dark lashes. "First of all, my style of jerkiness is very different than Leo's, and it's uniquely mine. I'm not like him in any way. And secondly, he's not my adoptive father, or my stepfather, or my anything. He was just the dude who was married to my mother when she got pregnant with me."

Darlene wanted to kick her son under the table, but since there was nothing covering it, Eric would see.

The mirth gone from his face, he turned to her. "You had an affair while you were married?"

"We were separated at the time."

"Why did you go back to him?"

Darlene closed her eyes. "It was a mistake I regretted for years." She opened them and leveled her gaze at him. "I should have filed for divorce and stayed with Roni's father. I met him at work, and he was the sweetest computer nerd ever. He worshiped the ground I walked on but was too shy to initiate anything, and I had to do the seducing. He thought that he'd died and gone to heaven."

"Did you tell him that you got pregnant?"

She shook her head. "I told no one. I went back to Leo and pretended that Roni was his. Leo suspected the truth for years, but he never had the guts to have it tested. Roni and Leo have the same coloring and are about the same height, so it wasn't obvious that they weren't related."

The question in Eric's eyes was so obvious that she didn't need to wait for him to ask it. "That wasn't what ruined our marriage. Leo was a controlling jerk from the start, and I enabled his behavior by giving in to his demands. He treated me badly when he still believed that Roni was his, and he treated me badly when he started suspecting that Roni was too smart to be his son."

"I'm sorry that you had to live through that." Eric reached for her hand. "But if not for those difficulties, you wouldn't be with me here today. You would be happily married to Roni's father. So, I'm not sorry for that."

"True." She lifted their joined hands and kissed his knuckles. "I'm also sorry that you were married to a cheating shrew, but I'm glad that she was horrible and that you divorced her, so you could be with me here today."

"Bravo." Roni clapped his hands. "You two are so sweet that it's nauseating." He pushed to his feet. "I need to get to the lab, but I'll see you tonight at the ceremony." He leaned to kiss Darlene's cheek. "I'll bring Sylvia along if that's okay with you."

"Of course, it is." She beamed up at him. "Maybe after the ceremony, the four of us could get coffee and talk about your initiation trials and how you met Sylvia." She chuckled. "That's one heck of a story." She turned to Eric. "The way Roni and Sylvia met is like a script from *Mission Impossible* combined with *American Pie*."

"I can't wait to hear it." Eric rose to his feet and clapped Roni on his back. "Wish me luck."

"Good luck, Eric," Roni sounded sincere. "May the Fates grant your wishes tonight." He clapped Eric on his back.

"Thank you."

Kaia

s yet another clan member stopped Kaia and William on the way to the lab, she already knew what he was going to say. She'd heard it from five other people in the last fifteen minutes, and if the pattern continued, it would take them another hour to get to a destination that was ten minutes away.

"Congratulations on finding each other," the guy said. "I wish you and your family the best of luck with your transitions."

"Thank you. I appreciate the support," she repeated the same answer she'd given all the other well-wishers.

"You must be very popular." She took William's hand. "I don't get how everyone already knows about my family and me being here. I just got here yesterday, and my family arrived the night before."

"Rumors spread fast in the village." William forced a tight smile.

For some reason he was a ball of stress, and she didn't know how to calm him down. Well, she knew the reason for his anxiety. He was afraid of her encountering problems while transitioning, but he shouldn't take so seriously the few moments of panic she'd experienced. It was natural for her to fear the unknown, and it hadn't been a premonition because she'd gotten over it. When a premonition was real, it held her in its grip until it came to pass.

William had met with Kian early this morning, and when he'd returned, he'd said that he would tell her about it later. Her suspicion was that the boss had refused to ask the goddess to shorten her trip to Scotland, and that was why William was so anxious.

When they finally made it to the elevator, and no one got inside with them, Kaia leaned against the wall and let out a breath. "Is everyone usually this friendly and welcoming toward potential Dormants?"

"People here are friendly, and since living here is like living on an island, new faces are welcome, but I've never seen them react like that to a newcomer." He smiled shyly. "I didn't know so many people were rooting for me to find my truelove mate."

"You are their lovable tech guy who makes their lives easier."

As she was about to pull him into her arms, the elevator door opened, and William took her hand. "Some would argue that I make their lives more complicated." He led her out of the elevator. "I designed the security measures in the village, and they are not easy to live with."

Things looked pretty utilitarian on the lab level, but there were no well-wishers lurking down the hall, and Kaia let out a relieved breath.

"They should be thankful for that." She lifted on her toes and kissed his cheek. "If not for your ingenious system, Kian wouldn't let them out of the village. Your security measures allow them the freedom to come and go as they please."

"Not everyone thinks things through like you do." He put his hands on her waist. "People, even immortals, only see what's in front of them, and they rarely bother to get to the bottom of things."

Kaia lifted her hand and stroked his cheek with the tips of her fingers. "They love you and appreciate you, so I don't think you are right about your fellow clan members. They are well aware of what you do for them." She pressed a soft kiss to his lips. "Are you ready to show me your domain?"

He nodded, but his brows remained drawn together.

"I thought you would be more excited about showing me your lab."

"I am excited, but my worry over your imminent transition puts a dark shadow over everything."

She sighed. "I assume that Kian said no to asking his mother to come back?"

"He didn't say no, but he didn't say yes either. He's going to tell her about you and your family, and hopefully, she'll be curious enough to shorten her trip to come to see you."

"That's good news, right?"

"It's not as good as if he called her right then and there, and she promised to return immediately. That was what I hoped for."

"It's just a silly blessing, and there is another god in the village who can give it to me. We can ask Darlene to ask her grandfather on my behalf."

"Kian assured me that Toven is just as capable as Annani in the blessing department and that he helped strengthen his mate even before her transition. She had a heart problem."

Kaia shook her head. "Toven's mate was a human?"

"She was a Dormant."

"Are you saying that Toven mystically healed her heart condition even before she attempted transition?"

"Correct."

All that talk about blessings made Kaia nervous.

Did the gods put their hands on those they blessed? Was that how they transferred their healing energy?

Suspending disbelief wasn't difficult for her on a theoretical level. The universe was full of mysteries yet to be discovered, and she didn't like to dismiss anything unless it was completely ridiculous. But it wasn't as easy to do when her life was on the line.

"Then we have nothing to worry about, right?" Kaia affected a bright smile and took William's hand. "Toven is obviously powerful enough to help me."

He gave her hand a light squeeze. "I can hear the uncertainty in your voice, Kaia. Don't try to be brave for my sake, and don't dismiss your premonitions. What are you feeling? Are you still apprehensive?"

She put her hand on her belly. "It's not as bad as it was yesterday, but it is still here."

Syssi

"I wonder if Bridget has the results already," Syssi said as Amanda's car drove itself into the tunnel.

"She would have called you if she did."

Syssi sighed. "Yeah, I know. I'm just anxious to find out whether Eric and Gilbert are Dormants. I prayed to the Fates to make it so."

She'd been checking her phone throughout the day and had even considered calling the doctor, but that would have been counterproductive. Bridget would have called her as soon as she found out whether Eric and Gilbert were related to her.

Unless Bridget had the results and they were negative, and she didn't want to deliver the bad news over the phone.

When her phone rang and Bridget's name appeared on the screen, Syssi's heart did an anxious little flip. "It's Bridget."

"Answer it." Amanda turned to look at their daughters who were sleeping in the backseat. "The ringing will wake up the babies."

With shaking hands, Syssi accepted the call. "Hello, Bridget. What's the verdict?"

"You are related to Gilbert and Eric. They are Dormants. Naturally, the same goes for their sister."

"Yay!" Amanda pumped her fist in the air. "We have twin boys for our girls."

"Thank you for letting me know," Syssi said. "Did you call them?"

"I called you first. I thought you would want to deliver the good news yourself."

Syssi cast a sidelong look at Amanda. "Can you take care of Allegra while I pay Gilbert and Karen a visit?"

"Sure thing. I have Dalhu and Onidu to help me at home."

Syssi was still uncomfortable leaving Allegra alone with Okidu even though Annani had told her the Odus had practically raised her children. Unlike her, Amanda seemed fine with Onidu watching Evie, which was surprising, given how anxious she'd been about having another child when she'd first discovered that she was pregnant.

Both of them couldn't wait for Annani to return and spend time with their daughters so they could transition and become indestructible.

Syssi nodded her thanks to Amanda before returning to Bridget. "We are minutes away from the village parking, and I can stop by their place on my way home."

"What about Eric?" Bridget asked.

"If he's not there, I'll ask Gilbert to call him. I don't want to deliver news like this over the phone."

It just didn't seem right. This would change their lives completely, and not all of it was positive.

Aside from the danger that everyone was aware of, there were other issues that needed to be addressed. Karen would need to quit a job that she loved because she couldn't bring her nanny to the village, Gilbert would need to change the way he managed his business or close it down, Cheryl would have to change schools, and so would Idina.

As Amanda eased her new Mercedes SUV into her parking spot, Onidu rushed over to take the double stroller and other baby paraphernalia out of the trunk.

By the time Syssi and Amanda got out of the car, he was already unbuckling Evie's car seat. A moment later, both baby carriers were on the stroller, and they were ready to go.

"I feel sorry for Karen." Amanda sauntered behind Onidu in her high heels. "Taking care of twins without help is going to be tough, especially since she's not used to it. She and Gilbert hired their nanny when Idina was born, and she has been with them ever since."

"When did you get a chance to talk to her?"

"I met her yesterday at the playground. She brought Idina and the boys to play with Phoenix and Ethan. It was heartwarming to see so many little ones at the playground. I wish Kian could have seen it."

He would have loved it.

When the playground had been incorporated into the village square's design, it had been pure wishful thinking on Kian's part that one day it would be teeming with children. Seeing his optimism pay off would make him happy.

"You should have called us." Syssi followed the butler with the stroller into the elevator. "We would have brought Allegra over."

Amanda was the last to enter and pressed the button for the ground level. "When I got to the playground, it was nearly seven in the evening, and they were getting ready to leave."

"Maybe we can organize another playground meetup later today."

"Count me in." Amanda waited for the door to open and stepped out into the pavilion. "I'll walk with you to their house."

They both lived in the newest part of the village, while Gilbert and Karen were staying in phase two, which wasn't on the way, but Syssi was glad for the company.

"What were you doing in the playground at seven in the evening?" she asked.

Amanda lifted a brow. "You seriously don't know?"

"Know what?"

Was Amanda planning a surprise party? And if she was, for whom?

Amanda shook her head. "The village rumor machine is strange. I was sure someone would spill and tell you about Eric's ceremony tonight."

Syssi stopped in her tracks. "What are you talking about? He doesn't even know that he's a Dormant yet."

"Apparently, Eric's so convinced that he's a Dormant that he didn't want to wait. Max volunteered to be his inducer and also to make all the arrangements for the ceremony. Naturally, he came to me for help, but I told him that I no longer had the energy to organize parties and gave him pointers on how to do it himself."

Shaking her head, Syssi resumed walking. "We rode together to work, we spent all day together, and you didn't think to mention it to me?"

Amanda winced. "I hoped you wouldn't hear about it until you got the results. I knew you would start stressing about it and try to talk Eric out of attempting it before he was confirmed as a Dormant."

"So what? You should have told me."

"I know." Amanda cast her an apologetic look. "Can you forgive me?" She added a quivering lower lip.

"Oh, stop it." Syssi slapped her arm. "I know that you're not sorry at all."

Eric

Eric's gut clenched as he read Gilbert's text. "The results are in." He looked up at Darlene.

Her hand flew to her chest. "Don't keep me in suspense. Are you related to Syssi or not?"

"Gilbert didn't say. Syssi is at their place, and she's waiting for me to get there so she can tell us together."

Darlene frowned. "Then it's probably a no. No one makes such a big deal out of good news." She gave him a small smile. "But that doesn't mean that you are not a Dormant. You might have the immortal genes without being related to Syssi."

"True." Eric pushed to his feet and offered her a hand up. "Let's find out."

She took it and let him pull her to her feet. "I need to tell William that I'm leaving."

"He and Kaia probably got the same text." He opened the door of her tiny office.

It was a converted closet, but Darlene didn't mind. She was just glad to have a space of her own to work in that was more than a desk tucked into some dusty corner of the main lab. She'd decorated it with two tiny plants, one large landscape painting that served as a fake window, and several framed photographs of Roni at different ages.

The guy hadn't been cute, even as a small boy.

Roni looked pissed in all his photos, and Eric wondered whether Darlene's ex had been as abusive toward him as he'd been toward her. It wasn't fun being around a person who tried to put you down, especially when you were much smarter than the jerk trying to make you feel bad about yourself.

Darlene's so-called office was inside William's larger one, and as they walked out of hers, they found William and Kaia getting ready to leave as well.

"Did you also get a text from Gilbert?" Eric asked Kaia.

"Yeah." She tucked her phone inside her wallet purse. "I don't know why Bridget told Syssi first. I hate the suspense."

Roni swiveled his Batman-like chair around. "You'll find out the results in five minutes. Text me when you do."

"You can come as well," Darlene said. "In a way, it involves you too."

He waved a dismissive hand. "I don't like family drama." Roni smiled at Eric. "Best of luck."

"Thank you," Eric said. "I appreciate it."

What he appreciated even more than the good-luck wish was the smile Roni gave him. He had a feeling that the guy didn't smile often, and never just to be nice to someone he didn't like.

It was a good sign that Roni was making an effort to be friendly, even if it was just for his mother's sake.

When they got to Karen and Gilbert's place, the door was wide open, and through it he saw his brother pacing while Syssi and Karen sat on the couch and talked quietly.

"Here you are." Gilbert threw his hands in the air. "What took you so long?"

"We came as soon as we received the text." Kaia entered the room and zeroed in on Syssi. "Now that we are all here, you can tell us the verdict."

Syssi grinned. "I'm happy to welcome you all into the family. Gilbert and Eric are my third cousins."

"Thank goodness." Kaia dropped into the chair William pulled out for her. "I had heart palpitations on the way here." She cast Syssi a mock glare. "Did you forget that we are still human? We can't take stress like that."

Syssi laughed. "You're nineteen. You can handle it."

"Yeah, I might be able to. But my mother, Gilbert, and Eric are no spring chickens, and neither is Darlene." Kaia slanted a look at Darlene. "You're still hot, though."

"Thank you." Darlene looked embarrassed. "I hope to look much hotter once I transition."

Eric pulled out a dining chair for her. "I think you're hot too, and I wouldn't mind keeping you just the way you are forever, but since that's not on the table, I'll have to resign myself to a younger version of you."

Looking unsure whether he meant it or not, Darlene narrowed her eyes at him. "Says the guy who dated twenty-year-olds up until two weeks ago. I'm sure you'll like the younger version of me better."

Kaia

E ric looked like he was about to spout more compliments for Darlene when Syssi lifted her hand to stop him. "Does your family know about the induction ceremony tonight?"

Gilbert chuckled. "I tried to talk him out of it before, but now that we know for sure that he's a confirmed Dormant, I'm glad he rushed to secure himself an inducer."

"I thought you were joking," Kaia said. "Is Max seriously arranging your ceremony and initiating you? Since when are the two of you best buddies?"

Max had his eye on Darlene, and he'd flirted with her even though he knew she was seeing Eric. There was no way he was now supporting Eric so enthusiastically. The Guardian was a nice guy, but no one was that selfless.

"They are not buddies." Darlene grimaced. "And it seems strange to me too that Max is doing all of that for a rival."

Syssi's lips lifted in a surprised smile. "Were you dating Max before you met Eric?"

"I wasn't, but Max was hopeful." Darlene looked at William. "Probably with your encouragement."

William lifted his hands in the universal peace sign. "In my defense, I didn't know that Eric would turn out to be Syssi's distant relative. I wanted you to find a nice immortal to partner with, and I happen to like Max. He's a good guy, and there is no way he's doing this for some nefarious motives. Maybe he feels guilty for trying to steal you away from Eric."

"When is the ceremony?" Kaia asked to stop the argument.

"It will start at eleven at night and end a little after midnight." Eric took Darlene's hand and brought it to his lap. "A nice lady at the café explained that it is done at that hour to symbolize a new beginning."

"Who did you talk to?" Syssi asked. "Was it Amanda?"

"It was the nurse," Darlene said. "I forgot her name."

"Gertrude?" William asked.

"Yeah, that's the one."

"Gertrude is very knowledgeable," Syssi said. "She worked with Doctor Bridget for many years, and now she also works with Doctor Merlin, helping him with his fertility potions. She grows herbs in her garden."

The name sounded familiar. Wasn't she the one William had said would run the clinic in Safe Haven?

If she worked with the other doctor to brew fertility potions, she might be helpful in more ways than one.

Except, Kaia was no longer in a rush to get pregnant.

She had to transition first. Heck, they also needed to get married before they had children, but throwing a wedding into a mix of explosive issues would create a nuclear bomb.

Her mother and Gilbert were finally warming up to William and accepting him as her partner, but if she threw in wedding plans, they would once again suspect that he had some kind of unhealthy influence on her.

In fact, she wondered why no one had brought it up yet. Now that they knew that immortals could thrall and compel humans, it must have occurred to them that William could have done it to her.

Not that he ever would, but they didn't know him as well as she did.

"I'll certainly plan to attend." Syssi flipped her long hair over her shoulder. "Is Max planning a party for you after the ceremony?"

"I don't know," Eric said. "We haven't spoken since yesterday. I should check with him."

"If he didn't, we could have a small party in here," Karen looked at Gilbert. "We should take a nap, or we will fall on our faces staying up so late."

He patted her knee. "If Cheryl agrees to watch the little ones, we might be able to steal an hour or two of shuteye before the ceremony."

As everyone turned to look at Cheryl, she shrugged. "Fine. Provided that you let me sleep as late as I want tomorrow."

"It's a deal," Gilbert said.

Syssi rose to her feet. "Kian will be there as well, and Amanda and her mate." She slung the strap of her purse over her shoulder. "I need to start looking for a babysitter." She smiled at Cheryl. "If Eric wasn't your uncle, and you didn't need to be at the ceremony, I would have paid you to babysit Allegra. We have a shortage of experienced babysitters in the village."

Cheryl's eyes widened with two dollar signs popping up on her irises. "Pencil me in for your future babysitting needs."

"I will." Syssi smiled. "I'll see you all later tonight."

When everyone rose to their feet, and a round of hugs and congratulations ensued, Kaia thought about the implications of her mother, Gilbert, and Eric transitioning. Except for Cheryl, who was eager to start a babysitting business in the village, no one was mentioning the future. What were they going to do about their living and work arrangements?

Perhaps it was time to discuss it.

William

After Syssi left, Kaia went to the kitchen and a moment later returned with a pack of Coke cans. "Anyone want a Coke?"

"I do," Cheryl said.

"I should check on the little ones." Karen rose to her feet. "It's way too quiet over there."

"I thought they were napping," Darlene said.

"They are watching a kids' show." Gilbert walked over to the fridge and took out a pack of beers. "Let's celebrate."

It was Coors Light, which was like drinking soda for William, but he didn't want to be the odd man out, so he accepted what Gilbert was offering.

"I should check with Max about his plans for the ceremony." Eric pulled out his phone. "I don't think I'll be in any state to celebrate after he beats me up and bites me, and I don't want you to organize a get-together if I'm going to be passed out." He looked at Gilbert. "Unless you want to do that regardless of my state."

"It's going to be way past midnight, and I'd rather go to sleep." Gilbert offered a can of beer to Karen, who'd returned from checking up on the kids. "Let's make a toast now." He clinked his can with hers. "To all of us making it through the transition."

"Hold on." Eric was still typing on his phone. "Okay, I'm ready." He put the device back in his pocket and lifted his beer. "To everyone successfully turning immortal." He clinked his can with Darlene's and then with Kaia's. "Did you and William start working on it?"

William felt his cheeks warm up, but Kaia remained unfazed. "Yeah." She cast him an apologetic smile. "Sometimes my family lacks boundaries."

He chuckled. "Mine is way worse. Wait until you get settled in the village, and people feel comfortable with you. Even your ears will catch fire hearing them talk. Immortals are not shy about their sexuality."

"That's actually refreshing." Kaia gave him a seductive look before turning to her mother. "Did any of you give any thought to what you'll be doing once everyone's transitioned? We can't go back to our old lives."

"I don't see why not." Karen put her beer down on the dining room table. "I talked with Nathalie, Syssi's sister-in-law, and she told me that Syssi's brother still works at the same Homeland Security department he did before his transition. If he can do that, so can I."

"Not really," Kaia said. "You can get away with suddenly looking younger with a story about an excellent plastic surgeon, but for how long?"

Karen chuckled. "At least a couple of decades. Just look at the actresses on the big screen and on television. Some of them are in their mid-fifties and look twenty years younger."

"You're deluding yourself." Kaia took a long sip from her coke. "You are forty-five, and in two decades, you will be sixty-five. Given how everyone here looks, you will look twenty years younger than you are now. Do you really think you could pull it off for that long? You couldn't do that even for one decade."

Karen grimaced. "I'm not the type who can be satisfied with staying home and raising kids. I'll go crazy."

"Perhaps you can work remotely?" Darlene suggested. "What is it that you do?"

"I'm a system administrator. I'm responsible for managing the IT infrastructure of the organization. Some of it can be done remotely, but not all."

"Maybe William could use your skills?" Darlene turned to him. "Do you need a system administrator?"

He shook his head. "We are a small operation. Only large organizations with many users need someone like that. Using Karen's skills for our network would be like getting a surgeon to put bandages on scraped knees. It's not going to be satisfying for her."

"I see." Darlene turned to Karen. "What about a change of careers? How much do you love what you do?"

"Love is not the right word for how I feel about my job. It's fascinating, I have access to revolutionary technologies the public has no idea about, and I'm very good at what I do. To give it up will be a big sacrifice for me."

Kaia groaned. "I know that it will be painful for you to give it up, but no job is worth giving up immortality for."

Karen smiled sadly. "That's absolutely true, but that's not the only reason I might not wish to transition." She tilted her head in the direction of the hallway. "I have three little kids to take care of and two lovely older daughters who have already lost a father and who I don't want to leave without a mother."

Kaia paled. "So, what are you saying? That you are not going to do it?"

"I need more time to think about it, and so does Gilbert." Karen took her mate's hand. "We talked about it, and we decided to go back home as soon as we know that you are no longer in danger."

"What if I transition smoothly?" Eric looked at Gilbert. "Will that convince you to give it a try?"

Gilbert turned to Karen. "Not without the love of my life. If Karen doesn't want to risk it, I won't either."

As William felt a wave of panic coming from Kaia, he gave her hand a squeeze. "I think that the dangers of transition are overstated. We haven't lost a transitioning

Dormant yet, and that was when we had only one goddess to give them her blessing. We have two now, and with their combined power, the chance we will lose one now is negligible."

Did he believe what he'd just said?

Not really.

If he did, he wouldn't be so stressed about Kaia's impending transition. It was true that the clan hadn't lost a transitioning Dormant yet, but there was always a first time for everything. That being said, he didn't think that Karen and Gilbert should give up immortality. Gilbert was a confirmed Dormant, and if Kaia transitioned, Karen would be confirmed as well. Their fears were not unjustified, but they were overblown.

Darlene

The crowd Eric and Darlene found in the gym surprised them both.

The place looked like a wedding venue, just without the nice tablecloths, the fancy dishes, or the decorations.

Large circular tables were arranged around a roped-off wrestling mat, and there were enough bottles of whiskey and beer on each one to get even a bunch of immortal males drunk. A few soft drink bottles and some bar-style snacks had been included as well, but they seemed like an afterthought.

Given the no-frills and plenty of booze theme, it was pretty obvious that the event had been organized by a guy, but given the time Max had to put the event together, it was admirable nonetheless.

"Why are all these people here?" Eric whispered in her ear. "Are they all eager to see the human get his butt kicked?"

"Maybe they are here for the free booze," Darlene offered an alternative. "These immortals like to drink. Roni often invites people over for barbecues on weekends, and I get drunk just from watching the quantities of alcohol they consume."

From the corner of her eye, Darlene saw Amanda heading their way and turned to greet her.

"Good evening." She extended her hand to Kian's sister. "I'm glad you could make it."

"I couldn't help but overhear." Amanda shook it lightly. "Neither the booze nor the wish to see the human getting his butt kicked is the reason for so many coming to watch the ceremony tonight." She turned to Eric and offered him her hand. "I'm Amanda, Kian's sister."

"Enchanted." He smiled at her way too brightly for Darlene's liking and lifted her hand to his lips for a kiss.

"Come and join Dalhu and me at our table, and I'll explain why half of the village is here tonight even though most of them don't know you."

They might not have known Eric, but it wasn't hard to guess that the new guy wearing track pants and a sleeveless sport shirt was the Dormant who was about to get induced, and they also knew Darlene and that he was her chosen. As they walked toward Amanda's table, people smiled and murmured words of encouragement, to which Eric responded with his usual charm.

Her guy knew how to work a room.

"This is Dalhu," Amanda introduced her hulking mate. "My better half."

He rose to his feet, towering over everyone, and offered Eric his hand. "Good luck."

"Thank you." Eric pulled out a chair for Darlene. "Am I allowed to drink before my initiation?"

"I don't see why not." Dalhu picked one of the whiskey bottles. "Are you familiar with this one?"

Eric nodded. "It's good."

Dalhu filled up a glass, handed it to Eric, and looked at Darlene. "Would you like some?"

"No, thank you. I don't like whiskey."

"Neither do I." Amanda waited for Eric to take a sip. "There are several reasons for the impressive turnout, and none are about seeing the poor human getting bested by an immortal, or the free drinks. We don't celebrate birthdays, and very few of us bother with wedding parties, so these initiation ceremonies are an excellent excuse for us to gather and celebrate."

"Sounds reasonable," Eric said. "But no one knows me."

Amanda smiled. "That brings me to reason number two. By now, everyone has heard about the family of potential Dormants visiting the village, and when the rumor spread about you and your brother being confirmed relatives of Syssi, they wanted to get to know you. Reason number three is Max, who's a Guardian, so naturally all of his Guardian friends are here for him. The ceremony is mostly about the Dormant, but it's also about his inducer. You and Max are about to pledge eternal friendship to each other, and it's a big deal. Most clan members don't have siblings, and the ceremony gives men a wonderful opportunity to form brotherly bonds."

Darlene stifled a wince.

Eric's idea of a threesome with Max was kinky enough. Adding to the mix, a brotherly bond between the two men she was supposed to have sex with was over the top.

"Where is Max?" Eric asked. "Is he hiding in seclusion like a bride, waiting for everyone to arrive so he can make a grand entrance?"

"Probably." Amanda took a bottle of tequila and poured herself a shot. "I'm so glad that I'm no longer breastfeeding. I can indulge in some alcohol now."

Darlene frowned. "If Max is waiting to make his entry, who will lead the ceremony?"

"Kian, of course." Amanda poured another glass for Darlene. "Well, he always leads the first attempt, but if a repeat is needed, the second event is much more casual, and someone else might lead the ceremony."

"I won't need a repeat." Eric crossed his arms over his chest. "It's happening tonight."

Amanda smiled indulgently. "Every Dormant thinks that, and yet some need to make several attempts to activate their immortal genes."

"So I've heard. But I can feel it in my gut that it's happening for me tonight." Eric tapped his washboard abs.

Not wanting to dampen his mood, Darlene chose to keep her mouth shut, but she doubted that tonight's initiation would work.

She didn't know Max's lineage and how far or close he was to the source. In any case, he wouldn't have been her first choice as an inducer for Eric.

Darlene would have preferred Kian or Orion to do that. But Orion was still with Alena and Annani in Scotland, and she couldn't ask Kian. If Max failed to induce Eric, though, she would beg Shai to plead with Kian on her behalf.

Could Toven induce him?

She wasn't sure. A god's venom might be too potent, or its aggressive formulation might not be suitable for inducing a male Dormant. She needed to ask Toven whether any of the male gods bothered with initiating Dormants back in the day, but she was quite sure that the answer was no. The immortals of that time had still been very close to the source, and there had been enough of them to induce all the Dormants.

The gods had most likely considered themselves too lofty to bother with their lowly descendants.

Kaia

"Look at this." Kaia waved a hand at the transformed gym. "It seems like the party started without us."

The exercise equipment had been pushed aside, and about fourteen round tables had been brought in and arranged around the fighting arena. With sixteen chairs surrounding each table, there was room for over two hundred people, and more than half of the seats were already taken.

"We are not late." William led her through the tables toward where Eric and Darlene were sitting with a stunning brunette and a dude with shoulders the size of an entry door.

He was so big that he probably needed to duck and turn sideways to fit through a standard-size doorway. Perhaps that was why no one else was sitting at their table. The guy looked intimidating.

Naturally, Eric was perfectly at ease with that mountain of a man, talking with the guy as if they had known each other from high school.

"Hello." The brunette smiled at Kaia. "I was wondering when I would get to meet the famous bioinformatician who stole our William's heart."

Kaia returned her smile. "So far, the only new clan members I've met have been in William's lab."

"Why am I not surprised?" The brunette cast William a mock angry glare and rose to her stiletto-clad feet.

She was so tall in those shoes that she towered over Kaia, which didn't happen often.

The woman pulled her into a tight embrace. "I'm Amanda. Kian's sister." She let go as quickly as she'd attacked and turned around. "This is Dalhu, my mate and the love of my life."

He let out a breath, looking embarrassed about the flowery introduction his mate had given him. "Nice to meet you. Good luck with your transition."

"Thank you." She sat on the chair William had pulled out for her.

"Did you start working on it already?" Amanda asked.

Kaia wanted to roll her eyes. William had warned her about his people's open attitudes toward sex, but she'd thought he was exaggerating so she wouldn't feel bad about Eric throwing that same question at them.

No wonder Eric felt right at home with these people. They also didn't have personal boundaries.

She gave Amanda a slight nod. "Is there an induction ceremony for girls? It would save everyone the trouble of asking if they'd started working on their transition. I'm not shy, but for some, it might be embarrassing."

Amanda snorted. "You are absolutely right. We should have a ceremony for females as well. The problem is that most of the adult female Dormants who have transitioned so far started working on it before knowing that they were Dormants, so maybe the party should be held after the transition."

"What about the clan girls? Don't they deserve to have a party?"

William had told her that they transitioned at a young age, but that didn't preclude throwing a party to celebrate the start of the process, especially since the clan didn't celebrate birthdays.

If Kaia transitioned and became a member, she would change that. Birthdays should be celebrated even if a person had thousands of them.

Amanda tapped a finger on her lower lip. "That's actually not a bad idea. The girls are too young to understand that their little bodies are going through a change, but that doesn't mean that their transition shouldn't be celebrated by those who love them and care for them. I'll talk it over with Syssi. Once my mother returns to the village, Allegra will start spending time with her, so that could count as the start of her transition. We should throw her a big party."

"What about Evie?" Dalhu asked. "Will she start spending time with your mother as well?"

"Of course, but she's too little to be affected by Annani's proximity. We need to wait a few more months."

"Syssi said that she and Kian would come." Kaia turned around to look at the gym's entrance. "My mother and Gilbert are also supposed to be here."

"Are they bringing your younger siblings along?" Amanda asked. "This may be frightening to them."

"Cheryl, my sister, agreed to babysit in exchange for a large sum of money and Gilbert's promise to record the entire match."

Amanda chuckled. "Tell your sister that she will have many clients willing to pay large sums for an experienced babysitter."

"Syssi told her that already," Kaia said.

William wrapped his arm around her shoulders. "You wanted to see a god." He motioned with his chin. "Toven just walked in with Mia."

Kaia's heart lurched into her throat, and she whipped her head around to get her first glimpse.

"Wow. I thought that Kian looked like a god. But this guy is the real thing."

Toven was so perfect that it was disturbing.

Amanda snorted. "My brother is more handsome than him, and I'm not saying that because of sisterly love. Kian is more manly. Toven is a little too soft."

There was nothing soft about the god's predatory gait or the way he scanned the room for danger. People skittered aside to let him and his mate through, and it wasn't just because of the motorized wheelchair she was driving.

There was an air of danger and power about him that Kaia could feel from more than a hundred feet away, and the lack of glow William had told her about wasn't enough to detract from Toven's otherworldly perfection.

Eric

E
ric stared at Darlene's grandfather, searching for the familial resemblance, but other than similar coloring, they had very little in common.

Darlene was a beautiful woman, but she was not in the same league as her grandfather. Toven was so damn perfect that Eric found it impossible to take his eyes off him.

Despite his willingness to experiment, Eric had never been attracted to other men, and even when his threesome adventures included another guy, they had always been about the woman. But if both he and Toven were single, and the god was interested, Eric wasn't sure he would have refused an invitation.

What was it like to be a god? To be so perfect that people just wanted to be near you, look at you, touch you? No wonder the mythological gods had been a bunch of entitled divas.

Except, that wasn't the vibe he was getting from Toven.

The guy didn't look stuck up or even aware of his physical superiority. Perhaps he was so used to the stares that he no longer noticed them.

Eric wasn't sure what he'd expected the god to look like, but in addition to physical perfection, he'd imagined his expression to be peaceful, maybe a little bored, and more than somewhat condescending. He didn't expect Toven to look discontented, especially since he had his mate by his side, and he hadn't expected him to look unhappy either.

The god proved what Eric had always suspected.

Happiness had very little to do with external factors. Everyone had their innate happiness setting, and even a god who had everything a human could ever dream of couldn't change it.

"I'm so glad the two of you could make it." Darlene rose to her feet and leaned to kiss Toven's mate on the cheek.

Eric followed Darlene up and stood next to her, waiting for her to introduce him.

"How could we have missed it?" The girl smiled at him. "This will be my first time witnessing an induction ceremony."

Darlene put her arm around him. "Let me introduce the star of tonight's main event. This is Eric Emerson."

Plastering his best smile on his face, Eric offered his hand to Toven's mate. "It's a pleasure to meet you."

"The feeling is mutual." She put her delicate hand in his. "I'm Mia."

"Enchanted." Eric skipped on kissing the back of her hand as he would usually do.

If Toven was the jealous type, he didn't want to anger him, and not just because the dude was a powerful god capable of smiting him. He was Darlene's grandfather, and she valued his opinion.

Straightening, Eric offered his hand to Toven. "I don't know what the protocol for greeting a god is. Should I bow?"

Toven surprised him with a genuine smile. "No bowing, please. Ever." He took Eric's hand and shook it lightly.

Amanda chuckled. "The rules are a little different with my mother. A dip of the head is expected, and you should address her as Clan Mother. When she gets to know you better, she will tell you to call her Annani, but until then you should stick with Clan Mother."

"Annani always liked fanfare." Toven removed one of the chairs to make room for Mia's wheelchair. "But since she actually has a clan of people who look up to her, I guess it's appropriate." He sat down next to Mia.

She put a hand on his arm. "You have people who look up to you too. Geraldine and Orion and their kids and grandkids and so on. Your clan will grow, but since it will be intertwined with Annani's descendants, you two will have to come up with proper titles to reflect that."

He took her hand and lifted it to his lips for a kiss. "Fates willing, you and I are going to have children as well, and since they will be born immortal, we might start a clan of our own."

"Fates willing indeed," Amanda said as she lifted her head. "Kian and Syssi are here." She waved them over.

"Karen and Gilbert are right behind them," William said. "They must have met outside."

Toven turned to look at the newcomers.

"Good evening." Eric rose to his feet to greet Kian and Syssi.

"Good evening, cousin." Syssi grinned. "I'm so glad that I can finally say that. I never had cousins before."

"We are a family of renown." Gilbert walked over to Eric and clapped him on the back. "Right, brother?"

"Now more than ever." Eric winked at Syssi.

"Are you ready to begin the ceremony?" Kian asked.

"Max is not here yet." Eric looked around. "We can't start without him."

"He's here." Kian pointed at the table near the entrance. "He was ambushed by his friends the moment he walked in. That's why you didn't see him."

Eric craned his neck. "I see him now."

Darlene took his hand. "Are you sure you want to go through with this? I don't mean the transition, I mean your initiator. I'm still not comfortable with Max doing it."

"I'm sure." He smiled at her. "Max is a good man, and I'm the guy whose talent is staying alive. I will come out victorious on the other side."

Kian

No matter how many times Kian had recited the ceremonial words, he hadn't grown tired of them. They still evoked in him a sense of pride and continuity.

Usually the initiates were teenage boys, but there hadn't been many in recent years. In fact, there had been only one, and Parker wasn't born to the clan.

The last initiation ceremony Kian had presided over for one of the clan's boys had been Jackson's and before him Vlad's, and before that Gordon's. The other initiation ceremonies had been for the adult male Dormants who'd joined the clan, but there hadn't been many of those either.

For some reason, there had been a dearth of children in the last couple of decades.

Before Syssi's arrival, Kian had nearly given up hope, but then the Fates had taken mercy on his clan and compensated for the lack of children with an influx of Dormants and had followed up with several pregnancies.

Kalugal's son was the latest arrival, but maybe Kaia's twin brothers would be next. It was still unclear whether she was a Dormant, but Kian had faith in the Fates.

William had dedicated his life to the clan and to humanity's advancement, working day and night to develop new technologies that made everyone's lives better.

He deserved his happily-ever-after.

Besides, Kaia was so perfect for him that there was no way she hadn't been handpicked for William by the Fates.

When everyone in the audience was holding a glass of the ceremonial wine, Kian lifted his and waited until they quieted down.

"Once again, I've changed a few words to adjust for the circumstances, so please don't correct me when you think that I forgot the correct wording."

There were a few chuckles, and when Eric smiled nervously, Max put a hand on his shoulder.

Kian held his glass up as he addressed the crowd. "We are gathered here tonight to present this fine man to our community. Eric is ready to attempt his transformation, and since he's Syssi's cousin, an accomplished fighter jet pilot, and more importantly, Darlene's chosen, he doesn't need anyone to vouch for him."

Kian waited for the chuckles and cheers to subside.

"Max has already volunteered to assume the burden of initiating Eric into his immortality, but I need to ask again." He turned to the Guardian. "Are you sure that you want to be bound to Eric for eternity?"

Max slanted a glance at Eric. "I'm sure."

Kian nodded. "Eric, do you accept Max as your initiator? As your mentor and protector, to honor him with your friendship, your respect, and your loyalty from now on?"

When Eric looked surprised, Kian realized that no one had told him the extent of the mutual commitment Max and he were assuming.

Max lifted a brow. "Now you're having second thoughts?" He batted his eyelashes and put a hand over his chest. "If you abandon me at the altar, I'm never going to forgive you."

People laughed, but as the seconds ticked off, Max's amused expression tightened.

Darlene looked at Eric as he shook his head as if to clear the stupor and offered his hand to the Guardian. "Buddies forever."

When Max clasped it, Eric pulled him into a bro hug, and the two clapped each other on their backs.

"Forever." Max grinned. "But you have to say, I do, or it doesn't count."

"I do."

Kian continued, "Does anyone object to Eric becoming Max's protégé?" He looked around at the faces of those standing closest to him, and for a moment, it looked like Darlene was going to object, but then she shook her head, and he let out a relieved breath.

Raising his wine glass, Kian turned back to Max and Eric. "As everyone present agrees that this is a good match, let's seal it with a toast. To Eric and Max."

As cheers and hoots erupted from the Guardian section of the room, Kian wondered why this particular pairing was making them so excited.

The only adult Dormant to receive such enthusiastic cheers had been Michael.

Was it because Eric was a former soldier, a fighter like them?

Or was it because of Max?

The cheering went on for several minutes, and then Kian lifted his hand to silence everyone again.

"Let's begin. Gentlemen, please take your positions."

Darlene

It was done, and there was no going back. Max was going to induce Eric, and Darlene had a lump in her throat the size of a tennis ball.

She wanted to be close to the ring, but the table she was seated at was a little farther away, and people's backs were blocking her view. She thought about getting up and getting closer to the ring, but no one was standing, and she was embarrassed to be the only one.

The most she could do was turn her chair so she was facing it, but since those sitting in front of her were taller, she had to crane her neck to see what was going on.

Seeing her distress, William tapped the shoulder of the guy sitting at the table in front of her and blocking her view. "Can you move your chair a little? Darlene needs to see her mate's initiation."

"Of course." The guy scooted his chair aside.

As others did the same, creating a path for her to see the ring clearly, she mouthed her thanks to them.

Kian waited until the commotion was over before giving the signal for Max and Eric to begin, and as soon as he did, Eric lunged forward, diving for Max.

The Guardian hadn't been prepared for the swift attack, and when Eric collided with him, he went down like a rock.

Max had either been distracted by someone in the crowd, or he'd just pretended for Eric's sake, but Darlene didn't care how it had happened as long as Eric had his victorious moment.

"Go, Eric!" She shot to her feet and clapped.

Gilbert, Karen, and Kaia joined her, and even some of the immortals clapped their hands.

As soon as Max was down, Eric started throwing his fists at him, but the element of surprise didn't last. He managed to deliver only two punches before Max threw him off with a roar and went after him.

Darlene's heart sank into her gut.

What if Eric provoked Max into a killing frenzy?

Would the others stop the Guardian in time to save Eric?

Eric didn't give up easily, and he fought ferociously to keep Max from pinning him down, but he was no match for the Guardian's superior strength and training.

Darlene doubted that even a minute had passed before Max had Eric pinned face down on the mat and immobilized. But instead of the fury she'd expected to see on the Guardian's face, Max was grinning.

It did nothing to assuage her fears, though. With his fangs fully elongated and dripping venom, the grin made Max look even more terrifying.

How could any woman find that arousing?

Was she expected to have sex with a monster like that? To let him bite her with those sharp fangs?

Not going to happen.

"I'm never transitioning," she murmured under her breath.

Still grinning, Max hissed through his fangs, "If you wanted to be on top, all you had to do was ask." He struck Eric's neck.

Eric didn't make a sound, but Darlene's breath caught in her throat.

She wasn't the only one.

Everyone in the audience was holding their breath with her, and as the seconds ticked off, the silence stretching over the gym became so oppressive that Darlene couldn't force air into her lungs.

She was getting lightheaded when Kian lifted his hand.

"That's enough," he broke the silence.

Max immediately retracted his fangs and treated the wounds with a long lick.

"You can go to Eric now," Syssi said. "It will take him a couple of minutes to wake up, and he will be loopy when he does."

As Darlene ran into the ring and ducked under the rope, Max turned Eric on his back with surprising gentleness.

"He did really well." The Guardian smiled at her. "You should be proud of him."

With his fangs already half-retracted, he looked a little less terrifying, but she didn't want him anywhere near Eric. "I got him now. You can go."

"What, no 'thank you'?" He leaned away to make room for her.

"Thank you," she gritted out as she checked that Eric was still breathing.

Max crouched next to her and said quietly. "You can sit on the mat and put his head in your lap. That's what mothers of transitioning boys usually do." He winked before pushing up to his feet.

Kicking her shoes off, she did as he'd suggested and sat cross-legged on the mat with Eric's head resting in her lap.

"Someone should have told me what I was supposed to do," she murmured as she stroked his hair.

Somehow, there wasn't a mark on him, and she wondered how that was possible. Had Max even punched him? Or had he just wrestled Eric down?

Bridget ducked under the rope and crouched next to them. "How are you doing?"

Darlene frowned. "You're asking me? Eric is the one who was just bitten."

"He's fine. I can hear his heartbeat and his breathing. But you're as white as a sheet."

"I'm okay now," she whispered.

Thankfully, now that the initiation was over, it was no longer quiet in the gym, and other than the doctor no one made a move to intrude on her and Eric's space. Was that also part of the custom?

"Max was very careful with Eric," Bridget said. "Which isn't easy for an immortal once they are provoked. He was a good choice."

"We didn't choose him. He volunteered." Darlene looked at Eric's smiling face in puzzlement. "Why does he look so happy after getting beaten?"

"It's the venom. It's the one time Eric gets to experience the euphoric high of a venom bite. Don't be surprised if he wakes up randy. The venom is also an aphrodisiac."

"I thought that it only worked like that on females."

"To a lesser extent, it has a similar effect on males. That's how they are incapacitated in a fight. The venom does not paralyze them. It's like a drug. They know what's going on, but they don't care. It takes away their will to do anything but soar on the euphoric cloud."

"So it's not deadly?"

"Oh, it definitely could be. If Max had kept pumping more venom into Eric's system, he could have stopped his heart. Kian stopped him just in time."

Kaia

"Have you talked with Eric today?" William leaned against the dresser as Kaia pulled her clothes out of the drawers and spread them over the bed.

She and William and her entire family were invited to Friday dinner at Kian and Syssi's home, and her mother wanted them all to dress nicely, but Kaia had nothing that would pass her mother's approval.

"I didn't. He was hiding in Darlene's office all day, and I didn't want to annoy him by asking him again if anything was happening. Why? Did Darlene say something to you?"

"No." William sighed. "It looks like Eric will have to choose another initiator and do it again."

Almost three days had passed since Eric's ceremony, and he was getting frustrated and taking it out on anyone who asked him if he was feeling anything.

Nothing was happening with Kaia either, but supposedly it took longer for females to start transitioning, so she wasn't worried yet.

Looking at the selection of clothes on the bed, she groaned. "I still don't have anything nice to wear. I should have ordered something."

William hugged her from behind, draping himself over her and looking at the meager spread. "You could borrow that dress from Darlene again. You looked hot in it." He kissed her neck.

"That's not a bad idea. She wanted me to keep it, so I don't think she would mind loaning it to me again."

"If you want to get it from her, you should hurry up. There isn't much time left."

"I'll call her. Maybe she can drop it off here on her way to Syssi and Kian's. They need to pass by the house anyway, and I don't need a lot of time to get ready. I'll just pull it on, and I'll be ready to go."

"That's my girl." He kissed her neck again. "Effortlessly beautiful."

Kaia pulled out of his arms and turned around. "What are you going to wear?"

He looked down at his slacks. "I thought that I would just shower, shave, and get a clean shirt. Why?"

Kaia walked into the closet and pulled down the tux that was encased in a plastic bag. "I want to see you in this."

William chuckled. "I'll be way overdressed. Besides, it's probably too big on me. I lost weight since the last time I wore it."

She pouted. "I just want to see you wearing it. You can take it off later." She put her hands on his chest. "I have a thing for men in tuxes."

His eyes blazing with an inner light, he banded his arms around her and pulled her against his body. "I'm the only man in a tux you will have a thing for. You're mine."

"Oooh, I love it when you get all bossy." She lifted on her toes and kissed him. "But the effect would be even sexier when you are in a tux."

"Give it to me." He pulled the hanger out of her hand. "I'm putting it on right now."

"Shower first." She kissed the tip of his nose and pulled out of his arms. "Hurry up, though. I want to have my way with you before Darlene and Eric get here."

"Give me three minutes." He moved so fast that he was a blur.

Laughing, Kaia sat on the bed with her phone and made the call.

"Hi," Darlene answered. "Let me guess. You need to borrow a dress."

"How did you know? Is telepathy your talent?"

Darlene chuckled. "I wish. Do you want to come over and check out my closet again?"

"I'll just borrow the same dress I wore to the restaurant, and I was hoping you and Eric could stop by William's house on the way to Syssi and Kian's and bring the dress with you. It will take me thirty seconds to pull it on, and we can continue together."

"No problem. We can come over a few minutes earlier."

"Thanks, Darlene." Kaia hesitated before asking, "Anything?"

Darlene sighed. "Nothing. It didn't work."

"Don't sound so defeated. Eric is a confirmed Dormant, so it's going to happen."

"Yeah, I know. That's why I'm not freaking out yet. I guess you have nothing to report either?"

"Nope. But I'm not worried. William says that it takes longer for female Dormants to enter transition. But I get why Eric is so disappointed, though. I also thought that I would beat the statistics and start transitioning right away."

Kaia had hoped that being young and healthy, she would enter transition a day or two after they had started working on it, but it didn't look like it was happening.

"Yeah, I also heard that it takes a long time for females," Darlene said.

"Who did you ask?"

"Amanda. After Bridget, she's the best source of information on everything that has to do with immortals and

Dormants. When I want to know something, I hang around the café about the time she returns from work, and I ambush her when I see her passing through."

Kaia laughed. "The human ambushing the demigoddess. It sounds funny."

"First of all, I am not just a human. I am a demi-demigoddess. And secondly, it works. I pretend to just happen to be there, and while I walk home with her, I ask her all the questions I have."

Kaia crossed her legs and leaned her elbow on her knee. "Why can't you ask Roni? He's been with the clan for a while, and I'm sure he knows everything there is to know by now."

"Roni has no patience with his old mother, while Amanda is a teacher at heart, and she loves explaining things. She never makes me feel stupid for not understanding something."

Did Roni make Darlene feel stupid?

If so, the guy needed a talking-to, and she was just the girl to do it.

"If Amanda is so good at teaching, she should run a class for potential Dormants."

"I'm way ahead of you. I'm writing down everything I'm learning, and once I have it organized and proofread, I'll put it up on the clan's virtual bulletin board for anyone who needs it."

"That's a great initiative. When did you start?"

Darlene sighed. "Yesterday. I need to occupy my mind with something or I'll go crazy. Waiting for Eric's transition is nerve-wracking." She chuckled. "The funny thing is that I want him to be immortal, but at the same time, I don't."

Kaia frowned. "Why wouldn't you want him to transition?"

"Because once he does, he will grow fangs, and I'm not looking forward to getting bitten."

"Why? It's amazing."

"Doesn't it hurt?"

Kaia rolled her eyes. "Didn't Amanda explain it to you?"

"I didn't ask her about it. She's Annani's daughter. I can't ask her a personal question like that."

"What about your mother?"

Darlene snorted. "Do you want to talk with your mother about sex?"

"Not really. Anyway, the bite hurts a little, but because it is usually delivered as you are having a mind-blowing orgasm, the endorphins in your body make it barely noticeable, and then the venom takes care of everything, and all you feel is an intense pleasure. Let me put it this way. None of the sex you have had so far can prepare you for that. I'm trying to think of an analogy, but nothing profound comes to mind."

Darlene laughed. "Doctor Kaia Locke, I haven't known you long, but I've never heard you stumped for words to describe anything. If you say that it's indescribable, I don't need you to come up with an analogy. I get it."

William

William stood in front of the mirror in his walk-in closet and examined his reflection. The tux jacket was loose on him, and he had to add a belt to the slacks to keep them from sliding down, but he still looked better in it now than the last time he'd worn it.

His closet was full of clothes that needed to go to charity. He'd gotten several new items already, but he needed to get more that were suitable for social outings.

Perhaps he and Kaia could go shopping on Sunday. If they were invited to more social events, they both needed to get some nicer stuff than what they wore to work every day.

William had been invited to Friday dinner at Syssi and Kian's only once before. Usually, those evenings were reserved for close family time, but from time to time Syssi also invited close friends and newcomers, like she'd done today.

He wasn't a big fan of dinner parties, but he was actually looking forward to this one. Perhaps what made it different was that he was going with Kaia. It wasn't fun attending social gatherings where he was often the only bachelor, but now he belonged to the exclusive club of mated couples, and he felt like a new man.

William hadn't expected the boost in confidence that having Kaia at his side would provide. They were a team, and she had his back as much as he had hers. There would be no more awkward moments when he would catch too late that people were looking at him with glazed eyes and polite smiles. If he went off on a tangent about some tech problem he was working on, she would nudge him to make him aware of boring his audience, and if he had nothing else that was interesting to the others, he could sit back and let her do the talking.

Being mated to Kaia was blissful, and he was grateful to the Fates for finding him the perfect companion for his life journey.

Kaia knocked on the door. "Can I come in now?"

"Not yet." He pulled the bowtie out of the tux pocket and tied it around his neck with practiced fingers. "Now you can."

He turned around as she opened the door. "What do you think?" He spread his arms and turned in a circle. "Does the tux do it for you?"

"Oh, yeah." Kaia sauntered over to him and gripped the lapels. "Come here, you sexy man." She smashed her lips over his.

Closing his hands over her lush bottom, William hoisted her up and kissed her back, his tongue pushing into her mouth and caressing hers lovingly.

The doorbell ringing pulled a groan out of his throat. "Couldn't they have come fifteen minutes later?"

Kaia pulled away from him with a sigh. "I thought we had more time. I'll keep them busy while you change."

"Why?" He made another turn. "Don't you want to drool over your sexy man throughout dinner?"

The doorbell rang again.

"Ugh. I have to get the door." She pointed a finger at him. "Get changed, but you are wearing this tux again when we get home tonight. I have plans for it."

The husky command combined with her hooded-eyed promise had his shaft swell and pulse. "Yes, ma'am."

After Kaia ducked out of the closet, William considered spending a few moments to take the edge off. Given that they were going to spend the evening with his boss and Kaia's family, sporting a painful erection throughout dinner would not only be tortuous, but also disastrous.

No more than five minutes later, William got out of the closet wearing one of his new pairs of slacks, the button-down shirt he'd worn to his interview with Kaia, and a much calmer disposition.

When he got to the living room, he found her with Eric and Darlene, already wearing the sexy black dress, and her long blond hair cascading in soft waves down her back and front.

That was all Kaia needed to look exquisite. She didn't need makeup or jewelry or high heels to change from a pretty girl to a goddess. Releasing her hair from its customary ponytail and wearing a nice dress was all it took.

"You're breathtaking." He pulled her into his arms for a quick kiss.

"You clean up nicely too." She leaned away to give him a once-over. "I remember this shirt."

"Do you like it?"

"I love it. It's the perfect blend of dorky and stylish."

He wasn't sure that was a compliment, but she'd said she loved it, and that was all he cared about.

"Shall we?" Eric pushed to his feet and offered Darlene a hand up. "It's five minutes to seven."

William took Kaia's hand and followed the two out the door. "It's a two-minute walk to Syssi and Kian's place."

"Being on time means arriving five minutes early," Darlene said. "So we are already late."

William chuckled. "Even if we are, you have nothing to worry about because we won't be the last to arrive. Amanda is never on time."

"My family also believes in the five minutes early rule," Kaia said. "But since my younger siblings' arrival, my mother never manages to actually pull it off. She has to turn into a drill sergeant to get everyone ready and out the door."

Hearing the smile in her tone, William squeezed her hand. "But it's worth it, right?"

"Absolutely. I wouldn't have it any other way, and I want to have a large family too." The smile slid off her face. "But as Darlene has so astutely pointed out, I need to adjust my dreams and aspirations to my new reality. Given how long I will live, my life can't be centered around having children. Even if a miracle happens and we manage to have as many as I want, raising them would only take a tiny fraction of my life."

They'd already reached Kian and Syssi's house, but William halted before taking the steps to their front door.

"You are a brilliant scientist, Kaia, and just like me, you are driven by curiosity and the need to make new discoveries. I know that you want a large family, but your work must be just as important to you."

"It is." She smiled. "I'm not sad about having to shift my thinking and adjust the way I imagined my future. I'm just acknowledging it out loud." She leaned closer and kissed his lips. "I love you, and I want to spend eternity with you making discoveries, raising children, and having fun with our grandchildren and great-grandchildren and so on. Our journey is going to be awesome."

Syssi

S yssi sat at the head of the table with Kian by her side and marveled at the blessing the Fates had bestowed on her.

She considered Kian's family her own, but it was so nice to add several from her side.

Gilbert and Eric were talking with Andrew, and watching them together, she could actually see the family resemblance. It was in the way they held their bodies and even in their speech patterns. It proved how powerful nature was versus nurture.

Despite the generations separating them from their original maternal ancestor, they still exhibited similar traits. As for their paranormal talents, Gilbert claimed to have a good nose for crooks, and Eric claimed that his talent was staying alive, but those weren't necessarily paranormal abilities. Even if they were, they weren't nearly as strong or unusual as her foresight or Andrew's lie detecting.

She'd invited Toven and Mia and Kalugal and Jacki, but Kalugal had politely declined her invitation. He and Jacki were concerned about their baby's exposure to humans who might be carrying viruses on them without showing symptoms.

Given that they'd planned to travel to Egypt two weeks before the baby had been due, it was funny that they were so worried about the humans infecting their newborn son. They had been fine with the possibility of delivering little Darius in a hospital teeming with humans in a Third-World country, but now they feared a family of humans who were all perfectly healthy.

Perspectives and priorities changed once people became parents, and in that regard, immortals were no different than humans.

Gilbert put his wine glass down and turned to Kian and her. "Karen and I want to thank you for your hospitality and for the warm welcome you've extended to us, but we've decided to go home Sunday night." He cast an apologetic glance at Kaia and then at his brother. "You two can stay and keep working on your transitions, and as soon as anything happens, we will rush back here. But since we don't know when or if it's going to happen, we can't just sit around and twiddle our thumbs. I have building projects that need my attention, and Karen's boss is about to tear all her hair out if Karen is not back at work by Monday."

It was understandable but disappointing nonetheless. Syssi had hoped that Eric and Kaia's successful transitions would encourage Karen and Gilbert to start theirs as well, and that they would decide to move permanently into the village.

It might still happen, but not as quickly as Syssi had hoped.

Kian emptied his whiskey glass and put it down on the table. "Either Onegus or I will have to sift through your memories and erase everything that has to do with the village and its location. I will also ask Kalugal to reinforce Emmett and Eleanor's compulsion to keep you from revealing what you know about the existence of immortals."

There was no way Kalugal would meet with the viruses-carrying humans in person, and doing it over the phone would be less effective. Kian should have asked Toven to do that, and Syssi wondered why he hadn't.

The god hadn't volunteered his services either.

"Is it really necessary to sift through our memories?" Karen asked. "The compulsion is very effective at keeping us from revealing anything even accidentally."

"Compulsion can be overridden by a stronger compeller," Kian said. "If you fall into our enemies' hands, their leader can get you to talk. I'm not worried about him finding out what he already knows, but I don't want him to have even a hint of a clue about where he can find us. Furthermore, the only reason I'm allowing you to leave with memories of the existence of gods and immortals is that Kaia and Eric need to remain here, and you need to know what's going on with them."

"I don't want you to leave," Kaia said. "My transition might start any time now."

Karen gave her daughter an apologetic smile. "I know, sweetie. But it could also take a week or two, and we can't wait that long. We will come back as soon as it starts."

Gilbert shook his head. "What I'm concerned about is a stranger getting in my head. It's not that I have secrets to hide, but like everyone else, I sometimes have thoughts that I don't want to share with anyone other than my better half." He winked at Karen.

Syssi put a hand over her mouth to stifle the laugh bubbling out of her.

What Gilbert needed to hide was most likely his visits to internet porn sites.

He was a healthy male in his prime, and since he was still human, she doubted that his sexual fantasies were limited to Karen. Humans could be in loving, committed relationships and still indulge in fantasies about other partners. Immortals who had been fortunate enough to be blessed with a truelove mate couldn't think about touching anyone else, even as a fantasy.

Kian laughed. "Don't worry. If I'm the one doing the sifting, I'll make sure to stay away from those kinds of memories, and if it's Onegus, he'll avoid them like the plague as well."

Kaia

K aia lifted the teacup to her lips and blew air on it to cool it down before taking a sip.

After Gilbert's announcement that he was taking the family home Sunday night, her mood had plummeted.

She barely listened to the conversations going on around the table and hid her face from her mother's watchful eyes by staring at her plate.

William put a hand on her thigh. "Are you feeling alright? You've been uncharacteristically quiet."

Kaia forced a smile. "Are you calling me a chatterbox?"

"No, that's me. But you usually have an opinion on everything, and you are never shy about sharing it." He leaned closer and whispered in her ear, "I was counting on you dominating the conversation so that I wouldn't have to contribute."

That was surprising. William's problem was that he sometimes talked too much, not too little. But that usually happened when he got excited about subjects that interested him. He didn't like to offer his opinion about subjects he didn't know much about.

Kaia tilted her head. "Since when are you shy about saying whatever?"

"I'm not shy. I just prefer to better utilize my neural synapses than wasting them on things that are irrelevant to me."

Nodding, she patted his arm. "Now that I know when you need me to shield you, I promise not to neglect my duties." She let out a breath. "Starting tomorrow. This meal has exhausted me, and all I can think about is getting into bed."

William frowned. "It's only ten at night. Even Idina is still full of energy."

"Idina had an afternoon nap. I didn't." Kaia leaned sideways, rested her head on William's arm, and closed her eyes. "When can we go?" she whispered as quietly as she could.

"Soon." He lifted his hand and put it on her forehead. "You are a little warm."

Kaia lifted her head and forced her eyes open. "Maybe I'm transitioning?"

His entire body stiffened. "I'm calling Bridget."

"What's going on?" Amanda pushed to her feet.

"William says that my forehead feels warm."

A grin spread over the woman's gorgeous face. "It could be the start of the transition. What do you feel?"

The expectant silence stretching over the room was like a thousand spotlights that were directed at Kaia, and the warm feeling she'd had before intensified tenfold, making her sweaty.

She fanned herself with her hand. "Is it hot in here, or is it me?"

"It's not any warmer than it was three hours ago." Amanda put her hand on Kaia's forehead. "You're definitely running a fever." She turned to William. "Did you call Bridget?"

"I texted her. She says we should go to the clinic. She'll meet us there in an hour."

"Why only in an hour?" her mother asked.

"Bridget is at a restaurant in town with Turner, but she's sending Hildegard to the clinic. The nurse can take Kaia's vitals and hook her up to the monitors if needed."

Kaia didn't feel bad enough to go anywhere. She'd gone to classes with a fever and had plodded through even though all she'd wanted to do was sleep.

"I don't need to go to the clinic," she protested. "And there is no need to rush the nurse over there either. I have a little fever that could be a cold or flu, and I'm tired. That's not serious enough to justify a doctor's visit. I can wait for Bridget to return to the village and check my vitals."

"You make a good point." Amanda put a hand on her hip and struck a pose. "Do you have a sore throat?"

"No."

"Runny nose?"

Kaia shook her head.

"Stomachache?"

"Just from stuffing too much food into it. Okidu is a great cook."

"Thank you, Mistress," he called from the kitchen.

"You're welcome," Kaia called back. "And thank you for a wonderful meal."

Smiling, Amanda walked back to her seat. "You might be transitioning, but I don't think you are about to faint and lose consciousness." She pulled her phone out of her purse. "I'll text Hildegard that you will be there in an hour."

As she typed on the glass, her long, manicured nails made clicking sounds that, for some reason, annoyed Kaia.

As a neuroscience professor, Amanda shouldn't have such long nails. It just didn't fit the image. She shouldn't be so beautiful, and she shouldn't be dressed like a fashion model, either.

Kaia was dimly aware that her annoyance had nothing to do with Amanda, who had been very nice to her and her family. She was antsy because all her senses were suddenly hypersensitive. The dress felt scratchy against her skin, the fabric was too thick and not breathable enough, and her bra was too tight, digging into her skin, and the sounds around her were amplified and irritating.

Perhaps she shouldn't have insisted on staying.

Instead of going to the clinic, though, Kaia wanted to go home to change out of the dress and discard her bra. But she'd made such a fuss about staying that it would be embarrassing to say that she'd changed her mind and now wanted to leave.

William

Once dinner was over, Kian rose to his feet. "Who wants to join me for a cigar outside?"

William wasn't a smoker, but he wanted to ask Kian whether he'd talked with Annani, and he hadn't had a chance to do it privately yet. Now that Kaia was possibly transitioning, he wanted the Clan Mother to be near.

She seemed fine, so it didn't seem urgent, but things could change in the blink of an eye.

Looking at Kaia across the table, he didn't know what to think. After dinner, she had moved to sit next to her mother, and she seemed a little better, but he had to make sure she would be okay without him for a few minutes.

He waited for a lull in the conversation before walking over and putting his hand on her shoulder. "I'm going outside with Kian. Will you be okay without me?"

She smiled weakly. "I'll manage. The question is, will you? You don't smoke."

Her smart eyes communicated that she knew his desire to join Kian had nothing to do with cigars.

"I'm going to keep Kian company while he smokes. Some of our best ideas have come to us over his cigars."

"Have fun." She blew him a kiss.

Gilbert rose to his feet. "I'll join you."

"Do you smoke?" William asked.

"Only occasionally." He put his hand on William's back. "If Kian is offering cigars, I'm not going to say no."

"Same here," Andrew grinned. "It's conducive to brotherly bonding. Right, Dalhu?"

"Right." William looked over his shoulder to see whether Toven and Eric were joining them as well, but they had chosen to stay behind.

Outside, Kian motioned to the four armchairs facing a fire pit table, where his cigar box lay open. "Help yourselves, gentlemen."

As the others got busy cutting the cigars, lighting them, and remarking on the quality, William leaned closer to Kian and asked quietly, "Did you have a chance to talk with the Clan Mother?"

Kian nodded. "They were supposed to return next Tuesday, but she said she would try to be back by Thursday. If she's needed earlier, though, she said to let her know, and she will come as soon as she can."

If there was an emergency, Kaia would need the goddess's help immediately and not eighteen hours later, which was how long it could take Annani to travel from the castle in Scotland to the village, and Thursday was nearly a week from now. If Kaia was transitioning, she would probably no longer need Annani's help by then.

Hopefully, Kian was right about Toven's ability to provide a blessing just as potent as Annani's.

William forced a smile. "Thank you."

"You're welcome."

Not to be rude, he stayed with the smokers a few more minutes and then excused himself and went back to Kaia, but she still wasn't ready to leave.

She was busy convincing her mother to stay and see her through the transition, but he could see on her face that she was suffering.

The girl was stubborn and too proud to admit that she wasn't feeling well.

It took another hour until Kian and the other cigar smokers returned, and then everyone said their thanks and goodnights to their hosts and headed out.

"Are you going to the clinic now?" Karen asked Kaia when they were outside.

"I want to change into something more comfortable." Kaia rubbed her arms. "My skin feels itchy all over, and this dress is not appropriate for a doctor's visit. William's house is right there." She pointed. "It will take me a minute."

He found it strange that she referred to their bungalow in Safe Haven as ours but not to the house.

"We will wait outside," Gilbert said. "The little ones are sleeping, and I don't want them to wake up until we get to the clinic."

Idina was sprawled over Eric's shoulder while the twins slept comfortably in their double stroller.

"I'll do it quickly." Kaia took William's hand and headed to their house.

Kaia

The moment the front door closed behind them, Kaia reached for the hem of her dress, pulled it over her head, and tossed it to William. "I'm sorry for the impromptu striptease, but I've been waiting to do this for hours." She unhooked her bra on the way to the bedroom.

"You should have said something. We could have come home earlier."

"I didn't want to spoil anyone's fun." She let the bra drop down her shoulders and tossed it into the laundry basket in the walk-in closet.

William followed her inside. "What should I do with the dress?"

"Just toss it into the basket as well. I'll check later if it needs dry cleaning."

Given what was awaiting her, it was such a mundane conversation, but that was precisely what both of them needed right now to keep from freaking out.

Kaia pulled on one of her most worn-out T-shirts that she usually wore to bed. It had been washed so many times that it was incredibly soft, and the fabric didn't irritate her over-sensitized skin. It was also loose and black, so she could get away with not wearing a bra.

She added a pair of old black leggings that had seen better days, pushed her feet back into the black flip-flops she'd worn before, and gathered her hair into a ponytail.

"I'm ready."

"What about an overnight bag?" William asked. "Should you pack something in case Bridget wants to keep you in the clinic?"

"I don't want to keep my family waiting. Besides, if I show up with nothing, Bridget will have to let me go back to pack, so I might get away with sleeping here tonight." She grimaced. "I really don't want to sleep in a hospital bed."

Kaia slung the strap of her small wallet purse across her body.

She didn't need the money or the credit cards, but she needed somewhere to put her phone. If she'd worn jeans, she could have put it in her pocket, but just thinking about the stiff fabric made her itch intensify.

On the way out, William stopped her before she opened the front door.

"I want one great kiss before we go." He wrapped his arms around her. "I have a feeling that from now on, we will have very few moments alone."

Kaia let herself melt into him for a moment. She had to stay strong, and leaning on William was a luxury she couldn't rely on.

There was nothing he could do to make her transition easier, and it was all up to her.

"I love you," he murmured against her lips.

"I love you too." She clung to him for a moment longer, absorbing his strength. "We need to go. They are waiting for us on the street."

He didn't let go. "Annani is coming back only on Thursday, but she told Kian that she would come as soon as you need her."

That was disappointing.

Kaia hadn't expected the goddess to cut her trip short for her, but she'd hoped Annani would do it for William.

"That's okay. Toven is here, and he seems like a nice guy who loves his granddaughter. If Darlene asks him to help me, he will."

William

As William opened the door to the clinic, Bridget eyed the crowd spilling into the small waiting room with a frown.

"Good evening. Is there a reason for all of you to be here?"

Karen assumed a battle position. "We are worried about Kaia," she said in a commanding tone.

"You can be worried outside in the café." Bridget shooed them out. "It's practically part of my clinic." She looked at Kaia. "Besides, you look fine to me. Most of the transitioning Dormants get here after they pass out."

Karen opened her mouth to argue, but Gilbert put his hand on her shoulder, and she closed it.

Kaia threw her hands in the air. "That's what I was trying to tell everyone. I'm fine. I just have a little fever, and I'm tired." She rubbed her arms. "The only thing that really bothers me is this itching. It feels as if my skin is too tight for my body. Am I going to get taller?"

Bridget frowned. "Let's get you into the exam room." She cast William a sidelong glance. "You can wait out here or with Kaia's family. It's your choice."

He wanted to come in with Kaia, but she hadn't asked him to accompany her, and he didn't want to be pushy. "I'll wait with the family."

Kaia turned around and gave him a quick peck on the cheek. "I'll call you as soon as I know anything."

He nodded. "I'll be waiting."

As they stepped outside and walked over to the nearest table, Karen huffed. "Bridget is way too bossy. She kicked us out so unceremoniously that it was rude."

Gilbert chuckled. "Takes one to know one."

"I'm not bossy, and I'm not rude." Karen glared at him. "I'm assertive."

"If you say so, dear." He pulled out a chair for her.

It was after eleven at night, and the café was deserted, but the vending machines were always on, providing decent coffee and something to eat for those who got stuck without access to anything better.

"Can I get you something to drink?" William waved his hand in the direction of the vending machines.

Karen groaned. "If I'm about to stay awake all night, I'd better have some coffee." She turned to Cheryl. "Can you take the little ones to the house? Eric can carry Idina and help you put them in their beds."

The boys were asleep in their stroller, and Idina was passed out on Eric's shoulder.

"Sure," Cheryl agreed without arguing or asking for payment. "But you have to promise to call me as soon as you know anything."

"I'll text you," Gilbert said. "I suggest that you go to sleep if you can. We might spend the night out here, and someone needs to wake up tomorrow and take care of the little ones."

"Yeah, someone." Cheryl gripped the handle of the double stroller. "That's my middle name. Cheryl Someone Locke."

"Come, munchkin." Eric hoisted Idina higher on his shoulder. Propping her up with one arm, he put his other one around Cheryl's waist. "I'll help you put them in bed."

"I'm coming with you." Darlene joined them. "You might need a third pair of hands. I didn't forget how to change diapers or rock babies to sleep yet."

When they walked away, William turned to Karen. "How do you like your coffee?"

"Black with a pinch of Splenda," Gilbert said. "I'll come with you. I know the precise measurement of that pinch. If you get it wrong, she won't like it." He winked at Karen.

At the vending machines, William inserted his clan card into the slot. "Long espresso?"

Gilbert nodded. "Tell me the truth, William. Is Kaia in danger?"

He let out a breath. "The truth is that I don't know. She should transition with ease, but there is a big difference between should and would. Shit happens, and I just pray that it doesn't happen to Kaia."

"Or to Eric." Gilbert took the cup and added a sprinkle of Splenda powder to it. "He will probably need to go for another round. Only this time, I suggest someone else does it." He looked pointedly at William.

"I can't." William pressed the button for a cappuccino. "It would take a lot to get me aggressive." He chuckled. "I think the only way it could happen would be if someone I love was in danger."

Gilbert tilted his head. "From what I've seen so far, that's not typical for immortal males. Those I met seemed to have testosterone in spades."

William pulled his cappuccino out and motioned for Gilbert to make his selection. "That's not true. It's just that so far, you've been exposed mostly to Guardians. Many of the civilian clan males are not the aggressor types, but if their loved ones are threatened, all of them will find their inner beast, and that includes even the females." He gave Gilbert a small smile. "It's a mistake to think that they could be easily subdued just because they look and act feminine. If the need arises, they will fight like tigresses to protect their family." He handed Gilbert the coffee. "We also have a Kra-ell female who can hand three trained warriors their asses, and Wonder is nearly as strong, but she doesn't like fighting."

In the back of his mind, William knew that he was saying too much and talking too fast, but he was too anxious to stop.

Kaia

B ridget had taken blood samples from Kaia on the first day of her arrival in the village. She'd also measured every inch of her body, including the length of her fingers and toes, had measured her weight with no clothes on, and checked her responses to stimuli.

She was repeating the entire process now and notating the measurements on her tablet and comparing them to the previous ones.

"Are there any changes?" Kaia asked.

Bridget nodded. "Aside from the low fever you are running, your blood pressure is elevated, and so is your pulse. Those, along with the fever, are usually the first signs. I had another transitioning Dormant who complained of itching, and that was Cassandra. We know that she descended directly from Geraldine, who born immortal and had only one other daughter, Darlene. But Roni, who is Darlene's son, didn't complain of itching when he transitioned, so it might be unrelated."

"What can cause the itching?"

Bridget shrugged. "There might be many reasons for it. Your nervous system might be overstimulated because of the changes happening in your body, it could be a reaction to stress, or it could be an allergic reaction to the venom. The good news is that it will stop in a few days. In the meantime, I'll give you something to ease it."

"Thanks. So, you are sure that I'm transitioning?"

Bridget nodded. "I suggest that you stay in the clinic tonight even though you seem fine. Things can change in a heartbeat, and I don't recommend taking chances. I'll hook you up to the monitoring equipment, and it will continually measure your blood pressure and your pulse. You don't need an IV, so no catheter. You can get up and use the bathroom whenever you want."

Kaia was all for taking her chances and spending the night in bed with William instead of a hospital bed, but Bridget didn't seem like the type who could be pressured into agreeing to something she was recommending against. Besides, William and her mother would side with the physician, and Kaia couldn't take them all on.

She didn't have the energy.

"Can I go out and tell my family? If I faint on the way, they will see me and bring me in."

Ignoring her sarcasm, Bridget smiled. "Of course. Did you pack an overnight bag?"

"I didn't, but William can do that for me."

She had so little with her that he could stuff all her belongings into a duffle. He wouldn't even need to figure out what to bring.

"You can go home, pack a bag, and come back here. As long as you have someone with you at all times, that's fine."

It was on the tip of her tongue to point out that William was with her twenty-four-seven and that at the first hint of trouble, he could rush her to the clinic, but she knew it would be futile to argue with Bridget, and she was too tired to even try.

Well, she could give it a tiny try.

"William is with me all the time. Why can't I sleep in a comfortable bed with him by my side?"

"Because he's going to fall asleep at some point, and he might miss the signs of you going into distress."

"Are you going to stay with me all night long?"

Bridget shook her head. "I'll supervise Hildegard while she hooks you up to the equipment, and then I'll go home to sleep. If there is no emergency, I'll check on you tomorrow morning." She patted Kaia's arm. "Count yourself lucky. It seems like you will have an easy transition."

"I hope so." Kaia hopped down from the exam table and pushed her feet into her flip-flops. "I don't want to keep you here longer than necessary, so I'll just go out to tell my family the good news, and I'll come back. William can pack a bag for me and bring it here later. Can he stay with me in the patient room?"

Bridget nodded. "We have a cot that we keep for the partners of transitioning Dormants."

"Awesome." Kaia faked a smile. "I'll be back shortly."

She had no intention of having William sleep on a cot. They were going to cuddle on the damn hospital bed, and if Bridget had a problem with that, Kaia would plead with her to let him stay. There was only so much she was willing to compromise on.

William

When Kaia walked out of the clinic, William was seized by two warring emotions. One was relief and the other was disappointment. Relief that she was safe and not transitioning after all and disappointment for the same reason.

"What did the doctor say?" Karen asked.

"I'm transitioning." Kaia sat down on the chair William pulled out for her.

"That's it?" Gilbert gaped at her. "No sirens going off and no loudspeakers announcing the news to the entire village?"

Kaia smiled tiredly. "Disappointing, right?"

William reached for her hand. "So, what now? Are we going home?"

"I wish. Bridget said that I could go home and pack a bag, but since she's waiting to hook me up before she can go home to sleep, I don't want to keep her waiting. I told her that you could pack a bag for me and bring it over." She squeezed his hand. "She said they have a cot for the partners of transitioning Dormants."

"I don't want to leave your side even for a moment."

"I can pack your bag." Karen turned to William. "If that's okay with you. Can I go into your house without Guardians descending on me?"

"I can let them know that you are coming. Do you know where Kaia's things are?"

They'd been to the house, and Kaia had shown them around, so Karen should have no problem finding her way around.

"Everything is in the dresser drawers," Kaia said. "I just need pajamas, underwear, and a change of clothes for when Bridget lets me go."

"The duffle bags are on the top shelf in the back," William added.

"Anyway." Kaia smiled reassuringly at her mother and Gilbert. "Bridget insists on me staying in the clinic out of caution. She expects my transition to be easy."

William didn't know what Bridget was basing her observation on, but he trusted that the doctor had told Kaia the truth.

"How did she determine that you are transitioning?" Gilbert asked. "What are the signs?"

"The fever is the most obvious one. Also, my blood pressure is slightly elevated compared to the reading she did when I arrived, and my pulse is faster." Kaia rubbed her arms. "I'm also itchy, which isn't a common symptom. The only other Dormant who experienced that was Cassandra, but there is no way we are related. Geraldine's line starts with her, and she only has two daughters."

William frowned. "Maybe she forgot about having a third one. She has memory issues."

"That's ridiculous." Karen huffed. "How can a woman forget she has a child?"

Evidently Darlene hadn't shared that part of her story with Eric yet, or maybe she had, but he hadn't told the others. In any case, it wasn't William's story to tell.

"Geraldine suffered from complete amnesia following a nearly fatal accident, but the timeline doesn't work. You can't be related."

"We couldn't be related even if Geraldine had a third daughter she forgot about. I wasn't adopted, and I know who my parents are." Karen sighed. "Were. It's still difficult to talk about them in the past tense."

"When did they pass away?" William asked.

"Two years ago. They were taken from me two months apart."

Gilbert reached for her hand. "That's when we decided to have another child. When the doctor told us that we were having twins, we hoped for a boy and a girl." He smiled sadly. "You know, a girl for Karen's mother and a boy for her father. But they are both boys, and we adore them."

"They healed my heart." Karen put a hand over her chest. "Idina healed the hole left by Kaia and Cheryl's father, and Evan and Ryan healed the one left by my parents."

Lost for words, William nodded.

"I assume that your mother is still around," Karen said.

"She is. She lives in Scotland."

"We would like to meet her," Gilbert said. "Does she know about Kaia?"

"She does, but my mother is a cautious type. She wished us both luck, but she said she would only come to visit after Kaia transitioned."

Kaia was in no rush to meet her future mother-in-law. It wasn't that she feared the woman would resent her for stealing her son, but she just couldn't deal with anything else right now. She had enough on her plate.

Perhaps William's mother had realized that and had decided not to add stress to an already stressful situation.

"I should get back." Kaia pushed to her feet. "Bridget is waiting for me." She hugged her mother. "After you bring me the bag, I want you to go to sleep. Nothing is going to happen tonight, and the boys will need you in the morning."

Kaia

Kaia drifted in and out of sleep throughout the night. Disturbing dreams of her past life had kept waking her up, but she wasn't sure whether they had been about real memories or her mind had conjured them from bits and pieces of stories she'd accumulated in her synapses.

If they were real, she'd been a misogynistic prick. Edgar had hated women. He'd lusted after them, but after several rejections, he'd developed a deep-seated hatred for women and had tried to avoid them.

It couldn't have been real. How could she be such a feminist if in a prior life she'd thought so little of women and their role in society?

Edgar believed that the only thing women were good for was satisfying male urges and popping out babies.

Ugh. What a jerk.

Had his punishment been to be reborn as a smart, successful woman?

Cuddled next to her, William was sleeping peacefully, his face looking so much younger when he was relaxed.

She loved him so much.

Thank goodness that he was so different from the way she'd been as a man.

"I love you," she murmured into his neck.

He smiled in his sleep, or so she thought, but then his hand traveled under her hospital Johnny to cup her naked butt.

"I love you too." He nuzzled her ear and, a moment later, was fast asleep again with his hand still draped over her bottom under her gown.

Kaia didn't mind the possessiveness it implied. It was born of love, not a need to dominate and subjugate like Edgar's.

Except, her butt was in full view of the door, and if Bridget or Hildegard walked in, it could be a little embarrassing.

After her mother had delivered the overnight bag, the nurse offered to take off the blood pressure cuff as well as the stickers and wires so Kaia could change into her pajamas and then put them back on, but Kaia had been too tired and decided to leave the hospital gown on.

As the pressure cuff inflated again, she waited for it to deflate, and when it did, she drifted off to sleep again.

The next time she opened her eyes, William wasn't in bed with her, the blanket was tucked snugly around her, and she could see daylight through the half-closed shutters.

She also needed to use the bathroom, but it wasn't urgent. It could wait for Hildegard to come and free her from the wiring.

A knock sounded on the door, and a moment later, Bridget walked in. "Good morning, Kaia. How are you feeling?"

"Good." She smiled, giving the doctor a thorough once-over.

Bridget was a beautiful woman, with a mane of red hair that was gathered in a loose bun on the top of her head and gorgeous eyes that shone with intelligence. Curly tendrils cascaded down the sides of her face and neck, framing her delicate features and providing color to her nearly translucent skin.

She was petite but had ample cleavage and the kind of ass that men salivated over—sizable but firm—perfect for holding on to.

"You are very pretty, Doctor Bridget." What was happening to her? Why had she said that? "I mean your hair. I love what you did with it. Have you had highlights added to it?"

"The highlights are natural." The physician frowned. "It's so nice of you to notice, but I wonder, did your vision improve?"

Had it?

There were hundreds of different hues in Bridget's red hair that Kaia hadn't noticed before, and there were tiny golden flakes in her blue-green eyes that she hadn't seen before, either.

Was it a change in vision, or was it a new appreciation for the female form? A remnant from her dreams of being Edgar?

"I didn't notice before that your hair had so many different shades of red, and you have tiny gold flakes floating in your irises."

"Your vision might have improved." Bridget walked over to the wall and flicked a switch on.

An eye exam chart appeared on the wall across from the bed.

"Can you read the bottom line for me?"

"I can't."

It hadn't occurred to Kaia before, but she had forgotten to put her glasses on.

Snatching them off the side table, she put them on.

"Can you read it with the glasses?"

Kaia shook her head. "It's still blurry."

"Try to read the line above it without the glasses."

The doctor hadn't checked her vision before, so how could she know if her vision had improved?

Surprisingly, though, she was able to recite the letters without her glasses.

"Your vision has improved by a lot." Bridget looked surprised. "That's unusual so early in the process."

"Awesome." Kaia grinned. "I won't mind losing the glasses. Can I ask you for a favor, though? Can you take off the wires and blood pressure cuff? I need to use the bathroom."

"Of course." Bridget put her tablet on the table and freed Kaia in seconds. "William went to get you breakfast. He should be back any moment now."

"Great. I'm starving." Kaia ducked into the bathroom.

Eric

It was Saturday, the fourth day following Eric's initiation ceremony, and he was not showing any signs of transitioning. It was time to concede failure and seek another initiator, but it could wait for Monday.

He wasn't looking forward to facing the pitying expressions of people as they asked the same stupid questions, inquiring about his transition that was obviously not happening.

Right now, he was spending a blissfully quiet afternoon with Darlene, watching *Top Gun* and eating pizza, the two of them enjoying each other's company without the family drama.

Kaia was doing well, but Karen and Gilbert were going back and forth about whether they should stay or leave, and Eric had gotten tired of that. He wasn't going anywhere, and he could keep an eye on Kaia until his own transition started.

As the doorbell rang, he turned to Darlene. "Did you invite someone?"

He'd been so contented, and he hated their time alone getting interrupted.

"I didn't, but my mother is just the type to come for a visit without calling first." Darlene untangled herself from his embrace and pushed her feet into her clogs. "It's probably her."

But when she opened up, it wasn't Geraldine at the door. It was Max, with a six-pack of Corona in one hand and a bag of nachos in the other.

"You are not watching the game?" The Guardian strode into the living room without waiting to be invited as if they were frat buddies.

"What game?" Eric asked.

"Never mind." Max plunked the beers on the coffee table and sat next to him on the couch. "I love *Top Gun*." He grinned at him. "Are you reminiscing about your days in the Air Force?"

"Yeah." Eric dropped his feet to the floor and leaned to reach for the nacho bag. "What happened? Did none of your Guardian buddies want to watch the game with you?"

Max smiled. "I'm taking my initiator duties seriously and taking care of my protégé." He pointed to the Corona. "Do you think any of my Guardian buddies would drink that? I got it for my still very human initiate because we are supposed to bond." He put his hand on Eric's shoulder and kneaded it.

That was a very familiar gesture from a guy that he barely knew, and Eric wished he had immortal senses already so he could figure out Max's agenda.

Was he coming on to him?

Or was it just his style of showing affection?

In either case, he had no problem playing along, provided that Max's expectations were reasonable. There was a limit to what Eric was willing to do with another man.

"I can bond over beers." He lifted his gaze to Darlene, who stood on the other side of the coffee table and seemed unsure about the scene unfolding before her. "Come back and sit next to me. We can share a beer."

She walked around the table and sat on his other side.

The movie was still playing, but none of them were paying attention. There was tension in the room, and it wasn't sexual. It was like the three of them were trying to form a friendship, but it wasn't a good fit.

Eric was reminded of Kian's ceremonial words, which talked about him and Max being a good match. Could lack of compatibility between the initiator and initiate hinder the success of the process?

It wouldn't be part of the traditional wording if it weren't important.

Could that be the reason he hadn't transitioned?

"Listen, Eric." Max rubbed the back of his neck. "It's Saturday, and nothing is happening. Perhaps you need another round."

"I'll give it another day."

Max nodded. "If it still doesn't happen, I have no problem giving you another dose."

"No offense, Max," Darlene said. "But this time we will try it with someone closer to the source."

"There is another possibility." Max made a face. "What if you have some disease you don't know about?" He looked at Darlene. "Roni is very close to the source, and he was initiated several times unsuccessfully because his body was too weak from pneumonia."

"I'm healthy." Eric took a sip from the beer. "Bridget ran a thorough physical on me yesterday, and she said that my biological markers are of a man ten years my junior."

Max frowned. "Maybe you are transitioning with no symptoms? What if your markers are so good because your body is reversing the clock? I heard that Kaia is transitioning so smoothly that she's barely feeling anything. Maybe you are the same."

"I wish." Eric took a long swig from his beer. "Bridget compared my results to those from the physical she had in my file, and the results were almost identical. I'm not changing."

Max put his hand on Eric's arm. "Well, at least you know that you're healthy. That's good, right?"

"Yeah. It is." He was so sick of talking about it. "So, Max, what's new in your life?"

"Not much. I'm going back on missions starting next Monday. For now, I'm on village security detail."

That piqued Eric's interest. "Tell me about those missions. How do you find the dens? What's your mode of operation? What do you do with the victims?"

"Why do you want to know? Are you interested in joining the Guardian force?"

"Maybe I am. After I transition, I will need something to do with my time." He smiled at Darlene. "Sitting in your office and watching you work is fun, but I'm not ready to retire yet."

"You are a pilot," Max said. "Kian will put you on the payroll as one."

"I don't know if that's all I want to do." Eric leaned back with the beer still clutched in his hand. "If I become immortal, I will want to try many different things, and rescuing trafficking victims sounds like a good place to start. It would be immensely satisfying to beat the shit out of the scum that ruined their lives."

He wouldn't kill them. That was too merciful, and he had no mercy for monsters. He would leave them maimed and castrated to live out the rest of their lives in agony.

"You don't have the training." Max pulled another beer from the pack.

"It has been a while, but I got very good training in the Air Force."

Max chuckled. "After you become immortal, and I mean fully immortal with operational fangs and venom, come to the gym to one of our training sessions, and you'll see what I mean. Your training is useless compared to ours."

"I still managed to take you by surprise and knock you off your feet." Eric took a swig from his beer.

Max grinned. "Maybe I let you do that to make you feel good."

"Yeah, right."

The Guardian shrugged. "Perhaps I got distracted."

William

As Bridget walked into the room with her tray, William winced.

This would be the third time she made a cut on Kaia's palm, and even though Kaia hadn't complained, he hated to see her in pain.

The other two times hadn't been a failure, but they hadn't been a complete success either.

The cut Bridget had made Saturday evening had taken four minutes and twenty-five seconds to heal, and the cut she'd inflicted on Sunday had taken four minutes and nineteen seconds. The healing was still much faster than it would have been if Kaia was fully human, but not nearly as fast as it would have been for an immortal.

"Ready for another test?" Bridget put her tray on the side table.

Kaia sighed. "It's not going to produce better results than the one you did yesterday. Let's face it. I'm only slightly immortal."

Bridget chuckled. "There is no such thing. It's like saying that you're slightly pregnant. You either are, or you're not. Besides, the second time the wound healed six seconds faster than the first time, so there is progress."

Kaia extended her hand. "Let's hope that it's my lucky Monday."

Bridget turned to look at William. "No other witnesses this time?"

He shook his head. "It's just us."

Karen, Gilbert, Eric, and Cheryl had come to witness the first and second tests, but since the progress was so slow, there was no point in making it a spectacle each and every time.

Bridget nodded. "Get ready with the stopwatch."

William took the device out of his pocket and turned it on. "I'm ready."

The moment Bridget made the cut with her tiny surgical knife, William started the counter.

Kaia winced but didn't even hiss, and as they watched the blood well over the cut, Bridget kept cleaning it with gauze so they could see the healing progress. By the time the bleeding stopped, and the last of the thin white line disappeared, there was a large pile of bloody gauze on her tray.

William stopped the watch. "Four minutes and fifteen seconds."

"Well, it is getting better, so that's good news." Bridget scrunched the pile of gauze and disposed of it. "I've never witnessed a transition like this, but then every Dormant is different." She smiled at Kaia. "At least the itching has stopped."

"Thank goodness for that." Kaia rubbed her arms.

William didn't mind that at all. As long as Kaia was okay and not in danger, he was fine with her transition taking as long as it needed to.

"I think it's time William and I went back to Safe Haven and continued our work." Kaia ran a finger over the cut area on her palm. "It doesn't look like I'm going to worsen, and at this rate, it will take months for me to get through the initial stage of the transition. There is no reason for me to stay in the clinic and waste your valuable time."

William had to agree even though he was anxious about Kaia being released.

Her blood pressure hadn't gone up beyond the initial rise, and Bridget had told Hildegard to take readings only twice a day and none during the night. The only monitor Kaia was still hooked up to was the one measuring her heart rate.

Bridget nodded. "You don't have to stay in the clinic, but I want you to stay in the village for at least another week. I want to keep monitoring your progress."

"I'm glad that you agree with me. My family extended their stay to see me through the transition, but they need to go home, and now that I'm officially out of danger, they can finally go."

After it had been established that Kaia was not going to lose consciousness and that her transition was progressing slowly but smoothly, there had been a lot of back and forth about whether they should leave or stay, and in the end, it had been Karen's decision to wait until Kaia got released from the clinic.

"That's up to you and them." Bridget removed the two wires still attached to Kaia's chest and collected her tray. "You can get dressed." She shook her head. "You don't even need pain medication. This is so strange," she murmured as she walked out the door.

Kaia let out a breath and flung the blanket off her. "Let's get out of here. I've been going stir-crazy staying in bed all day."

William chuckled. "You were watching television and catching up on your favorite shows. You weren't going crazy at all."

"It was fun for one day." Kaia took her pajama shirt off and dropped it on the bed. "I'll shower at home. I need to get out of here." She reached into the duffle bag he'd handed her and pulled out a T-shirt.

It was a struggle to keep his eyes on her face and not stare at her breasts.

Kaia hadn't changed physically, but then there had been nothing to improve, and other than a few stolen kisses and caresses under the blanket, they hadn't done much. He missed having her naked under him and over him, and in every position imaginable.

But more than that, William wanted his old Kaia back—the one who had a spark in her eyes and a zest for life and who had thrived on challenges—the one who had been like a breath of fresh air in his stagnant life.

The new Kaia seemed subdued and unhappy, and he didn't know why or how to fix it.

The transition hadn't taken a physical toll on her like it had taken on other Dormants, but it had taken a psychological one.

He assumed it was disappointment, and it was understandable to some extent. But the bottom line was that Kaia was transitioning, which meant that she was becoming immortal, and they would be able to spend eternity together.

That should be enough, right?

What did it matter how long it took?

And yet, Kaia seemed troubled and somewhat muted, and she avoided looking into his eyes. It was as if her spark had dimmed, and she'd lost some of the self-confidence that had been such a huge part of her personality.

He wished he knew how to help her, but the only thing he could think of was arranging for her to meet with

Vanessa. The therapist had much better tools to help Kaia than he did.

"I'm ready to go." Kaia collected her glasses from the side table and dropped them into the duffle bag. "At least I've gotten rid of those. I have perfect eyesight now."

"You got immortality." He took the duffle bag from her. "Is it really so important to you how fast you heal? Your body's self-repairing mechanism might be a little slow, but it works, and it's good enough to keep you alive forever."

"I know." She gave him a tight smile. "It doesn't bother me. It's just that I get restless when I have nothing to do. I want to get back to the research."

Kaia

As they walked out of the clinic, Kaia pulled her phone out of her purse. "I should call my mom to tell her the good news."

William wrapped his arm around her waist. "How about you call her over a cappuccino and a sandwich? You haven't had breakfast yet."

As her stomach growled in response, she nodded. "Sounds good to me."

"Excellent. I haven't had breakfast yet, either." He led her to a table, pulled out a chair for her, and put her duffle bag on the ground by her feet.

"I thought that you grabbed something when you went home to shower and change."

"No way. I wanted to eat with you. The roast beef sandwich?"

Kaia shook her head. "I'm in the mood for a pastry or a Danish. Or both."

He tilted his head. "Since when have you been craving sweet things?"

She was more of a savory kind of girl, but ever since the Edgar persona had surfaced in all of its tainted glory, even her taste in food had changed.

Kaia forced a smile. "I'm celebrating going home."

"That's indeed a cause for celebration." William leaned and kissed her forehead. "I can't wait to have you all to myself again."

"I can't wait either."

"I'll get us cappuccinos and an assortment of pastries."

"Yummy." She licked her lips.

When William turned his back to her and walked to the counter, Kaia let the smile slide off her face and leaned back in her chair. If she wasn't hungry, she would have preferred to go home, get in the shower, scrub away the sticky film from her body, and if possible, wash away the slimy feeling clinging to her from the disturbing dreams of living the life of a misogynistic jerk.

Heck, it wouldn't have been so bad if it was limited to memories and dreams, but Edgar clung to her even while she was wide awake. She was seeing the world through the prism of his eyes, and it wasn't a pleasant sight.

What the hell was she going to do about that?

How could she tell William that she was suddenly attracted to women when she wasn't supposed to be attracted to anyone but him?

Wasn't that one of the main tenets of being truelove mates?

With a sigh, she took out her phone again and placed a call to her mother.

"Kaia, sweetie. How are you doing this morning?"

"I'm out of the clinic, sitting in the café and waiting for William to bring me coffee and pastries, so I'm feeling great."

Hopefully, her mother's bullshit radar didn't work as well over the phone.

There was a moment of silence, and Kaia tensed for the inevitable 'what's wrong' question.

"Did Bridget test you again today?"

She let out a breath. It seemed that her mother didn't suspect anything. "She did, and there was a slight improvement. The cut healed five seconds faster than it did yesterday. I begged Bridget to let me go back to Safe Haven, but she only agreed to let me out of the clinic if I promised to stay in the village for another week. She wants to keep testing me every day to see if the gradual improvement continues."

"That's good news, right?"

"Yeah." Kaia closed her eyes. "My transition is the oddest one Bridget has witnessed, but as William pointed out, the end result is still immortality, and it doesn't matter if I'm going slower than all the others before me."

Her mother chuckled. "My sweet, competitive Kaia. You can't tolerate not being the best at everything."

So that's why her mother's bullshit detector had failed to penetrate Kaia's cheerful facade. Karen thought that she sounded a little off because her pride had been hurt by her underwhelming transition.

Perhaps she could throw in some more misdirection.

"It's not about that." Kaia moved the phone to her other ear. "Well, it's a little about that, but that's not why I'm not jumping for joy. I'm tired, and bored, and I want to go back to work. I got so sick of being stuck in that clinic with nothing to do, and I felt uncomfortable about Bridget and Hildegard coming to the clinic just to look after me while I didn't need looking after. I'm fine, and hopefully, I will continue to improve, but I can do that while working on the project." She sighed. "I really want to return to Safe Haven. The village is nice, but I miss our bungalow over there. It's small and cozy. William's house is too big and too formal. It doesn't feel homey."

"Oh, sweetie. You didn't have enough time to get used to the house. William's place is much smaller than our home in the city, and you never complained about it not being cozy."

"That's because it's full of people, and kids, and toys, and it's always noisy."

"I miss home," her mother said. "If Bridget believes that you are out of the danger zone, there is no reason for us to stay. We can go back."

Kaia had been expecting that, but her gut clenched nonetheless.

"Here is your coffee." William put a paper cup in front of her.

She smiled at him. "Thanks."

Her mother huffed. "Was that sarcasm?"

Kaia rolled her eyes. "I thanked William for bringing me coffee, not you for abandoning me."

"We are not abandoning you. Whenever you need us, we will come running."

"I know." Kaia removed the lid and took a sip. "I agree that you need to go home, but it doesn't make me happy. I enjoyed having you here with me, and I hoped we were all going to stay for good."

Her mother released a breath. "You know it's not that easy. We have a life back home. I have a job that I love doing, and Gilbert runs a profitable business. We can't just leave everything behind."

"Yeah, I bet Berta can't wait for you to return. She misses the boys."

The nanny had been with them since Idina had been born, and she loved the little ones as if they were her own.

"I'm sure she's enjoying the time off. Naturally, I'm paying her regardless of our absence."

"What about Eric?" Kaia asked. "Is he going home as well? Or is he making another attempt?"

"Eric is a big boy, and he makes his own decisions."

William

Kaia was quiet as they walked out of the café, probably thinking about her family going home. She hadn't tried to convince them to stay, which William thought was a mistake, but perhaps she just didn't have the energy.

Maybe he should try to convince Gilbert and Karen not to leave.

Eric hadn't transitioned yet, and he wasn't going to unless he made another attempt. But that didn't preclude Gilbert from going for it. And since Kaia was transitioning, there was no longer a question of whether Karen was a Dormant, so she shouldn't wait either.

"Why isn't Gilbert attempting transition? He doesn't need to wait for Eric to succeed, and if he wants to induce your mother, he shouldn't wait."

Kaia shrugged. "They are aware of their options, and they will decide what they want to do. I don't want to push them."

He opened the front door for her. "Maybe you should. I know that you don't want them to leave."

"Naturally, but since I'm going to leave as soon as Bridget okays it, I can't expect them to stay here without me."

She dropped her purse on the entry table and continued to the bedroom.

He followed behind. "Why are you in such a rush to go back to Safe Haven? We can work from here."

Kaia lifted a brow. "Neither of us has done much work since we got here. There are too many distractions, and I'm not talking just about my transition. In Safe Haven, there is nothing to do other than work on our project and make love."

"Speaking of making love." He reached for her waist and pulled her against his body. "I missed you."

He hadn't expected her to react with a grimace or to push on his chest.

"I'm gross. I need to get in the shower and wash off all the sticky gunk from where the wires were attached to me, and you need to get back to the lab. You've missed so much work because of me that it will take you weeks to catch up."

It was all true, but the old Kaia would have jumped in bed with him nonetheless.

Perhaps she needed some time to rest. Or maybe she was right about needing to go back to Safe Haven. She might feel more at home there. Safer.

He let go of her. "I can work from here while you get cleaned up. Once you feel like yourself again, we can go to the lab together."

Kaia cast a longing look at the bed. "I was hoping to take a nap after the shower. I'm still weak."

Alone.

Kaia didn't want him to get in bed with her.

She hadn't said it, but that's what she meant.

"I'll stay right here until you are done in the shower, tuck you in bed, and work from the armchair." He pointed to the bedroom's sitting area. "I'm not leaving you alone at home while you are still transitioning. You might need my help."

"I can call Cheryl and ask her to stay with me while you are gone."

Kaia might have fooled a human, but he was an immortal, and even though she was transitioning, she was still emitting human scents. Before her transition, the scents were so strong and multifaceted that he couldn't take them apart to decipher singular emotions aside from arousal and love. Those were strong emotions that tended to overpower most others.

Anger and hate were also powerful, but Kaia hadn't manifested them before, or at least not strongly enough to be distinguishable from the others.

Now she was emitting both, and he prayed that they were not directed at him.

Who could be the object of her hatred, though?

Perhaps it was just intense frustration, and Kaia was angry at her situation and hated being in the village.

What could he do to make it better?

Right now, it seemed that what Kaia needed was to be alone, and he doubted she wanted even Cheryl to be with her.

"I'll make a deal with you. I'll stay just until you are done with the shower. You can ask your sister to come over and keep an eye on you, but if you want to be alone, I can work with that. I'll send you texts every thirty minutes, and if you don't answer them within five minutes, I'll rush over to check on you."

The relieved breath Kaia let out confirmed his suspicions. "Thank you for being you." She wound her arms around his neck. "I need some time to process what's going on with me, and I need to be alone. I'm glad that you're so understanding, and your feelings aren't hurt."

He pressed a soft kiss to her forehead. "Take as long as you need, and when you are ready, talk to me. We are a team, and I want to help you in whatever way I can."

"I appreciate it, and I wish you could help, but only I can reorganize the mess in my own head."

Darlene

Darlene shifted her gaze away from her computer screen and glanced at Eric.

He'd dragged a chair into her office and was working on the laptop William had lent him, using a flat cardboard box as his lap desk and a bigger one as a footstool. He didn't look comfortable, but when she'd offered to order a proper lap desk for him, he'd said that he was fine and that he didn't want her to spend money on it.

From being convinced that he would transition right away, he now wasn't sure he would transition at all.

It was probably just a temporary slump, and knowing Eric, he would bounce back to being his cocky, optimistic self in no time.

But even when he was brooding, she loved having him in her office.

In the short time they'd known each other, he'd become such an integral part of her that she hated every moment she was away from him. Fortunately, he seemed to feel the same and followed her wherever she needed to go.

They were inseparable.

"What are you working on?" she asked.

He looked up. "I'm exchanging emails with a couple of other operators who are interested in leasing my planes. I have one of them doing me a favor and managing what I already had booked and couldn't cancel, but I'm not making any new bookings, and I still need a source of income."

"Right. We are not original clan members, and we are not mated to one of them, so we don't get a share in the clan profits. Kian gave me an allowance when I moved into the village, but I didn't like getting paid for doing nothing. As soon as William hired me, I asked for the allowance to be canceled."

"How much is William paying you, if I may ask?"

"You may, and it's $4,500 a month."

He arched a brow. "Is that enough? Or let me rephrase. Is that what someone with your skills would be paid in the human world?"

"My skills are rusty, and I'm not sure anyone outside of here would have hired me. I asked for $4,500 expecting to get less, but I got exactly what I asked for, and it's more than enough. Don't forget that we don't pay for housing or utilities or any kind of insurance. I even got a car for free. I offered to pay for it in installments, but Kian refused to hear of it."

Eric smirked. "Then I can afford to do nothing if I want. My pension from the Air Force and what I'll get in lease payments for the planes is more than enough to live on."

She shook her head. "At some point, you will have to fake your own death, and the pension payments will stop. Besides, you need something to do, or you'll go nuts."

"I was just joking. Once I turn immortal, I'll fly planes for the clan. Max said that they could use another pilot. But until then, you are stuck with me in your shoebox of an office."

"Hey, I like my little office. Don't insult it." She looked at the cardboard boxes he used. "Perhaps I can replace my desk with one of those that don't have a back panel, so we can both work on it."

Eric shook his head. "You need a larger office. It's deplorable that William keeps you in this closet." He looked at the door that they had to leave open because when it was closed, there wasn't enough air circulation for both of them in there. "It's not healthy for you to work in here, and you are not immortal yet."

"Neither are you." She sighed. "Have you given any thought to who you want to induce you next?"

He nodded. "I like Andrew. He's been immortal long enough to have his fangs and venom glands functioning properly, but since we are related on our maternal side, it might be a problem given the clan taboo."

"The taboo is only on mating between members of the same matrilineal descent. Kian induced Alena's sons, so it's obviously not a problem for your purposes. But Andrew is not your best choice because he's just as far from the source as you are. You need a stronger immortal."

"What about Dalhu?" Eric winced. "On second thought, forget that I said that. The dude is the size of a mountain, and he's scary. Anandur falls into the same category of being too big, and Brundar might kill me just because he likes killing things. Aside from them, I don't know any other immortals."

He knew Toven, but Darlene wasn't sure they could ask the god to do that or if Toven could even induce a male Dormant. Her uncle, on the other hand, was the perfect candidate for the job.

"Orion is coming back on Thursday, and he's your best choice. He's a demigod, so his genes are the most potent, and he's a very nice guy who's not intimidating at all. You will like him."

"Then it's settled. I'll wait for your uncle."

As the door to the outer office opened, William walked in and headed straight toward her and Eric.

"Good morning, boss." She smiled at him. "I didn't expect you here today."

"Good morning to you both." He put his hand on Eric's shoulder. "You probably heard already that Kaia was released from the clinic earlier today."

"I didn't." He put his laptop and cardboard on the desk and got to his feet. "Congratulations." He offered William his hand.

Eric

"Congratulations to you too." William pulled him into a quick bro embrace. "After all, Kaia is your step-niece."

"That she is." Eric clapped him on the back, and then the two of them took a step away from each other.

In Eric's heart, Kaia was his niece, but no one had thought to inform him that she'd been released from the clinic, and it hurt more than he was willing to admit. What was the deal with Gilbert? Did he forget that he had a brother? Or maybe he'd thought that Eric would begrudge Kaia her successful transition?

If he did, he was dumber than an ox. He sure was as stubborn as one.

Realizing that William and Darlene were staring at him, Eric planted a smile on his face that he hoped looked at least somewhat genuine. "So, what's the next step? Are you going back to Safe Haven?"

"Not yet." William leaned against the doorframe. "Bridget wants Kaia to stay in the village for another week so she can monitor her progress. Her transition is very unusual." He let out a breath. "I'm just glad that she didn't lose consciousness and that it's going smoothly. I don't care how long it takes."

"You were so worried for nothing," Darlene said.

Eric didn't think that William's worry had been excessive. They had all been anxious for Kaia, and he had been anxious for himself as well.

Still was.

His journey into immortality wasn't over yet.

William pushed away from the doorframe. "Kaia had a bad feeling, and as someone who is surrounded by people with paranormal abilities, I don't take premonitions lightly, and I'm not done worrying yet."

"I'm with you on that," Eric said. "I'm crossing my fingers for Kaia."

"Thank you." William smiled, but there was tension in his expression that he didn't even try to hide. "I need to check on what's going on in the lab. I'll see you later."

When William left, and the door to the outer office closed, Eric sat back and took his borrowed laptop from Darlene's desk. "When William and Kaia return to Safe Haven, are you going with them?"

"If William still needs me." She smiled. "You'll come with me, of course."

"What about my transition? I need to stay in the village to be near the clinic."

"Right. I forgot about that for a moment." Darlene pushed a strand of hair behind her ear. "I'll ask William if I can do my work remotely. He'll understand why I can't go."

"What about the new clinic in Safe Haven? Hildegard said that Gertrude was already there setting things up. Maybe it's ready."

"I can check." Darlene turned to her computer screen. "If they got the shipment, it will be notated."

While he waited for her to find out, his phone rang.

"Finally, someone's thinking to let me know that Kaia is out." He accepted the call. "Good morning, Gilbert. Are you calling to share the good news? If you are, you're too late. I just saw William, and he told me about Kaia."

"Where are you?"

"In Darlene's office."

"What is William doing in the lab? He's supposed to be watching Kaia."

Eric frowned. "Why? Did Bridget tell him to watch her?"

"No, but it's obvious. Kaia is still in the initial stages of her transition, and she needs to be monitored." He groaned. "Karen and I asked Kian to arrange for transportation back home tomorrow, but now I'm starting to think that we've been too hasty."

They'd been talking about going home for days, and their scheduled return had been postponed several times before. But now that they'd arranged for transportation, it seemed to be final.

Still, perhaps he could change their minds.

"Darlene's uncle is returning to the village on Thursday, and we are going to ask him to induce me. Can't you stay for my second ceremony?"

"I wish we could, but Karen is right here beside me, and she's shaking her head. She really needs to go back to work."

"Can you come back on the weekend? We can ask the dude to induce me on Sunday."

They hadn't taken into consideration that Darlene's uncle might refuse, but if he did, there were other candidates Eric could ask. He hadn't thought about Shai before, but as Darlene's stepdad, he should be willing to help her. And her sister's mate was the chief of security and a head Guardian, so he was an excellent candidate as well. He wouldn't refuse his sister-in-law's request.

"Maybe I'll come by myself," Gilbert said. "We can't drag the little ones back and forth like that."

"What about you? When are you going for it? You are a proven Dormant, and you don't have to wait for me to transition. Karen is proven too, and she doesn't have all the time in the world to wait either."

"We know, but we need time to think it through."

"What's to think about? You need to do it."

Gilbert and Karen had been going round in circles, one day deciding that they needed to go for it and the next deciding that they couldn't. In his gut, Eric knew that they would eventually get over their fear and attempt transition, but he was tired of the merry-go-round.

Gilbert sighed. "It's not as simple as that. Karen and I are thinking about passing on the offer. We have three small children that we don't want to orphan."

Eric sighed. "You can't be serious."

"We are very serious."

"Look, you and Karen aren't attempting transition simultaneously. If anything happens to you, they will still have Karen, Kaia, Cheryl, and me. It's not like they would have no one to raise them with love and care. And if you make it and then Karen doesn't, they'll have you and all of the above."

"Karen and I discussed all of those scenarios, and both of us agreed that we don't want to go on without the other. Though if your transition goes smoothly, we might reconsider."

Darlene

E ric ended the call with a groan. "No pressure. No pressure at all."

Darlene had an idea of what Gilbert had said based on Eric's side of the conversation, but she hadn't heard Gilbert's last words that had Eric feeling pressured.

"What did he say?"

"If my transition goes smoothly, they will reconsider."

"That's not fair of Gilbert to put it all on your shoulders."

It was stressful enough for Eric to deal with his own transition and his odds of survival. He didn't need the added worry of his brother conditioning his own transition on how well Eric's went.

On the other hand, she could understand Karen and Gilbert as well. It wasn't an easy decision for a bachelor like Eric or for the mother of a grown son like her, so it must be tenfold more difficult for the parents of two babies and a toddler.

"Maybe we shouldn't wait for Orion," she said. "Kian and Kalugal are also demigods, and they are both here. Perhaps they will agree to induce you. And as for the equipment, some of it was delivered to the clinic in Safe Haven, and some is still in transit, but it doesn't really matter. Your inducers are here in the village."

He leveled his gaze at her. "You didn't suggest either of them before, and I assumed that there was a good reason for it."

She shrugged. "I didn't feel comfortable asking Kian, and Kalugal has a new baby and is not seeing anyone, especially not humans, because he's afraid of bringing viruses to his son. He might refuse because of that. And Kian, well, he's Kian. Not the most approachable of guys. But we can ask Syssi to ask him on your behalf. After all, you are her cousin."

For a long moment, Eric just looked at her, and then he reached for her hand over the desk. "What about your grandfather? A god's genes are the most powerful of all."

"That's what I'm afraid of. Maybe his venom is too powerful. I doubt that the gods bothered inducing Dormants back in the day."

"It doesn't hurt to ask." Eric pushed away the box he used as his footstool and put the laptop on her desk. "Can we go see him?"

"What, right now?"

Darlene didn't like the idea of asking Toven for anything. He might be her grandfather, but he was a stranger to her. During the dinner at Syssi and Kian's, he'd barely exchanged two words with her.

"Yeah, why not?"

"I don't know if he's home."

"Check. Send him a text."

She swallowed. "I'll send my mother a text and ask her to call him."

Toven and Geraldine weren't close either, but her mother had a way with people. If the god could induce Eric without killing him in the process, Geraldine could get him to agree.

Eric regarded her with an amused expression on his handsome face. "I don't think Toven will appreciate the request coming from your mother, your sister, or your son. It needs to come from you and, better yet, from both of us. We can go to his house and knock on the door, saying that we stopped by to say hello on the way to see your mother. If he's not there, we will stay to chat with Mia and wait for him to come home. I bet he doesn't leave her alone for long."

"That's actually a good plan. It's almost noon, so it won't look strange that I'm visiting my mother on my lunch break." She swiveled her chair around and got to her feet. "He will find it much harder to refuse us with Mia around. He likes showing her how good he is." She took her purse and slung the strap over her shoulder.

"So, he isn't good for real?" Eric circled his arm around her waist.

"I don't know. I think he means well. He bought half of the Perfect Match company from Syssi and the two other partners, not because he wanted the business but because he believed that the service should be made available for people with disabilities who can't afford the sessions. That's a philanthropic endeavor, and it implies that he wants to do what's right for people. But he's a god, and he's aloof, intimidating, and impossible to read."

Eric leaned away to look at her. "Are you talking about the Perfect Match virtual reality studios?"

"Have you heard of them?"

"Who hasn't? Since your grandfather and Syssi own it, do you think we can get a discount?"

"We can go for free. The clan has two machines in the village, and I can put our names on the waiting list. Those machines are very popular."

"I bet." Eric snorted. "It's the best porn anyone could have ever imagined. You get a fantasy built to your specifications and a virtual partner to share it with. Sign me up."

Darlene laughed. "It's not just for hookups. People go on solo adventures, and friends go to have fun in exotic locales and do crazy things. The possibilities are endless."

"Did you try it?"

She shook her head. "I'm not very adventurous, and if I had the guts to try it, I would only do it with someone I know and like. What about you? Why didn't you try it yet?"

"Who said I haven't?"

"I would be very surprised if you had. You're too cocky to use a service like that."

"How well do you know me, my love." He drew her against his body and kissed her temple. "I wanted to try it, but spending so much money on a virtual experience seemed frivolous to me, especially since I had no trouble finding real women to hook up with. I thought that it was only good for rich guys who couldn't get sex in real life because they were unattractive or didn't have time. It sure beats employing the services of professional sex providers."

She arched a brow. "Are you sure about that? Those providers, as you call them, are not just in the business of sex. They are also in the business of fantasy fulfillment, and they are real. I doubt a virtual experience can be as good as the real thing."

Darlene had heard people talking about it and singing its praises, but she assumed the claims were exaggerated.

Eric leaned to whisper in her ear. "There is only one way to find out. Do you think they have a threesome adventure? If they do, we could try it out in the virtual world first and see if you like it."

She shook her head vehemently. "Not here, that's for sure. We don't have the same level of anonymity in the village as they have in the commercial studios, and I don't want to become the next piece of gossip to sweep over the entire clan, including those in Scotland and in the sanctuary."

Eric

怀—	

When they reached Toven's house, Eric knocked on the door, took Darlene's hand, and plastered a wide smile on his face.

She chuckled quietly. "You look like a Tupperware salesman."

"Then let's hope Toven loves Tupperware," Eric said while maintaining his grin.

Unexpectedly, the god opened the door himself.

His brows rose in a surprised expression. "Hello."

"Good afternoon," Eric said. "We are on our way to Geraldine's for lunch, and we thought to stop by for a visit."

The god was still frowning when an elderly lady stepped out from behind him. "That's so nice of you. Please, come in. We were about to sit down for lunch, but if you are on your way to Geraldine's, we can have tea first. We don't get as many visitors now as we did when we just moved in, and it's a shame. I enjoyed it."

The god's frown turned into an indulgent smile as he put his hand on the woman's shoulder. "You've heard the lady. Come on in. I'll get Mia."

Eric had heard that Mia's grandparents were staying in the village despite being human, but seeing her grandmother in person warmed something in his heart.

His mind must have registered the apparent lack of older people, or rather older-looking individuals, and it had bothered him on a subconscious level.

He'd never liked the idea of senior communities or neighborhoods just for young couples. That wasn't how humans were wired. Humans were tribe animals, and they functioned best in blended communities where several generations coexisted and contributed to each other.

Appearances were misleading, though, and in reality, the clan was a tribe with a staggering number of generations coexisting in the village. They just all looked the same age.

The dearth of children, however, was depressing.

"We don't want to inconvenience you," Darlene didn't budge from the doorstep. "We can stop by after lunch."

"You are not going anywhere," Mia's grandmother said. "I can call Geraldine and tell her to bring whatever she made over here, and we can all have a nice lunch together." She waved her hand to encourage them to come in.

"We don't get enough visitors, and it gets boring." She laughed. "Who would have thought that a village full of immortals could be boring."

Darlene raised a pair of panicked eyes to him. They hadn't even told her mother that they were coming over.

He leaned closer to Mia's grandmother's ear and said in a conspiratorial voice, "The truth is that we didn't tell Geraldine that we were coming over for lunch, so we can accept your invitation without hurting her feelings."

"Wonderful." She offered him her hand. "I'm Rosalyn."

"I'm Eric." He lifted her hand and kissed the back of it.

"Oh, I know who you are. Mia told me that you were very handsome and charming, and she didn't exaggerate one bit. You are all that and more."

"Thank you."

"Hi." Mia drove into the living room in her motorized wheelchair. "What a wonderful surprise."

"I apologize for the intrusion," Darlene said. "I should have called ahead." She looked at Eric. "My mate is much more impulsive than I am."

"I like that in a man," Mia's grandfather said from the couch. "Assertiveness and boldness are the markers of a winner."

Eric chuckled. "That's what I keep telling Darlene."

From behind Mia, Toven was still regarding them with a raised brow.

He knew that they hadn't come on a social call, but he was waiting patiently for them to state the reason for their visit.

"I heard that Kaia was released from the clinic this morning," Mia said. "Is she out of the woods, so to speak?"

"Not yet." Eric sat on the couch next to Mia's grandfather. "I'm Eric." He offered his hand to the man.

"Curtis. Welcome to the family." He shook his hand with surprising strength for an older gentleman.

"Kaia's transition is unlike any of the others." Darlene sat on Eric's other side. "She's progressing very slowly, but thankfully, very smoothly as well. That's why she was allowed to go home. But Bridget wants to keep testing her for a few more days."

"That's interesting." Toven pulled out one of the dining chairs and sat next to Mia. "What do you mean by slow?"

Normally, Eric wouldn't have shared medical information about his niece, but this wasn't a normal situation. Toven had information that they didn't, and he might have helpful suggestions.

Besides, they needed to ask him for a big favor.

"I don't know the results of today's tests, but Saturday and Sunday, it took her over four minutes to heal from the cut test. It's much faster than it would have taken a human to heal a cut like that completely, so it indicates that she's transitioning, but slowly. Also, her eyesight corrected itself, and she now sees perfectly, so that's another proof that things are changing in her body. It's just taking longer than it did for other Dormants."

"That's interesting." Toven rubbed his jaw with his thumb and finger. "I wonder why Kaia's transition is so different."

Darlene

~

It was the opening Darlene needed. "I hoped you would know more about it. Back in the days of the gods, so many Dormants were initiated, and someone must have collected that data. Were there any anomalies back then?"

Toven shrugged. "I wasn't involved with Dormants." He draped his arm over Mia's shoulders. "Mia is the first Dormant I ever initiated."

Darlene's heart sank.

"Did any of the other gods induce male Dormants?" Eric asked. "Or was it beneath them?"

"To the best of my knowledge, it was always done by immortals. Don't forget that in those days, Dormants were initiated when they reached puberty, so they were still children. The idea was to make the process as fun and as exciting as possible for them, so their initiators were immortals who were just a little older than them."

That wasn't good. No one knew what a god's venom would do to a male Dormant. But if Toven had successfully induced Mia's transition, a fragile girl with a lot of health problems, he should be able to do that for Eric as well.

Still, it was more prudent to wait for Orion's return. Gilbert would just have to come back to the village for the ceremony on Sunday.

Looking at Eric, Darlene waited until he felt her gaze and turned to look at her. "We should wait for Orion to return or ask Kian," she said.

"What do you need to ask of Kian?" Toven asked as if he didn't know.

"Eric is obviously not transitioning, and we need to find a new initiator for him. I suggested that we find someone closer to the source. I thought that Orion would be the best choice. He's as close to the source as it gets, and he's not too intimidating, but he's not here, so we will have to wait for him."

Toven smiled knowingly. "Do you want me to do it?"

"Yes, please," Eric said.

"No." Darlene shook her head. "We don't know what your venom can do when you get aggressive. It might be too potent and kill Eric instead of initiating his transition."

"It won't. That's not how the venom works, and I have excellent control over the amount of venom I inject. The moment Eric's heart starts to slow down, I'll stop."

"Are you sure?" Darlene asked.

"I'm positive." He leaned and kissed Mia's temple. "I was very careful with Mia, injecting her with only a minimal amount of venom at a time. If I could do that while aroused, I can do that while aggressing on a male." He smiled at her. "I wouldn't do that for anyone else, but you are my granddaughter, and your happiness is important to me. I still regret not being around to help your mother and you. If I hadn't been such a jaded wreck, I wouldn't have turned Orion away, and we could have found your mother much sooner. Perhaps even before she met her husband."

Darlene chuckled. "Then I wouldn't have been born. I should be thankful to you that you threw Orion out, but at the same time, I regret all the years we all missed as a family."

They still weren't as close as she would have liked, but things didn't happen overnight, and she needed to give it time.

Her mother was doing her best to bring everyone together, but with Orion gone, everything had been put on hold, awaiting his return.

"When do you want me to induce you?" Toven asked Eric.

"As soon as possible. My brother is taking his family back home tomorrow, and I hoped that they would get to watch my second initiation ceremony." He grinned. "As the middle child, I'm always hungry for attention."

"We can do it tonight." Toven leaned back and crossed his feet at the ankles. "But there is no time to arrange for another ceremony and no need. We can meet up at the gym, Kian can say the ceremonial words again, and if you want, your family can witness the match."

Mia lifted her hand. "Before you rush off to do that, did you check with Bridget whether it's okay to try again after such a short time?"

Darlene looked at Eric. "We didn't, and we should."

"Call her now," Toven suggested.

"Can it wait for after lunch?" Rosalyn asked. "My casserole is getting dry sitting in the warming drawer."

"It can wait." Eric rose to his feet and offered a hand up to Darlene.

She didn't agree, but since everyone had gotten up and headed to the dining table, she couldn't voice her objection without sounding rude.

"So, Eric." Toven draped a napkin over his slacks. "Tell us about yourself."

"What would you like to know?"

"Everything. My granddaughter chose you as her mate, and you are about to become part of our family. I would like to get to know you better."

Eric

After lunch was over and Toven had learned everything there was to know about Eric aside from his shoe size, they all returned to the living room, and Eric texted Bridget.

A quick question, if I may. How soon after the first initiation can I have another?

Instead of replying to his text, she called. "First of all, tell me, how are you feeling?"

"I feel the same as I did before Max bit me. There is absolutely no change."

"Do you feel well overall?"

"I do." He chuckled. "As you've seen, according to the results of my latest physical, I'm in perfect health."

"Is Max going to initiate you again?"

"Nope. This time I'm getting the highest and purest octane available. Darlene's grandfather agreed to induce me. In fact, he is here with me, and I'm going to switch the speaker on, so he can join the conversation."

Toven smiled. "I don't need that to hear perfectly well, but thank you for the consideration."

After a long moment of stunned silence, the physician said, "Good afternoon, Toven."

"Hello, Bridget."

"When is the event going to take place?" she asked.

"Tonight at the gym, but without all the fanfare," Eric said. "Toven hinted that one ceremony was enough for a schlump like me."

His attempt at self-deprecating humor didn't garner even a chuckle.

Tough crowd.

"I'll be there," Bridget said. "Seeing a god in action should be a sight to behold. In fact, I want to film the event."

Toven laughed. "Now you're giving me performance anxiety. Gods and immortals are not that different as far as brute strength goes. In fact, I've never needed to engage in hand-to-hand combat, and I'm so untrained that Eric might best me. I've always relied on my mental powers to defend myself."

"I have no doubt that you will be spectacular," Bridget said. "If that's okay with you, I will bring a professional camera."

"Be my guest," Toven said.

"Thank you. I'll meet you at the gym tonight at eleven-thirty." She ended the call.

Eric lifted a brow. "You've never fought with your hands? Not even as a boy?"

Toven shook his head. "My upbringing was very formal, and I spent most of my time studying. My mother would have disowned me if I was caught fighting with other boys."

"That's sad." Eric made a face. "You missed out on male bonding. Gilbert is seven years older than me, so we didn't get to fight much, but I found plenty of partners in crime at school."

Toven smiled. "It sounds like you had a great childhood. I'm happy for you."

"I did." Eric smiled as the memories flashed through his head.

Suddenly, it occurred to him that the ceremony was about more than just getting bitten, and that he and Toven would also exchange vows of friendship and loyalty. Would he be bound to both his initiators?

"I have a question. Since Max failed to induce me, am I still bound to him for eternity?"

Toven laughed softly. "The promise is not as binding as the ceremonial words make it sound. If you don't like Max, you don't have to be friends with him."

"What about loyalty?" Darlene asked. "Will Eric have to protect Max if the need arises?"

"If Eric transitions and becomes a member of the clan, he will owe loyalty to everyone in his new family, and if we are attacked, he will be expected to join our defense efforts."

"How do you know that?" Mia asked. "You are not even an official member of the clan."

"I am not, but I pledged my loyalty to Annani and her descendants. Do you think Kian would have allowed me to live in the village without that? I'm not subordinate to him or his mother, but I will stand with them if the need arises."

"Got it." Eric leaned back and wrapped his arm around Darlene's shoulders. "I have no problem with that. I like the idea of being part of a community of people who look out for each other. It's just that I feel uncomfortable asking a god to be my buddy."

Toven chuckled. "If you transition, you will be mated to my granddaughter. We will be more than buddies. We will be a family."

"Awesome." Eric grinned. "Wait until Gilbert hears about that. He always wanted us to have a big family, and now that he can have it, he's playing chicken."

"What do you mean?" Curtis asked.

"He and Karen are afraid of attempting transition because they have three little kids they don't want to orphan. They are seriously considering giving up on the opportunity to become immortal."

"I'll talk to them after the ceremony tonight," Toven said. "They have nothing to fear."

Eric wondered why Toven sounded so sure when everyone else kept warning them about the dangers to older Dormants. Was it because he'd managed to successfully induce a sick young woman? Or was he just cocky because he was a god?

"What makes you so sure that they will make it?" Darlene asked.

Toven smiled. "I'm sure you've heard about the blessings Annani gives to transitioning Dormants." When they nodded, he continued, "She's coming back to the village this Thursday, and I'm here to assist her. If your brother and his wife need help transitioning, they will get blessings from two gods, not just one. They are practically guaranteed to come out immortal on the other side."

"Forgive me." Eric dipped his head. "I don't want to sound disrespectful, but isn't that putting too much faith in blessings?"

Toven smiled indulgently. "Not when they are coming from a god." He snapped his fingers, and suddenly, his skin was glowing. "We command energy that we don't understand." He snapped his fingers again, and his skin stopped glowing.

"How did you do that?" Darlene asked. "I thought that you lost your glow."

"I did, but Mia helped me find it again." He leaned toward his mate and kissed her cheek.

Eric was impressed but not convinced. The glow was a neat trick, but it didn't prove anything. Nevertheless, it might be enough to convince Gilbert and Karen to stop fretting and embrace the incredible opportunity they were being given.

William

As William opened the door to his house, he was greeted by a happy-looking Kaia and the aromas of cooked food.

Both made him salivate.

"Welcome home, my darling." Kaia wrapped her arms around his neck and pulled him to her for a kiss.

As his hands roamed over the curve of her bottom, he was conflicted about what he wanted to do first, make love to Kaia or eat what she'd made.

Somewhere in the back of his mind, an annoying thought floated to the surface. Kaia was doing a great impression of a 1950s wife, and it was so uncharacteristic of her that it had gotten his attention despite the haze of lust and hunger clouding his brain.

Letting go of his mouth, Kaia took his hand. "I made dinner." She led him to the kitchen.

"I can smell it."

He had no idea what she could have possibly found in his refrigerator to cook with.

William made sandwiches, but he never cooked, so he didn't buy groceries to prepare meals with. Other than cold cuts, cheeses, and frozen buns, whatever was in his kitchen had been brought over by Darlene weeks ago. After she'd visited him, she'd gone to the supermarket and gotten him a load of dry and frozen goods that he could prepare quick meals from. With the exception of the occasional frozen pizza that they popped in the oven, he and Kaia had been eating mostly in the café and other people's houses.

"Sit." Kaia motioned to the kitchen bistro table. "I'm going to serve you."

He shook his head. "I will do that. You cooked, I'll serve."

"Not today." She shoved him toward the chair. "I want to do something nice for you, so don't argue."

William stifled a chuckle.

That was the Kaia he knew and loved. Bossy and assertive even when she was playing housewife.

The baking dish she put on the table had a roasted chicken resting on top of rice pilaf and was decorated with baby carrots and green beans.

William's mouth watered. "Where did you get the ingredients to make this?"

"From Geraldine. She came over to check on me, and when I told her that there was nothing to make dinner from, she asked what I wanted to make and brought everything I needed from her house." Kaia handed him the chicken shears. "Can you do the cutting?"

"Of course." He got to work on the bird. "It smells so good."

"I hope you like it." She sat across from him.

"Did you get any rest at all?" he asked.

He'd been texting every thirty minutes to ask Kaia how she felt, and she'd answered right away, but she hadn't told him that she was making dinner.

"My mother and Gilbert came over with Cheryl and the little ones, and they made a mess, I mean the little ones. I cleaned the house after they left, and then Geraldine came, and then I cooked dinner, and here we are. I feel great."

Maybe giving her brain a rest and doing simple physical work was just what she'd needed.

Some claimed that it was therapeutic, and others claimed that exercise was great for mood improvement, but he'd never experienced either. Everything that took time away from his work annoyed him and made him anxious.

Well, not everything.

Time spent with Kaia was wonderful.

"I'm glad." He put half of the chicken on her plate and half on his.

She looked at the portion and laughed. "I can't eat all that."

"Eat as much as you can, and I'll finish the rest." He put rice pilaf on her plate and then on his and finished with the baby carrots and green beans.

"I don't have Coke." Kaia pouted. "And I can't drink that horrible beer you have in the fridge. It's the same one you had in Safe Haven."

"How about wine?" He got to his feet. "I should have a couple of bottles somewhere."

They were there when he'd moved into the house, part of a welcome basket that Ingrid had prepared.

"Found it." He pulled a bottle from the top shelf. "Now I just need to find a bottle opener." He started rummaging through the kitchen drawers until he found it.

"I'll get the glasses." Kaia pushed away from the table. "I know where they are."

After William uncorked the wine and poured it into two glasses, he raised his glass to Kaia's. "Cheers, my love. To your immortality."

Kaia

"To immortality." Kaia clinked her glass with William's and leaned over the table to meet him halfway for a kiss.

She still enjoyed kissing him, still felt desire for him, but it was tainted by the other part of her that had lain dormant along with her immortal genes and had been awakened alongside them.

She'd hoped that fussing with her looks and playing house would make her feel more like a woman, but Edgar was still there in the background, and she couldn't keep pretending that she was alright when she was anything but.

But how could she tell William that the transition had brought the male side of her to the forefront and that she was no longer the woman he'd fallen in love with?

Would it be a deal breaker for him?

Even if it was, she couldn't continue like this. She had to tell him and get it off her chest. Maybe he could even help her.

Kaia put her glass down. "Something strange happened to me during my transition. I hoped it would go away, but it's still here, and it's driving me crazy."

His eyes clouding with worry, William put his glass down as well. "What is it?"

"Remember what I told you about remembering my past life?"

"Vividly."

"For some reason, the transition awakened way too many of those memories. I dreamt about being Edgar, and I found much more about who I used to be than I ever wanted to know. He wasn't a nice man." She shook her head. "I mean, I wasn't a nice man. I was a misogynistic jerk who hated women, put them down, and believed that they were good only for pleasuring men and bearing children."

"You shouldn't beat yourself up over that. Many men of that generation held the same beliefs. Changing those attitudes was one of the clan's missions, and it's been extremely difficult to undo hundreds of years of patriarchal indoctrination. We are still not where the Clan Mother would like us to be. Large portions of the world are still stuck in the Dark Ages in that regard, and even the West still has a long way to go before true equality can be achieved."

"Don't try to make light of it. I was much worse than the average chauvinist. But my deplorable attitudes toward women are not the worst of it." She picked up the glass and emptied the rest of the wine down her throat. "Suddenly being attracted to women is."

William chuckled. "I don't think that's so bad. After all, I'm attracted to a woman as well."

Kaia could have throttled him.

He was usually so understanding, so willing to listen, but now he was belittling a very serious problem.

There was a good reason why the vast majority of people didn't remember their past lives. It was a curse, an affliction, and she wanted those memories and their influence gone.

"You don't get it. I found myself lusting after Bridget and thinking how perfect her ass and her boobs were. And then I lusted after Hildegard, thinking that her husky voice was so damn sexy. Those thoughts weren't kind, though, like an appreciation of their feminine beauty. They were nasty and lewd, and they weren't Kaia's. They were all Edgar's. I don't know what to do."

William's smile faded away. "I'll call Nathalie. She knows how to deal with invading spirits and how to prevent them from taking over."

"Edgar is not an invading spirit, and I don't need an exorcist. I need someone to erase those memories, but now that I'm immortal, I can't be thralled."

But she could still be compelled.

"That's why I want to go back to Safe Haven as soon as possible. Emmett and Eleanor might be able to compel me to forget Edgar's life."

"I'm not sure they can do that. Those are not your own memories, not as Kaia, and you have no control over them. Compulsion forces you to do or not to do things, but you need to be able to do them in the first place for it to work."

"What do you mean?"

"Emmett can compel you to sing opera, but he can't compel you to do it well if you don't have the ability to do that. Or he can try to compel you to shoot a bullseye on a target that's two miles away. You won't be able to do that no matter what. Do you get what I'm saying?"

"I think so. How about thralling? Would that work?"

"If you were still human, perhaps someone very skilled and very powerful could do it. But since those are very old memories, even then it might not be possible. Thralling works best on recent memories."

Slumping in her chair, Kaia groaned. "Then I'm screwed. I don't want to live forever with Edgar in my head. I'll go insane."

William leaned forward and put his hand over hers. "A god or a goddess can thrall other immortals, and Annani is an excellent thraller. She might be able to thrall away even old memories. But first, you need to meet with

Nathalie, if only to eliminate the possibility that Edgar is not you in a prior life, but someone who hitched a ride on your brain."

"Fine. I'll talk to her, but I know it's not an invading spirit regardless of what that aura guy said."

Darlene

"Are you excited?" Darlene asked as she and Eric got out of the elevator on the gym level.

After their lunch meeting with Toven, they'd gone back to her office, and Eric had gone back to working on a lease deal with his buddies. He'd seemed calm, and when they'd gone home, they'd made love and had fallen asleep.

It had been a good day, and hopefully, it would end well too.

"I am enthusiastic and, for some reason, less apprehensive than I was with Max." He chuckled. "Toven's claim about his lack of training is giving me hope."

"I wouldn't count on it. He's still a god with strength and speed you can't match."

"I know." He stopped and pulled her against him. "This time, it's going to work." He smiled. "It has to because there is nowhere to go from here. I jumped from the bottom of the ladder all the way to the top rung."

"Max wasn't the bottom rung, but I get what you're saying." She stretched on her toes and kissed his lips. "Ready?"

"Ready." He took her hand and pushed the gym doors open.

The place hadn't been rearranged this time, and only the family and a few others were there to witness Eric's second initiation attempt. It was underwhelming for such a monumental event, and Darlene regretted listening to Toven and not arranging another grand ceremony.

There were no tables, not even chairs to sit on, and they were all standing around the mat like spectators in an underground fight club.

Then again, if Toven's preference was to keep it low-key, she couldn't repay his kindness by disregarding his wishes.

"Good evening," Eric greeted their guests. "Thank you for coming to cheer me on." He smiled at Toven. "And thank you for agreeing to bite me."

"You're welcome." The god turned to Kian. "Shall we begin?"

"Bridget is not here yet," Kian said. "We also need the ceremonial wine, and Okidu is not done."

Kian's butler was using one of the treadmills as his table. He'd put the tray with small wine glasses on the track and was filling them from the two bottles he'd brought with him.

Gilbert patted Eric's back. "It's going to work this time. I feel it in my gut."

"Of course, it's going to work." Eric glanced at Toven. "I have a god inducing me. No other male Dormant has gotten induced by him before. I'm making history."

Toven put his hand on his shoulder. "First, you need to spur my aggression, and that's not going to be easy. I don't remember the last time my fangs elongated in response to a challenge by another male. I think it was when Mortdh irritated me. Since then, I have only used them to bring pleasure. But I have to admit that every time I think of him, which I try not to do too often, my fangs itch with the need to kill him, and I have to remind myself that he's already dead."

"Did you ever fight Mortdh?" Kian asked.

Toven chuckled. "I was too smart for that. He would have won, and he would have killed me." He sighed. "If I provoked him, and he *accidentally* killed me in the heat of the fight, it wouldn't have counted as murder. He was insane, but he wasn't stupid. In fact, he was very smart and calculating."

"I would love to hear more about him one day." Kian leaned against an elliptical machine. "It might provide me with a better understanding of his son." He smiled. "The more I know about my enemy, the better I'll be prepared to fight him if needed. Maybe we can meet and talk about Mortdh and your history with him over cigars."

Toven shook his head. "I don't like talking about him, or the other gods for that matter. Even after five thousand years, it's still painful."

"I thought that you'd grown numb," Darlene blurted. "That's what you told Orion."

"Guilty," he admitted. "When the pain and disappointment become intolerable, the only way to carry on is to become numb. But the moment I allowed myself to feel again, the pain returned along with the joy."

"Was it because of me?" Mia asked in a small voice.

"It was thanks to you. You brought me back to life."

The doors to the gym flew open, and Bridget rushed in with a big movie camera hoisted on her shoulder. "I'm sorry I'm late, but I was waiting for this." She patted the camera. "Brandon promised to get it for me, but he was stuck in traffic."

Syssi tilted her head. "At eleven-thirty at night? That's unusual even for Los Angeles."

"There was an accident on the 405." Bridget smiled at Toven. "I hope you're still okay with starring in this historical document."

"As long as no one outside the clan ever sees the recording, I don't mind." He looked at the camera. "Do you know how to use it?'

"It's not complicated." She patted the sleek device. "This thing does everything automatically. I just need to point the lens in the right direction and shoot."

Toven cast the camera another skeptical glance before turning to Kian. "Can we begin now that Bridget is here?"

"In a moment. I'm just waiting for Okidu to distribute the wine."

From the corner of her eye, Darlene saw the gym door open and then Max walked in. She nodded at him, and he nodded back, then leaned against the wall and crossed his arms over his chest.

Eric

Kian and Toven's conversation about the god's rivalry with his dead brother had given Eric an idea for how to spur Toven's aggression.

He could taunt him by mentioning Mortdh and how he had been stronger and smarter than Toven. But what if the mention of the hated brother got the god so enraged that he accidentally killed him?

Nah. Toven claimed to have excellent control over his fangs and venom glands. Besides, he was too calm and collected to lose control, especially in front of his mate.

Mia looked up to him like the god he was, and Toven basked in her adoration. He wouldn't want to lose that by killing his granddaughter's mate.

Potential mate.

If, for some reason, this induction failed as well, there would be no point in trying again.

Who knew? Maybe he and Gilbert weren't related to Syssi after all? Those tests weren't always reliable.

When Okidu was done distributing the wine, Kian lifted his glass. "Eric is ready to attempt his transformation for the second time, and we are gathered here to witness his initiation. He's incredibly fortunate to have Toven as his initiator, which will probably earn him the envy of many. Having a god as your initiator is not only an honor and a privilege, it also dramatically increases your chances of transitioning quickly. In addition, you are gaining a powerful friend."

Eric bowed his head to Toven. "I'm honored and grateful beyond words, and naturally, I accept you as my mentor, initiator, and protector. I was told that after the ceremony, the role of the initiator is similar to that of a godfather, so I'm pleased to pledge my loyalty and eternal friendship to my god-brother." He offered his hand to Toven. "Shall we shake on it?"

Taking his hand, Toven smiled without a hint of fang in sight. "I accept your pledge and intend to hold you to it, my young god-brother." He turned to Kian. "Let's conclude the ceremony and get it done."

Kian nodded. "Is there anyone here who objects to Eric becoming Toven's protégé?"

Eric glanced at the small crowd and was surprised to see Max. The Guardian stood apart from everyone else, leaning against the gym wall with his arms crossed over his chest.

Max lifted a thumbs up and mouthed something that Eric didn't understand but assumed was good luck.

When no one voiced an objection, Kian nodded. "As everyone here agrees that it's a good match, let's seal it with a toast. To Toven and Eric."

Gilbert hooted, Karen and William said good luck, and Kaia gave him the thumbs up. Cheryl, who'd stayed just outside the door with Idina and the twins asleep in their strollers, blew him a kiss.

Eric blew one back.

"Let's do it." Toven toed off his shoes and turned to Eric. "Ready?"

"As ready as I'll ever be to challenge a god."

As they took their positions on the mat, Eric reconsidered his idea of taunting Toven with talk about Mortdh.

Having a god as his god-brother was a cherished privilege, and he didn't want to tarnish it from the get-go by saying something hurtful.

The god might hold a grudge.

"Well?" Toven beckoned him with his hand. "Unless you attack me, my fangs won't come out."

"What if I insult your mother instead? Will that work?"

Eric had intended it as a joke, but Toven tilted his head in contemplation. "You can try, but I can't think of an insult that would be relevant to a goddess. My mother was very beautiful, regal, and proper."

Toven's sense of humor needed some work, and Eric was just the guy the god needed to sharpen his funny bone.

"Right. So that's a no-go." Eric shook out his arms to loosen them.

He was well-trained, and he was in good shape. He might be able to get the god to punch back.

Lurching forward, Eric threw a roundhouse kick at Toven, but his foot never made contact with the god's chest. With lightning-fast reflexes, Toven caught it and held on.

Eric lost his balance and fell on his ass, but his foot remained in Toven's clasp.

"You will have to try harder," the god said.

"How? I move in slow motion compared to you."

Toven let go of his foot. "Maybe insulting my mother will work after all."

"It's worth a try." Eric got to his feet and thought of something that was insulting but not vulgar. "Why did your mother play hard to get when she was so hard to want?"

For a moment, Toven just gaped at him, and Eric was sure that an assault was imminent, but then the god burst out laughing. "That's so true. How did you know?"

Great. So, he managed to make Toven laugh, but he failed to spur his aggression.

That insult was as vanilla as they got, but Eric didn't want to go overboard and dip into vulgarity. There were too many witnesses to the show who he wanted to impress with his wit and charm rather than his ability to use crass language.

"Well, looking at you, it wasn't hard to guess." Eric waved a hand in Toven's direction. "You are stiffer than a broomstick and have no sense of humor. No wonder you had to resort to virtual match-making."

That was such a blatant untruth that it shouldn't have worked to rile Toven, but when he smiled, his fangs were a little longer than they had been before.

"Go on," Toven said.

"Mortdh should be thankful that he was born to a different mother, but given how he turned out, your entire family's tainted gene pool could use a disinfectant."

Hopefully, Toven would accept his apology when this was over. Darlene belonged to the same gene pool, and she was wonderful.

His eyes blazing, the god advanced on him unhurriedly but with menacing intent.

Fear slithering down his spine, Eric lifted his fists in self-defense, but Toven swiped them aside as if they belonged to a newborn baby, grabbed Eric by the back of his neck, and struck with his fangs.

The bite was brutal, and it burned, but a moment later, a cooling sensation washed over Eric, along with the kind of calm he'd only experienced once when his friends had tricked him into eating a muffin baked with psychedelic mushrooms.

In the back of his mind, Eric was aware of the cool venom being pumped into his veins and that it was dangerous if it went on for too long, but he couldn't bring himself to care.

Kian

Kian had to admit that Toven's control was admirable. The god hadn't hurt a hair on Eric's head, and he retracted his fangs after thirty seconds, which was probably long enough for a god's potent venom to activate Eric's dormant genes.

He hadn't needed a full minute like Max had, and no one had to tell him.

Bridget kept filming as Toven laid Eric gently on the mat and turned to Darlene. "He's all yours."

"Thank you." She rushed to her mate, sat on the mat, and lifted his head to rest in her lap.

Toven pushed his feet into his shoes and glanced at the camera. "This concludes tonight's festivities. Goodnight, everyone."

Getting the hint, Bridget turned the camera off and handed the device to Kian. "I should check on Eric."

"He's fine." Toven walked over to stand beside Mia, who was congratulating Gilbert and Karen. "I heard that you are hesitant to attempt transition."

Gilbert nodded. "But before we talk about that, I just wanted to say that Eric didn't mean any of the nasty things he said. He was just trying to rile you."

"I know." Toven smiled. "He loves my granddaughter, who comes from the same gene pool, so he couldn't have meant what he said about disinfecting it." He rubbed his chin with his thumb and finger. "Mortdh inherited his insanity from his mother, not our father, so Darlene doesn't carry it. Your brother shouldn't fear that his children will be predisposed to mental health issues."

"It never even crossed my mind," Gilbert said. "Or Eric's. Darlene is a wonderful lady, and I'm happy that she and my brother clicked. I wish them all the best." He looked at the mat where Darlene was cradling Eric's head in her lap and murmuring words of love and encouragement to him. "How long is he supposed to be out? Is it going to be like last time?"

Toven shrugged. "I don't know. That was my first time inducing a male Dormant."

Kian glanced to where Max had been standing only minutes ago, but the Guardian was no longer there. He must have slipped out when everyone's attention was on Darlene and Eric.

"I saw the whole thing." Kaia's sister appeared right beside them, then looked at the god and blushed. "Good evening, your Excellence."

Chuckling, he gently patted the girl's back. "I'm no one's excellence. I'm just Toven."

"You are incredibly strong." She looked up at him as if he was a movie star. "Are you stronger than the immortals?"

"I might be slightly stronger and a tad faster, but don't worry. I've had thousands of years to practice moderating my strength. I didn't hurt your uncle."

"I know. It's just that it was scary to watch you bat away his hands as if he was a puppet on a string. Eric is strong."

"You should go back," her mother said. "You can't leave the babies alone in the vestibule."

"They are not alone. Max is watching them."

Kian wasn't sure whether Max knew what to do with a crying baby, but if either of them woke up, he could just open the door and call their parents.

Karen didn't look comfortable with the guy watching her children either, but she was too polite to say that. Instead, she glared at her daughter. "The match is over, and there is nothing more to see. Please, go back and let Max go home. He has work tomorrow."

"Fine." Cheryl glanced at the mat. "Is Eric going to be okay?"

Bridget was busy taking Eric's vitals, but she didn't seem worried.

"I'm sure he will be," Kian said. "Our doctor is with him."

When Cheryl left, Toven turned his attention back to Karen and Gilbert. "If you're not too tired, we can find a place to sit, and I'll try to convince you not to go home."

"We have to," Karen said. "Even if we decide to go for it, we can't just stay here. We need to figure out what to do with our house, my work, Gilbert's business, Cheryl's school, Idina's preschool, and the list goes on."

Toven just smiled. "I understand. It was much easier for me because I led the life of a nomad, but it was much more difficult for Mia, even though she's a freelancer and works from home. We've just recently moved into the village, and it's an adjustment, but we love it here."

"The village is lovely." Karen sighed. "But we have children to think of."

"I have a daughter," Kian said. "And I wouldn't want her to be anywhere else. This is the safest place for her." He put his arm around Syssi's shoulders. "There is a saying that it takes a village to raise a child, and it's never been truer than right here right now."

Syssi cast him one of her indulgent looks, communicating that he should let her take over. "The only way to address so many challenges is one at a time." She looked at Toven. "Can you meet with Karen and Gilbert tomorrow? We can all have a nice lunch in our backyard and discuss their options at leisure."

"I can, but you work in the morning, and they plan to leave in the afternoon."

"About that." She looked at Karen. "Aren't you curious to meet the goddess? She returns to the village on Thursday. Besides, Eric's transition might start as early as tomorrow. He was induced by a god."

Karen gave Syssi an apologetic look. "I wish we could stay, but we really need to go back. If it's okay with you, we can come back for another visit during the weekend."

Syssi let out a breath. "I want us to have a clear plan of action before you leave, and I also want us to have a proper goodbye lunch. I'll take a day off tomorrow." She looked up at Kian. "Our place at one in the afternoon. Does that work for you?"

"I'll make it work."

William

Kaia had talked a mile a minute on the way home from Eric's second initiation ceremony, and William hadn't interrupted her. He'd limited his responses to the occasional nod or a word here and there, and she hadn't even noticed that he was quieter than usual.

He wanted her so badly that his body ached all over, but she was in a funk, disturbed by urges she didn't welcome, and he wasn't sure she still desired him.

What should he do?

Should he let her take control and get her male urges out?

Or should he do the opposite, assume the dominant role, and hope that it would make her feel more feminine, more like her old self?

When they got to the house, he reached for her, sliding his arm around her waist. "Are you tired?"

It was after one o'clock in the morning, and she was still in the initial stages of her transition, but since her transition wasn't following the traditional path, he didn't know what to expect.

Kaia shook her head. "I'm immortal now."

"You're not over the initial stage of your transition yet. You don't have the energy of an immortal."

She looked at him with defiance in her eyes. "If you've already decided that I'm tired, why did you ask?"

He cupped her cheek and smiled. "There are degrees of tiredness. Do you want to sleep, or do you want to play?"

A smirk lifted the left corner of her lush lips, and she lifted her arms to his shoulders. "I want to play."

"That was the correct answer." He turned her around, pressing his erection to her backside. "Hands on the wall, Kaia."

She looked at him over her shoulder. "What kind of game are we playing?"

Caging her against the wall, he slipped his hand under her T-shirt and caressed her stomach. "The kind you're going to like." He added his other hand to the play, sliding it down between her thighs.

"How do you know that I'm going to like it?" She let her head drop back against his shoulder.

"Because I can smell your arousal." He nuzzled the side of her neck.

He could also feel the heat coming off her center, and as he rubbed her through the fabrics of her tights and panties, her thighs shivered deliciously.

"I think you like this game very much." He nipped her ear as he pulled her flimsy bra down and under her breasts. "Let's up the ante." He pinched her nipple.

Moaning, she bucked against him, rubbing her ass over his aching shaft in a blatant demand.

"Not yet, love." He left the heat of her center and added his other hand to the assault on her breasts.

Teasing her mercilessly, he caressed one breast while pinching the other and then switching it up. When he grazed her neck with his fangs, she lifted up on her toes.

Kaia was close to the edge, but he wasn't about to let her reach climax yet.

He took a moment to caress her tormented breasts and then slid his hands down her ribcage to her stomach and pushed them under the elastic of her tights to cup her center.

"William," she breathed. "Please." She pressed her core to his palm.

"Since you ask so nicely." He nipped her neck and pushed two fingers inside her, rubbing her clit with his thumb at the same time.

As the climax tore through her, Kaia gasped and arched back, her legs trembling from the force of it.

William pulled his fingers out and brought them to her mouth. "Open."

She obeyed, and as he thrust them between her lips, another tremor shook her body.

Evidently his gamble had paid off, and this was precisely what Kaia had needed to forget all about the male side of her.

When she was done sucking on his fingers, he hooked them under her chin, tilted her head, and kissed her.

As the taste of her exploded over his tongue, his eyes rolled back in his head, and he kissed her like a man possessed, sucking on her tongue and licking inside her mouth until he got it all.

Kaia

Kaia was still boneless from her climax when William went down to his knees and started peeling her leggings off. If not for the wall her hands and forehead were pressed against, she would have collapsed in a heap on the floor.

As her pants and panties cleared her bottom, he nipped one buttock and then the other and then lifted one leg at a time to tug the garments off.

When she was naked from the waist down, William gripped her hips and reached with his tongue between her legs, lapping up her juices as if they were the most delicious thing he'd ever tasted.

A shiver ran through her, but it wasn't one of arousal.

Suddenly Kaia was Edgar again, and the thought of licking a woman down there was repulsive to him.

Her.

Him.

Them.

No, it was only repulsive to the jerk she used to be. She was Kaia now, and Kaia loved cunnilingus.

Except, that nasty invading tone had ruined her fun, and it didn't take William long to realize that she wasn't enjoying his tongue as much as she usually did.

After pressing two soft kisses to her butt cheeks, he pushed up to his feet, enveloped her from behind with his big body, and ground his erection against her backside.

As he nuzzled and kissed her neck, Kaia shut her eyes tightly, stifling the frustrated groan that threatened to leave her throat.

William would misinterpret it, thinking that she didn't want him inside of her, when the opposite was true. She was just angry at those damn memories that had ruined their fun.

Her defenses had been momentarily down when Edgar had intruded on her pleasure, but she'd gotten rid of him quickly enough and could have continued enjoying William's talented tongue, but he was so attuned to her that he'd caught that one moment and decided that she didn't want him to continue.

Turning her head, she offered him her lips. "Kiss me."

William kissed her gently and yet ardently, and when he let go of her mouth, he turned her around, lifted her into his arms, and kissed her again.

Kaia wound her legs around his torso as he walked back to the couch and dropped down.

When they came up for air once again, they looked at each other as if they were reconnecting after being lost, or maybe it was just her. His face was so familiar, so precious to her, and the love shining in his glowing eyes nourished her battered soul.

He was beautiful to her, fangs and all.

As love for William swelled in Kaia's chest, a tear slid out of the corner of her eye. "I love you so much." She shifted up to her knees, unbuckled his belt, and lowered his zipper.

He whipped his shirt over his head, buttons flying as they were ripped off, and tossed it behind him. In the next moment, he arched up between her spread knees and pushed his pants and boxers down his thighs.

Kaia didn't wait for him to get rid of them all the way. Gripping his hard length, she sank down on it until they were merged.

William groaned, and as his shaft swelled inside of her, it filled her so deliciously that it was almost too much, but he didn't move, and his hands were gentle on her back. "I love you, Kaia, in any shape or form. You are mine, and I'm yours, and there is no obstacle we can't overcome together."

His words were like a gentle balm on her frayed nerves, and if not for the hard length pulsing inside of her and demanding her attention, Kaia could have melted with all the emotions he was evoking in her, but sex wasn't about soft and cuddly, at least not this time. She needed it rough and wild to chase away the last vestiges of those unwelcome urges and ugly thoughts.

Bracing her hands on William's shoulders, Kaia lifted and then sank back down, and when she did it again, he gripped her hips and took over.

Driving into her, he was no longer the gentle lover she was used to. He was a ferocious beast, his thrusts so powerful that the couch groaned under the force of them.

Kaia hung on for dear life, her fingers digging into William's shoulders, and as he hissed and sank his fangs into her neck, a climax erupted out of her with a magnitude of eight on the Richter scale.

Darlene

W hen Darlene's alarm went off at five in the morning, she groaned, found her phone, and shut it up.

There would be no swimming for her this morning.

The ceremony had ended late last night, and it had taken Eric nearly an hour to float down from his cloud of bliss and open his eyes.

He'd smiled up at her and said groggily, "I love you."

She still felt all warm and fuzzy as she thought about that. Regrettably, Bridget hadn't recorded that part of the event, so she would have to replay it over and over in her head until it was etched forever in her memory.

No one had ever looked at her like that. There had been more than love in Eric's eyes, there had also been fondness and warmth, and those were just as important.

When she and Leo had dated, he'd told her that he loved her, but there had been no warmth in his eyes when he had. Only lust. She should have known that it wasn't the real thing, but she'd wanted it to be, so she'd silenced the small voice in her head that had told her to walk away.

Turning to her side, she looked at the man sleeping soundly beside her. His stubble had grown overnight, darkening his jaw and making him look even more sexy and roguish.

Darlene used her finger to move aside a lock of dark hair that had fallen over Eric's forehead and cupped his cheek before pressing a kiss to his parted lips.

She'd done it several times during the night to check up on him, and each time he'd sleepily kissed her back. But this time, he didn't return her kiss, and when she kissed him again, and he didn't respond, Darlene's heartbeat went into overdrive mode.

"Oh, my God. You're transitioning." She shook his shoulder to make sure. "If you are just pretending to be asleep to mess with me, I will never forgive you."

He kept on sleeping, his rising and falling chest reassuring her that he was still alive and there was no need to panic.

"Yeah, right." She reached for the phone with trembling hands and searched for Bridget's contact.

The doctor answered on the fourth ring. "What happened?"

"Eric is not responding. He's breathing, so I'm not freaking out yet. What should I do?"

"If you are still in bed, get dressed. I'm sending a couple of Guardians with a gurney to bring him to the clinic."

"Thank you." Darlene let out a breath.

It was such a relief to let someone who knew what to do take charge of the situation.

Rushing into the bathroom, she left the door open so she could keep an eye on Eric while she took care of the morning necessities. It occurred to her that it was futile since she was still human and couldn't see whether his chest was rising and falling from even a few feet away, and she couldn't hear his heartbeat like any immortal could either, but that was all she could do, and logic was in low supply at the moment.

The knock on the door came when Darlene was pulling her pants on, and she nearly fell on her face when she tried to run to the door while tugging them over her ass.

Throwing the door open, she waved Max and the other Guardian in. "Thank you for coming so quickly. Eric is in the bedroom."

As the Guardians pushed the gurney through the door and rolled it to the bedroom, it suddenly occurred to her that Eric slept in the nude. In her rush, she hadn't thought to put at least underwear on him, and now that the Guardians were there, she felt embarrassed for the both of them.

"Can you put some clothes on him?" Darlene asked Max.

"No need." He and the other Guardian picked Eric up together with the blanket and transferred him to the gurney. "Bridget will need to get him naked anyway to hook him up to the monitors."

Darlene nodded. "I'll pack a bag for him and follow you."

"See you there." Max gave her a reassuring smile. "Don't worry. Eric is a fighter. He's going to make it."

"Thanks," she murmured.

When they rushed out, she went looking for her phone.

Gilbert would want to know that his brother was transitioning, and so would Kaia. She needed to call them, but she also needed to pack a bag for Eric and get to the clinic.

"Pack a bag first. I can make the phone calls on the way."

Talking herself through the packing helped keep her mind from panicking, and she reminded herself to put Eric's phone and laptop into the duffle bag. It might be a bit of wishful thinking that he would need them any time soon, but Darlene had to stay hopeful, or she would lose it.

Kaia

"Please." Bridget shooed Kaia and William out the door. "As I said before, you should all go home or to the lab and continue with whatever you had planned for today. Eric is doing well, and he's not going anywhere anytime soon. Darlene can keep you updated."

Kaia opened her mouth to argue, but William took her hand and gave it a gentle squeeze. "Your family is at the café. Let's join them and get some breakfast."

What she needed was coffee. After the phone call from Darlene had woken them up, Kaia and William had gotten dressed in a hurry and rushed to the clinic without having anything to drink.

She let out a breath. "Fine."

Arguing wouldn't have helped anyway. Bridget hadn't let her family loiter in the waiting room when Kaia had been staying in the clinic, so there was no way the doctor would soften up now.

Besides, Eric didn't even know they were there for him.

That being said, if he remained unconscious, they should take turns sitting with him and talking to him. Supposedly, it was helpful.

Gilbert waved them over. "I got a mountain of sandwiches. There is enough for everyone."

The café wasn't open yet, but nearly everything that was served during the day could be bought in the vending machines. Someone must be refilling them several times a day for them to always be so well stocked.

William pulled out a chair for Kaia. "I'll get us coffees."

"Thank you." She sat down and smiled up at him. "Don't forget a packet of sugar for me."

"I won't." He leaned down and kissed her forehead.

She felt much better after making love last night, more like herself and less like Edgar. Her entire mood had improved, and it wasn't just thanks to the orgasm and the venom-induced euphoric trip.

Last night had shown her that there was hope, and that as long as she dug her heels in as Kaia and made love to the man she loved, Edgar could be shoved back to the small corner of her brain he'd occupied before.

Perhaps she should cancel the meeting with Nathalie that had been scheduled for later today and use Eric's transition as an excuse.

Kaia wasn't looking forward to sharing with a stranger all the sordid details she remembered from her life as Edgar, and if she was getting better at suppressing that part of herself, maybe she didn't need to.

"I'm amazed that Eric started transitioning right away," her mother said. "I was sure it would take at least a couple of days."

"He had a god induce him." Gilbert put his arm on the back of her chair. "That's some potent mojo."

"Are you going to stay longer now?" Kaia asked.

Her mother sighed. "We don't know how long it will take Eric to go through the initial stage of his transition. Bridget said that it might take two days or two weeks, and given that he's unconscious, she thinks it will most likely be closer to the two weeks than two days."

"She says that his vitals are good." Gilbert unwrapped a sandwich and handed it to Kaia. "But I don't know why she says that. He is running a fever of 102, and his blood pressure is 180 over 90. Even I know that is high."

"His heart is strong." Karen put a hand on Gilbert's arm. "He might be forty-two, but he's in such good shape that his biological markers are of a guy ten years younger."

"I don't know if that's true." Gilbert motioned to Kaia to eat her sandwich. "Eric likes to boast, and he might have made that up."

"Eric is not a liar," Kaia said. "He might sometimes exaggerate, mostly to make a joke or to tease, but I've never caught him lying."

As a good liar herself, Kaia knew how to spot the telltale signs, and Eric was mostly honest. If he lied, it was by omission.

"In any case, Gilbert has to stay for sure." Her mother cradled her coffee cup between her palms. "But I should take the kids home. Cheryl needs to go back to school, and I need to go back to work." She smiled. "You have no idea how much I miss Berta. Cheryl has been a great help, but I feel bad about asking her to babysit so many times."

Gilbert snorted. "You shouldn't feel bad. The girl's eyes sparkle with glee every time you ask her to take care of the little ones, and then they spark with even more glee when I pull out the twenties and pay her. The little capitalist loves seeing her wallet swell."

"You shouldn't pay her in cash. We should deposit the money into her savings account."

He laughed. "That would be a poor incentive for our young businesswoman, if at all. She likes to get paid right away and see her money grow. I think it's a good lesson for her. It feels more visceral to her when she gets the money she earns without delay and holds it in her hands."

William returned with two paper cups and handed one to Kaia. "Here is your cappuccino, my love. One packet of sugar already mixed in."

"Thank you."

Kaia loved it when William called her his love. She wished she had a great term of endearment for him, but so far, she'd only come up with my prince, which was a little lame and unoriginal. She liked honey bear, but William would hate it. Maybe hunky bear?

"What are you smiling about?" William asked.

"Nothing important. Are we still meeting with Toven at Syssi and Kian's?"

"Maybe we can move the meeting to the café," her mother suggested. "That way, we can be close to the clinic and discuss our options at the same time."

"I would advise against it." William removed the lid from his coffee cup. "Toven might want privacy for what he has to tell you, and the café is usually overcrowded at lunchtime. Besides, Syssi took a day off to prepare a goodbye luncheon for you."

Karen nodded. "You are right. It's just that their part of the village is the farthest from the clinic. In case of an emergency, we won't be able to get here fast enough."

"Fast enough for what?" Gilbert asked.

"You know." Karen waved a hand. "Toven's blessing. If he's with us at Syssi and Kian's, it will take him fifteen minutes to get here."

"Maybe we should ask him to give Eric a preemptive blessing." Kaia looked at William. "Can you text Darlene and suggest it to her? She should be the one to ask Toven to do it now instead of waiting for Eric to get worse."

"I'll text her right away."

Darlene

⁀⁀⁀

Darlene sat on a chair next to Eric's bed and read on her phone to distract herself from worrying. Around her, the medical equipment hummed and occasionally beeped, the blood pressure cuff inflated and deflated, and Eric breathed on his own, which according to Bridget was a good sign.

William had texted her, suggesting that she ask her grandfather to bless Eric preemptively, but she didn't. Toven might get upset with her for asking him to do that while Eric was doing well, and she needed to remain in his good graces.

Eric's family and William were meeting Toven later for lunch, so they might hint at it casually and let him decide for himself.

If only William could come in and sit with her for a little while.

Heck, she wouldn't have minded her mother or sister coming over, either. Sitting there with nothing to do and no way to help Eric, Darlene felt small and useless, and she could have used the support of someone who cared about her.

She'd left the door to Eric's room slightly ajar, so she could hear what was going on in the waiting room, but so far the doctor had done an excellent job of keeping everyone out of the clinic.

It was unnecessarily cruel, and Darlene wished Bridget would allow at least one additional person in Eric's patient room to keep her company. When the doctor came in again, she was going to ask her to relax the restrictions, and then she would call her mother and Cassandra.

It was early in the morning, so her mother was probably still sleeping. Despite never having been human, Geraldine kept to a human sleep schedule. In a way, it was like Toven's missing glow. After a lifetime of hiding their abnormalities, they had a hard time letting go of the restrictions they'd put on themselves.

Darlene had read an article about the plasticity of the brain and how areas that were used extensively grew more neural synapses, while those in neglected areas shriveled and died. Maybe it was true for immortal abilities as well.

As the clinic's front door opened, she tilted her chair back to get a look and was surprised to see Max come in with a cardboard tray and a paper bag.

"I brought you a coffee and a sandwich." He stood in the doorway. "Do you want to come out to the waiting room?"

That was so nice of him. No one else had thought that she might be thirsty or hungry, and the truth was that she'd been so stressed out that she hadn't felt it until Max showed up.

She cast a quick glance at Eric, expecting what? That he would wake up and invite Max to sit in the room with them?

He hadn't even twitched in the past couple of hours, and his face was frozen in a peaceful expression. He looked like he was sleeping, but that was sadly deceptive.

If she left the door open, she could still hear the monitoring equipment from the waiting room. Besides, Bridget was in her office, and she could see all the readouts on her computer screen.

"I'll come out." Darlene pushed to her feet.

When she stepped out, he handed her the coffee.

"Thank you." She took the paper cup. "How come you were on duty this early today? I thought you'd get half a day off after attending the ceremony last night."

He chuckled. "I'm immortal. I don't need eight hours of sleep. My shift started at four in the morning."

As she sat on one of the chairs in the waiting room, Max sat right beside her. "How are you doing?"

"I'm not the one transitioning." She removed the lid and took a sip.

"You must be worried."

"Of course, I'm worried. He's unconscious."

"That's not unusual for a transitioning Dormant. Kaia was the anomaly, not the norm." He shook his head. "She's going through the strangest transition to date. I wonder what makes her different."

"It's not a question for us mere mortals to ponder." Darlene chuckled. "But wait, you are not a mere mortal."

"Neither are you, but I'm glad that you still have your sense of humor. And just as an aside, you should have transitioned by now, and you certainly shouldn't wait."

He hadn't added that she shouldn't wait for Eric to complete his transition in six months, but that was what he'd meant by his comment.

"Yeah, that's what everyone keeps telling me, including Eric."

That got his brows dipping into a deep V. "What is he suggesting you do about it? Leave him and find another male to induce you?"

She hadn't missed the hopeful tone in his voice.

"No, that's not what he's suggesting."

"Then what other option is there?"

If Max couldn't figure it out, she wasn't going to spell it out for him.

"Something creative, I guess." Darlene looked at the white paper bag. "What do you have in there?"

"A couple of chocolate croissants."

Her mouth watered. "Those are my favorite."

"I know." He handed her the bag.

"How do you know that? We've never shared croissants."

"I've seen you ordering them a couple of times. I figured you liked them."

That was such a lie. There had been no chocolate croissants in Safe Haven, and the two of them hadn't even exchanged helloes before being stationed there.

He must have noticed what she'd been ordering in the café since they had returned, but she'd never seen him there.

What was Max's deal?

Was he stalking her?

It made no sense.

She was with Eric, and Max couldn't know about Eric's idea for a threesome with him. If he knew, he wouldn't have asked how she was supposed to get induced while still being with Eric.

Maybe he hoped that Eric wouldn't make it.

It didn't seem like that. The Guardian seemed to genuinely care about him.

Whatever.

Shrugging, Darlene bit into the croissant.

When Eric woke up, they would sort it out. Right now, she didn't have the mental bandwidth to deal with Max, his peculiarities, or what Eric had in mind for the three of them.

Kian

Ever since Syssi had returned to work, she and Kian had rarely enjoyed lunch together during the workweek. She'd taken a day off to organize the goodbye luncheon for Kaia's family, and even though he didn't expect them to actually leave now that Eric was transitioning, he was still glad for the excuse to go home in the middle of the day and enjoy time with Syssi and Allegra again.

Perhaps he could take the rest of the day off and spend it with his wife and daughter?

It was tempting but impractical. If he did that, he would have to spend more hours in the office the following day. He and Shai had already planned on staying in the office later than usual today because of the long break he was taking.

Walking into the dining room, Kian gave the nicely set table a cursory look, but as the number of place settings registered, he looked again.

Had Syssi forgotten that Eric and Darlene weren't joining them?

He counted the guests he knew had been invited. Kaia and William were two, adding six members of Kaia's family, including the babies was eight, together with Toven and Mia, him and Syssi, that was twelve.

Kian counted again to make sure, but he'd been right the first time. There were fourteen place settings.

Perhaps Syssi had invited Mia's grandparents. Curtis didn't like late dinners, but he wouldn't mind a lunch invitation.

As Syssi walked into the dining room, he asked, "Did you invite Rosalyn and Curtis?"

Her eyes widened. "I didn't. Do you think I should have?"

"Not really. This lunch is dedicated to Kaia's family, and she's of no interest to them. Who are the extra two seats for?"

He'd seen Amanda leave for work this morning, so it couldn't be her and Dalhu.

"I invited Nathalie and Phoenix. Idina and Phoenix became best friends from day one, and I thought that having Phoenix with her would keep Idina occupied while we talked. Some of what needs to be said is not for her young ears."

"Good thinking." He pulled her into his arms. "My brilliant wife." He dipped his head to kiss her.

The doorbell ringing cut the kiss short, and a moment later, a loud demanding 'Da-da' sounded from Allegra's bedroom.

He chuckled. "I'll get our daughter while you get the door."

Their little one must have inherited her mother's foresight. How else could she have known that he was in the house?

Maybe she overheard him?

They never closed the door to her room so they could hear her, so it was possible that she'd heard him.

He found his daughter standing in her crib and holding on to the bars like a little prisoner.

"Da-da!" She started bouncing on the mattress, demanding to be picked up—her little tush going up and down.

"Come to Daddy, sweetness." He lifted her by the waist and started peppering her soft cheeks with kisses until she grabbed his nose and yanked. "Okay, I get it. No more kisses."

She was very good at communicating her wishes clearly and directly, which was an excellent trait for a future leader.

Ambiguity served no one's best interest, and the smell coming off her diaper didn't leave room for misinterpretation either.

"Let's clean you up." He carried her to the changing table in her bathroom.

As Kian disposed of the dirty diaper in the special pail that blocked the odors from spreading, cleaned her up, and put a fresh diaper on her, Allegra was quiet and didn't look into his eyes as if she was embarrassed about having to be changed.

Once he was done, though, she leveled her intense gaze at him and said, "Da-da," in a tone that sounded a lot like a thank-you.

"You're welcome, my little princess."

When he returned with her to the dining room, all of their guests were seated around the table, including the twins who sat on boosters that were strapped to the dining chairs.

"Good afternoon, everyone."

Kian walked over to the head of the table where Okidu had put Allegra's highchair between his and Syssi's seats, but Allegra refused to be seated in it.

When he tried to sit down with her, she twisted around, pointed at the boys, and commanded, "Da-da!"

Syssi laughed. "Oh, boy. We are going to have our hands full with this one. She's already interested in boys."

"We can make a match right now," Gilbert said. "Let's see which of my boys she fancies."

Okidu bowed. "Shall I move the highchair, master?"

"Yes, please. I'm curious to see if that's what she wants."

The twins were sitting between their parents, and it took a few moments to move everyone's chairs a few inches to the side to make room for Allegra's highchair to be placed between the twins.

When her throne was ready, she happily agreed to be seated and grinned triumphantly at Evan and then at Ryan.

"Your daughter is assertive," Karen observed.

"Thank you. I've noticed." He patted her blond curls. "Daddy is going to sit in his chair. Will you be okay here by yourself?"

"Da-da."

Since this da-da sounded like an affirmation, Kian smiled at his daughter, kissed her cheek one more time, and walked to the head of the table to sit next to Syssi.

Allegra preferred to eat unaided, and she was a good eater. There was no need to feed her. She made a mess, but thankfully, they had Okidu to clean after her, as well as cook and do everything else around the house.

"Shall I serve lunch now, mistress?" Okidu asked.

"Yes, please." Syssi smiled at him and then turned to her guests. "I suggest that we eat first and keep the discussion for later." She glanced at the two little girls that were seated next to each other and totally absorbed in a conversation about a cartoon character. "After lunch,

Okidu can keep an eye on the little ones in the den while we talk."

"I can watch them," Cheryl offered.

"You should stay," Kaia said. "Today's decisions are going to affect you as well."

Cheryl shrugged. "I can live with whatever as long as I have a good internet connection."

"Any news on Eric?" Syssi asked.

Kian knew that there had been no change, and so did Syssi, but he assumed she wanted to express her concern and let the family know that she was worried along with them.

Gilbert shook his head. "No news is good news, right?" He looked at Toven. "Eric is currently stable, but maybe a preemptive blessing could prevent him from deteriorating?"

Toven nodded graciously. "I will stop by the clinic this evening. After all, I'm Eric's mentor and protector now. I need to take care of my protégé."

"Thank you," Gilbert said. "I'm forever in your debt."

"I appreciate your gratitude, but I'm doing this for my granddaughter as much as I'm doing it for you. She chose Eric as her mate, and he seems to make her happy." The god smiled. "I also like your brother. I would have given Eric my blessing even if he wasn't Darlene's chosen and my protégé."

William

After they were done with lunch, Okidu cleaned up the table along with the disaster area created by the three babies, and then Syssi and Karen took the little ones to the den.

As Nathalie followed with Phoenix and Idina, holding one little hand in each of hers, William leaned closer to Kaia and whispered in her ear, "Maybe later you can talk to Nathalie."

She shook her head. "Not in front of everyone," she whispered. "No one knows, and I want it to stay that way."

He nodded. "I meant if you get a chance to be alone with her."

For some reason, Kaia viewed Edgar's resurfacing as a personal failure, and she hadn't even told her mother or Cheryl about it.

After serving coffee and desserts, Okidu bowed to Kian, turned on his heel, and headed to the den.

When Syssi and Karen returned with Nathalie, Karen didn't look happy.

"Are you sure the cyborg butler can take care of all the babies?" she said quietly to Syssi.

"We can see the den from here," Nathalie said. "Besides, Okidu raised Kian, so I'm sure he can handle a bunch of human children and one immortal girl who is very mature for her age."

"Idina is also mature." Karen sat next to Gilbert, shifted her chair a few inches to the side, and let out a breath. "I can see them from here."

"Then let's begin," Kian said.

When all eyes turned to Toven, he put his coffee cup down. "I probably don't have anything new to tell you, but I can emphasize what you already know and clarify things."

Karen nodded. "I would appreciate some clarity. Usually, I have no problem making decisions, but this time there are so many factors to consider, all of them life-altering, and I find myself vacillating between two extremes. One moment I decide that Gilbert and I should do it, and the next, I decide that it's not worth the risk." She looked at Cheryl. "When you are ready, I'll encourage you to seek an immortal mate and transition at a young age, and I'll do the same for Idina and the boys. It's enough for me to know that my children will never die. My own life is less important."

Cheryl turned red as a beet. "Don't talk like that. I want you and Gilbert to always be part of my life, so don't you dare give up on immortality because you are scared. If you need more time to reorganize everything, that's fine, but don't decide to never try." She said it so quickly that she ran out of air and had to suck in a breath. "And on another note, I was told that the age of consent is seventeen in the clan, and I know that it is sixteen in most countries around the world, not just the backward ones. So, if I want, I can turn immortal now."

Karen glared back at Cheryl. "You know my opinion on that, so I will not repeat it here and waste everyone's time." She forced an apologetic smile at Toven. "Forgive me for my long-winded speech and for my daughter's outburst."

"That's okay." He gave her a reassuring smile. "Your daughter said some of the things I intended to say. What I want to add is that your fears are uncalled for. I know that Syssi and Andrew had a hard time transitioning, but they both made it with the help of Annani's blessings. Now that there are two gods in the village to bless you, you are practically guaranteed to make it. The other issue is Idina. She's still young enough to transition just from being around Annani. Don't you want the peace of mind of knowing that your child is indestructible? And by the way, the same goes for Cheryl. She's right about the age of consent. If she were my daughter, and if she was mature enough to engage in sexual relations, I would rather she turned immortal as soon as possible."

"Not happening," Gilbert grumbled. "She's not mature enough, and that's the end of this discussion."

William tensed.

Gilbert might be entitled to his indignation, but that was not how he should talk to a god.

Toven smiled, in that part indulgent, part condescending way of his. "Cheryl might be too young to engage in sexual activity by American standards, but let's be practical. Most young women do not concern themselves with the age of consent when they feel ready to explore their sexuality. Besides, eighteen is an arbitrary number, and it is much lower in many countries."

"It's thirteen in Japan," Cheryl murmured under her breath.

"That's terrible," Karen said. "They are still kids, and so is Cheryl. I don't care what the age of consent is in Japan or in Germany."

"It's fourteen in Germany," Cheryl grumbled. "Provided that both partners are under eighteen."

William stifled a chuckle.

It seemed that Cheryl had investigated the issue thoroughly, and the question was whether she'd done it before or after learning what was required for her to transition.

Kian lifted his hand. "This is not constructive. Karen and Cheryl can argue about it when they get home. We need to address the bigger issues."

Kaia

Kaia had been trying to catch Cheryl's attention and signal her sister to shut up, but she'd been avoiding Kaia's eyes on purpose.

Cheryl might talk a big talk, and she liked to push their mother's buttons, but she wasn't ready for sex, so the entire argument was for naught.

Toven reached for the carafe and refilled his and Mia's cups. "So now that we've removed the fear of death from the equation, let's address the issues of gainful employment and business endeavors."

"I'm not sure that the fear of death is a done issue," Karen said. "Eric is unconscious, and he's younger than Gilbert and me."

Toven leaned forward. "You have my word that your successful transitions are 99.9% guaranteed. Take the odds of a fatal accident or a terminal disease and factor those in for your age, and you get much worse odds than that."

Once again, Kaia was struck by the differences in opinions between Kian and Toven and the rest of the immortals, including the doctor who was an expert on the subject. Those two knew something that the others didn't, and she was going to find out what it was.

Obviously, it was a big secret if Kian was keeping it even from his wife, but with the help of the journals, she might find the answer.

"You are right if the number you're citing is accurate," Gilbert said. "Why is everyone else so concerned while you are not?"

Go, Gilbert. He had noticed the same thing she had.

Toven leaned back in his chair. "I am new to the village, and they don't realize yet what an asset I am for transitioning Dormants. Mia, Kaia, and Eric are the first Dormants to transition since my arrival at the village." He cast Kian a challenging smile.

Kian didn't smile back. "We are all aware of you being a tremendous asset. Now let's keep going."

Interesting. Maybe Toven didn't want to keep guarding the secret he shared only with Kian. If Kaia didn't find the answer in the journals, Toven might be a good candidate to coerce the information from.

Right. As if she stood a chance of manipulating a seven-thousand-year-old being.

"Let's talk about your job." Toven turned to Karen. "I understand that you enjoy it. Could you find a similar job in Los Angeles?"

"Easily."

"Problem solved." He turned to Gilbert. "I understand that you are a builder. How many projects do you currently have running?"

"Only two, but they are big. I'm building two gated communities. I have about five months to completion on one and seven on the other, and then I need to sell them."

"I'm sure you have people working for you that can handle most of it without you looking over their shoulders."

Gilbert shook his head. "They need constant hand-holding. I can't leave all the decisions to employees. It would be a disaster."

"I can help you with that," Kian said. "We run multiple building projects here and in other states and even abroad, and I rarely see any of them. I have systems in place that allow me to run all of those projects with human contractors with practically no in-person supervision. The architect is a clan member, and so is the interior designer, and we have one member who launches new hotels and another who inspects the building projects. I can teach you our system so you can do everything from the village and only inspect your properties from time to time."

"I know that it's possible to run projects that way." Gilbert crossed his arms over his chest. "But my margins are slim, and I can't afford to hire big honchos who will do everything for me. I would have no profit left."

"Trust me," Kian said. "You'll make more profit than you do now because you will be able to run more projects simultaneously."

That had been the right thing to say to Gilbert.

He uncrossed his arms and put his hands on the table. "If you can show me how and convince me that I can make more money, we are moving into the village."

"What about me?" Cheryl said. "Where am I going to go to school?"

Kaia snorted. "Only minutes ago, you were arguing with Mom about hooking up with an immortal, and now you are concerned about school?"

"That was a hypothetical discussion about a principle, and I have no intention of hooking up with anyone anytime soon." Cheryl let out a breath. "I'm going to miss my friends, but this is more important. I guess I can finish high school online."

"Our young ones go to an excellent private school in Los Angeles," Syssi said. "I can introduce you to Lisa and Parker, who are about your age. They can tell you about the school."

"Thank you." Cheryl clutched her phone like a lifeline, and Kaia was sure she would check her Instatock stats under the tablecloth the moment she was no longer the center of attention.

"Any other objections?" Toven asked.

"Our house and our nanny." Gilbert took Karen's hand. "We are a big family, and we love our house. We also love our nanny. I'm not saying that those are reasons for refusing immortality, but I need help coming up with appropriate solutions. We need a bigger house than what you have available in the village, and we need help with the little ones so Karen can work." He looked at her. "Unless you want to take a sabbatical for a few years."

"I don't. You know that I need to work. It's not about the money."

"I know, love."

Syssi

Syssi hadn't contributed to the discussion yet, but maybe she should suggest that Karen and Gilbert be given a house in the newest section of the village where the houses were bigger. Gilbert and Eric were her family, so maybe Kian wouldn't mind.

Andrew and Nathalie had gotten one just because Andrew was her brother and not for any strategic reasons, and there were still a few new houses that weren't occupied.

"I might have a solution," Kian said. "If you are willing to be a little cramped for a couple of weeks, I can build an extension to one of the existing homes."

Gilbert's eyes widened. "How can you do that so fast?"

Kian smirked. "No time wasted on pulling permits and waiting on inspections, and a 3D printer."

"Can I build a custom house in the village?" Gilbert glanced at Karen. "I prefer to start from scratch and design a house I like rather than add patches to an existing structure, and so does Karen. Our current house was as much her design as mine and the architect's."

Kian shook his head. "We have a plot of land we didn't build on yet, but the plans for it are done, and I don't intend to put in the utilities for just one home. When that section goes up, I might allow some customization, but as it stands now, we have so many vacant houses that there is no reason to build more."

"I get it." Gilbert rubbed his jaw. "If I may ask, why did you build so many if you didn't need them?"

"I hoped that clan members who currently live in Europe would join us, and I also wanted to have homes ready for future couples and their families." Kian smiled. "The Fates have been good to our clan lately, and we've been blessed with many new Dormants." He waved a hand. "Just look how fortunate we were to find your family."

Syssi cleared her throat. "The houses in the newest section are a little bigger. Maybe Kaia's family can stay in one of the remaining ones."

"They are bigger, but they also have only three bedrooms each." Kian frowned. "I have an idea." He looked at Cheryl. "What do you think about having your own guesthouse?"

"I'd love it."

Kian looked at Syssi. "They can have Amanda's old place, and Cheryl can use Onidu's guesthouse. The house originally had three bedrooms, but Amanda converted one into a closet for her wardrobe and another one for Dalhu's studio. We just need to convert them back into bedrooms."

"That's a great idea." Syssi could imagine how it would look with an extension in the back that connected the main structure to the guest house. "It sits on a larger plot, so it has room for an addition."

"Can we see it?" Cheryl asked.

"Sure." Syssi grinned. "It's been empty since Amanda moved into the new section."

"That leaves the nanny problem." Gilbert let out a breath. "I understand that you don't have any available in the village."

"We don't." Syssi sighed. "Many of the ladies are willing to babysit when needed, but they don't want to do it full time. To be able to work, I have to take Allegra with me to the university. Amanda converted her office into a nursery, and we hired a human nanny who takes care of Evie and Allegra there."

"Maybe your university needs a system administrator?" Karen asked jokingly. "Then I could add my boys to your nursery. Idina can go to the same preschool Phoenix goes to."

Syssi pursed her lips. "I can ask. Maybe we will get lucky, and the university needs a new system administrator. It's not as exciting a job as your current one, but there are advantages to working for an academic institution. The environment is much more relaxed."

Karen nodded. "That would be wonderful, but I can't just quit my job without training a replacement. I still need to go back home." She sighed. "I'm going to miss Berta so much. Do you have any idea how hard it was to find a great nanny who could also cook?"

"I'll cook," Gilbert said. "If Kian's system works as smoothly as he claims, I'll have a lot of free time on my hands. I can get into cooking." He patted his stomach. "A man who loves to eat should know how to cook."

Karen rolled her eyes. "We will live on things off the grill."

"What's wrong with that?"

"Nothing." She smiled at her mate. "It's a small price to pay considering all the benefits." She cupped his cheek. "You'll be home when I return from work, and we will spend more time together as a family. That alone is worth the price of admission."

"Let's sum up," Toven said. "All the objections have been addressed, and solutions for them were found. The last thing we need to discuss is the timeline." He turned to Karen. "How long do you need to train a replacement?"

"Ideally, a couple of months, but contractually, I'm only obligated to give it two weeks."

"Excellent." Toven leaned back in his chair. "Here is the plan. Gilbert needs to stay until Eric wakes up, and Karen needs to go back and give her notice. But instead of going today, I suggest that you leave Sunday. What's the worst that could happen? They'd fire you?"

"I still need them to give me a letter of recommendation. Why do I need to stay until Sunday?"

"Annani is arriving on Thursday, and I'm sure you want to meet the head of the clan you are about to join. The next day is Friday, so there is no point in you leaving before the weekend. And who knows, maybe Eric will wake up by then."

Karen looked at Gilbert. "What do you think?"

"I think you should do what Toven is suggesting. In the meantime, Syssi can check if they need a system admin at the university, we can check out the house and decide what we want to do with it, and I'll spend some time with Kian learning his hands-off building method. If Eric wakes up by Sunday, I'll go home with you, and we will spend a couple of weeks getting everything ready for the move. If he takes longer, I'll join you as soon as I can."

Kaia

L unch had ended over an hour ago, Gilbert and Karen had taken the boys back to the house, and William had gone back to the lab, but Kaia had volunteered to stay with Idina and walk her home when she was done playing.

Her objective had been to have a word alone with Nathalie, but so far, it hadn't been possible.

Kian headed back to his office, but Syssi had the day off, and Allegra was enjoying the company of the two little girls, so Syssi joined Nathalie and Kaia in the den, and the three of them had been chatting about this and that.

She considered asking both women for their advice.

Nathalie and Syssi were both super nice, and neither would look down their nose at her because of what she was going through, even if it was ugly.

It wasn't as if she'd invited those damn memories and unwanted urges. Her transition had somehow unlocked them, and although she'd managed to shove them back into their little corner in her mind, they were still floating up at random times and making her feel contaminated.

Eric's analogy of using a disinfectant on Toven's gene pool came to mind, only in her case, it wasn't a gene pool. It was a soul pool.

Ugh. Why me?

"I'd better head home and start on dinner." Nathalie offered Phoenix her hand.

The girl shook her head and hid her hands behind her back so her mother couldn't grip them. "I don't want to go home. I want to play with Idina."

Idina looked up at Kaia. "Can I stay to play with Phoenix?"

"You've already got to play for a long time. It's time to go."

Syssi regarded the two little girls with a fond smile. "You don't have to go yet. They can play for a little while longer. Allegra is so happy to have friends over who talk and do interesting things."

Allegra was sitting on a baby mat, surrounded by a mountain of toys, but she found Idina and Phoenix much more interesting than the inanimate objects.

"I have a better idea." Nathalie started collecting Phoenix's toys and putting them into her Disney princess backpack. "We can invite Idina and Kaia to our house, and the two of you can keep playing while I make dinner."

"No!" Phoenix shook her head, her beautiful long curls bouncing from side to side. "I want to stay at Syssi's house and eat waffles. Okidu's are the best."

The butler suddenly appeared in the den as if summoned by a magic wand. "I shall get to it right away, mistress." He dipped his head.

Syssi laughed. "Now you have to stay. I'll make us cappuccinos."

That was the opportunity Kaia had been waiting for to be alone with Nathalie, but with Syssi's immortal hearing and the house's open floor plan, Syssi might hear them talking and feel left out.

Besides, there was no harm in sharing her problems with both. Syssi was a seer, so maybe she would have a vision that would provide a solution to Kaia's problem.

When Syssi returned with a tray loaded with cappuccinos and snacks for the girls, Kaia sat down on the couch between the two women and picked up one of the cups. "I need your advice on something that has been bothering me since my transition started."

Syssi frowned. "What is it?"

"Well, the truth is that it didn't start with the transition, but it certainly intensified to an uncomfortable level. Since I was about six or seven, I've been able to access memories of my prior life."

Neither of the women looked shocked.

"That's awesome," Syssi said. "What do you remember?"

"It's not awesome. Well, it used to be, but it no longer is."

The two women listened intently as she told them about Edgar, using words that were appropriate for the young ears in the room and only hinting at what the problem was, but Nathalie and Syssi were both intelligent ladies, and she didn't need to spell anything out for them.

Kaia turned to Nathalie. "Because of what Spencer said about my double auras, William thinks that they are not memories from a prior life but an invading spirit, and he suggested that I talk to you because you have experience dealing with ghosts and blocking them from taking over your mind."

Nathalie shook her head. "I don't think Edgar is a ghost. He doesn't talk to you, and he doesn't take over and block you. You are fully aware of him at all times, but you don't converse with him. The way you understand mathematics is also an indication that it's not a foreign entity. I didn't know what my invading spirit knew, and he told me things only when I asked." She snorted. "More often than not, he refused to answer my questions."

"That's what I thought." Kaia let out a breath. "One last question. You keep referring to the ghost who lived in your head as he. Did you ever have a female ghost?"

"I had many trying to get in, and some might have been females, but the two who spent the most time in my head were both males."

"Did they make you feel more masculine in any way?"

Nathalie shook her head. "Never. It was like having an annoying friend squatting in my head. We talked, and we argued, but we never merged."

Kaia slumped against the back of the couch. "I sometimes catch myself thinking as Edgar, and it's terrible because he's a jerk." She sighed. "I loved remembering the mathematics he was so good at, but I hate everything else I remember about him."

It was easier to think of Edgar as him and not as who she used to be.

"Sari's mate remembers his past life," Syssi said. "I can put you on a call with him. Maybe he can help you."

Kaia turned to Syssi. "Was he a horrible person in his past life as well?"

Syssi tilted her head. "He wasn't horrible, but he did a horrible thing, and he certainly wasn't the wonderful man that he is now. I think that's the whole point of reincarnation. You are supposed to fix the bad things."

"Yeah, I get it, but I want to forget being him. Do you think the goddess will agree to thrall me? William said that she's the only one who can do that."

Syssi smiled. "Of course, she would. When Annani heard that William found his truelove mate, she was overjoyed. You are one of the reasons she's cutting her trip a little short. She wants to meet you."

"Awesome." Kaia felt a weight lift off her chest.

If the goddess was happy for William, she wouldn't deny his request to help his mate.

Kian

As Okidu eased the limousine into the parking spot, Kian and Syssi walked over, and Kian opened the back door for Annani.

Amanda had tasked them with keeping their mother and sister in the parking garage for a few minutes, so she could finish putting the last decorating touches on the Welcome Home sign she'd bought on the way back from the university.

It wasn't necessary to receive Annani and Alena with much fanfare, but Amanda had insisted.

"Welcome home, Mother." Kian bent nearly in half to embrace her.

Annani kissed both his cheeks and then gave him a gentle nudge to signal that she wanted him to let go. When he did, she turned to hug Syssi, who had finished embracing Alena and was waiting patiently for her turn.

"Welcome home, sister." Kian wrapped Alena in his arms, careful of her growing belly. "You look rested."

Alena also looked much more pregnant than she had been when she'd left, but he knew better than to comment on it.

"I had lots of fun," Alena said. "I enjoyed spending time with my children. It had been such a long time since we made an effort to be together as a family." She looked lovingly at her mate. "Thanks to Orion's insistence on getting to know them, I got to reconnect with them as well. I would have stayed longer, but Mother was impatient because she wanted to meet William's mate."

"Whatever the reason, I'm glad to have you back." Kian turned to Orion and clasped his hand in greeting. "Welcome home, brother-in-law."

Orion pulled him into a one-armed bro hug and clapped him on the back. "Not yet, but soon. How is the cruise ship renovation going?"

"It's on schedule despite all the shipment delays and worker shortages. I'm doing my best to have it ready on time."

"As long as it's on schedule, I have no problem waiting for its completion. Any longer than that, and we will need to wheel Alena to the altar. I think we are having twins."

"We are not." She slapped his arm playfully. "He's just a big baby."

"Do you know that the baby is a boy?" Syssi asked.

"Not for sure, but I think so."

"Didn't you get an ultrasound?"

"I did, and everything is fine, but I asked not to be told. I like the suspense of not knowing ahead of time." She patted her rounded belly. "Just like back in the day when there was no way to know."

"I bet they were correct fifty percent of the time," Kian murmured. "Shall we get out of here and head to your new homes?"

Okidu had finished unloading their luggage from the limo, and there was a lot of it.

Alena frowned. "What new homes?"

"I moved you and Mother to the new secure section of the village. Your things are already there."

"You should have asked if we wanted to move," Alena grumbled. "Orion enjoyed being close to Toven and Geraldine, and so did I."

"If you want, I can move you back, but I think you are going to like your new homes better. They are more upscale, and they are closer to Syssi and me."

His plan had been to lure his sister and mother into staying in the village by providing them with nicer homes, but apparently he'd been mistaken.

"I do not mind where I stay." Annani threaded her arms through his as they walked into the elevator. "My home is the sanctuary. I am just a guest here."

"We hope to change your mind about that," Syssi said from behind them. "And I want Alena to stay as well. We have a new family moving into the village that has twin boys who just recently turned one year old and an adorable toddler girl."

Kian snorted. "Idina is adorable in a devilish kind of way." He pressed the button for the elevator.

"She's just a feisty little girl," Syssi said. "Which, in my opinion, makes her even more adorable. They also have a sixteen-year-old who shows potential as a future businesswoman."

"I have heard all about the new family of Dormants." Annani floated into the elevator. "I also heard that Kaia's transition was unusual and that Eric is unconscious. Has there been any change in that?"

"No, but he's doing fine." Kian put his hand on the small of his mother's back. "Toven has been giving Eric his blessing, and it seems to be helpful." He tapped her back twice, letting her know that Toven had given Eric two transfusions.

Annani nodded sagely. "I am glad. I wonder what would happen if I added my blessing to Toven's. Do you think Eric would wake up sooner?"

Kian smiled at his mother's attempt at innocence. "It's worth a try."

As the elevator doors opened and Annani beheld Amanda and the banner, her glow doubled in its intensity. "I am so touched." She walked into Amanda's outstretched arms. "What is the occasion?"

"I'm just glad to have you back."

"I hope you are aware that Eve is still too young to turn immortal."

Amanda cast her a mock glare. "That's not why I'm happy. I just missed my mom and my sister." She hugged Alena and then Orion. "I missed you too."

"Right." He chuckled. "I'm just an accessory to Alena, and I'm fine with that. I miss my sister and nieces too. How is Darlene holding up? I bet she's stressing over her mate."

"She is, but Eric is doing really well with the help of your father's blessings."

"When can I meet the rest of the family?" Annani asked.

"This evening, if you wish." Kian took Allegra out of her stroller. "They extended their stay so they could meet you."

"I will be delighted to meet them, and especially William's mate." Annani smiled at Allegra. "Now, let me have my granddaughter."

"Na-na." Allegra reached for her grandmother.

"That was a new word," Kian marveled. "My daughter is a genius."

Kaia

Kaia had thought that no one could impress her as much as Toven had, but Annani was in a league of her own.

Toven was a gorgeous male, but the goddess was so beautiful that it was painful to look at her and yet impossible not to, and while Toven tried to subdue his natural sense of superiority, Annani flaunted it like a queen.

There was nothing apologetic about her.

And yet, despite the diva attitude, the otherworldly beauty, and the power that emanated from her in waves, she wasn't scary or even intimidating. Annani was warm, kind, and full of good humor, a real benevolent goddess who aimed to do good but didn't shy away from using her power when needed.

Not that Kaia knew that for a fact, but that was her impression of the goddess.

After the introductions had been made and Idina had charmed the goddess with her cute little curtsey, Annani turned her attention to Kaia.

"Come sit with me outside for a few moments, child." The goddess threaded her arm through Kaia's. Annani was tiny, more than half a foot shorter than her, and yet Kaia felt small and insignificant next to the powerhouse seemingly gliding on air beside her.

How did she walk like that?

She stole a glance at the bottom of the Clan Mother's gown. It was floor length, but it didn't actually touch the floor, and her feet were hidden under it. She couldn't really float, could she?

As Annani got to the glass doors leading to Syssi and Kian's backyard, one of her Odus rushed to her with a shawl and a pair of sunglasses.

"It is still sunny outside, Clan Mother."

"Yes, it is." She took the sunglasses and put them on her tiny nose.

They were huge and shaped like goggles, dwarfing her small face.

Unable to help herself, Kaia snorted and immediately slapped a hand over her mouth. "I'm sorry. I had something in my nose."

Annani laughed, the sound raising goose bumps all over Kaia's arms. It was the most beautiful sound she'd ever heard, and she made a mental note to keep amusing the goddess so she would laugh again.

Was it Edgar's thought, though, or hers?

It was so confusing.

"I know these glasses look funny." Annani allowed the Odu to wrap the shawl around her shoulders. "My eyes are sensitive to the sun, and if I do not wear these ugly sunglasses, they get red." She threaded her arm through Kaia's again. "But I am a fast healer, and as soon as I get back inside, my eyes return to normal, so I only wear them not to scare people away." She leaned against Kaia's arm. "I have a feeling that a god's red eyes was how the vampire stories started."

As the Odu opened the sliding door and Annani stepped out, Kaia caught sight of a tiny foot. It was clad in a soft ballet-style shoe, the fabric the same emerald green color as the goddess's gown. Annani's feet were so small that she could probably wear Idina's shoes.

"I didn't see Toven wearing sunglasses," Kaia said, to distract herself from hunting for another peek at the goddess's tiny feet.

It was the oddest thing to get fixated on, and Kaia had a feeling that it was Edgar's fault. Heck, lately she was blaming everything that bothered her on him, but maybe some of the weird thoughts she had belonged to Kaia herself.

"Did you get to see Toven during the day?" Annani asked as she led Kaia to a comfortable-looking outdoor couch.

"I did, but it must have been indoors."

"That is the most likely explanation. His eyes should be as sensitive as mine, but then he is a male, and you know how they are. They have to be macho even if it means suffering."

"I know all too well how men are." Kaia winced. "I was one in my prior life."

It felt odd to confess her secret to the goddess mere minutes after meeting her, but she needed the Clan Mother's help to banish Edgar, so there was no point in dragging it out.

Who knew if she would get another chance to ask?

"How very interesting. It is more common to reincarnate as the same gender." Annani rearranged the folds of her gown, making sure that they were all even. "My son-in-law is an expert on the subject, and during my visit, we spent many fascinating hours talking about his research."

"I heard that he remembers his previous life as well."

"He does, but not the one that came right before this one. He remembers an older version of himself, a much cruder one that needed a lot of polishing." Annani lifted her head and smiled in the direction of the house. "Come join us, William."

"Thank you, Clan Mother." He came out holding a tray with a pitcher of lemonade and three glasses. "I thought you might get thirsty out here."

"I am a little thirsty." She took the tall glass he poured for her. "But you did not need to use an excuse to come out and join us. I am always glad of your company."

Annani

Young love was so sweet.

Annani sipped on her lemonade and observed the loving glances between William and Kaia.

It was about time the Fates found a truelove mate for William, and she could not be happier with their choice despite the little hitch in the form of disturbing memories.

Annani could sense Kaia's distress, the male urges she was fighting against, and the desperation with which she was clinging to her femininity.

The girl needed help, and she had come to the one person who could do that.

"Kaia was telling me about her past life as a man." Annani put her glass down. "That must be very confusing for you, child."

"It is." Kaia sighed. "Before my transition, it wasn't as bad. I only remembered the math skills and Edgar's self-image, which wasn't great. He was a big man, both in height and build, and he felt self-conscious about his size. I always thought that he was this gentle giant who did his best not to intimidate people, but it turned out that those were selective memories. After my transition, more of them surfaced, and I found out that he was a misogynist." She sighed and looked at William. "But the worst part is that I feel tainted by the combination of lust and hate he felt for females. I want things to return to the way they were before or eliminate those memories altogether. Is there a chance the Clan Mother could thrall them out of existence?"

Annani laughed. "Please, there is no need to refer to me in the third person. It is so contrived. And yes, I might be able to help you." She looked at William. "I will need you to go back to the house. I cannot have any distractions while I am doing this."

"Of course." He pushed to his feet, dipped his head, and turned on his heel.

When he closed the sliding doors behind him, Annani smiled to reassure Kaia.

The girl's eyes were darting nervously, and her breathing was shallow. She was too anxious to allow a deep thrall.

"Give me your hands, Kaia, and close your eyes." Annani clasped the girl's clammy hands. "I am going to look through your memories and try to push them back below the barrier of your subconscious mind. Hopefully, they will stay there, but if not, I can do it again until I succeed in keeping them there. Not everything needs to be achieved in one go."

Kaia let out a breath and opened her eyes. "Edgar was a nasty man. I don't want to remember anything of his personal life. But he was a gifted mathematician, and if possible, I would like to retain the memories of his craft. They've helped me a lot over the years, and I wouldn't have been nearly as successful without them."

Annani smiled. "As with everything else in life, things are rarely black and white, and most gifts come with a price. I hope I can allow you to retain the gift while freeing you from the burden of having to endure the less pleasant aspects of it."

"That would be awesome. Thank you." Kaia closed her eyes again, took a deep breath, and let it out slowly. "I'm ready."

As Annani gently entered the girl's mind, she did not encounter any resistance at first, but as she dove deeper, the male aspect hiding in the recesses of Kaia's mind tried to resist the invasion. It was as if her soul had split into two fragments.

Could that be the explanation for the split personality disorder? Nowadays, it was called dissociative identity disorder, and it was believed to be caused by trauma. Back in the day, it was called possession and was believed to be caused by invading demons or evil spirits. But perhaps a splintered soul was the real cause.

The question was how to banish the less desirable fragment and fill up the void that its absence would create so that what was left would be whole and not broken.

Perhaps instead of banishing it, she could mold it into something positive.

What if she could change Edgar's experiences of rejection and let him see them in a different light? If she eliminated that pain, or at least diminished it, the memories of his other emotions would lose their intensity, and Kaia would be able to push them back into the recesses of her mind.

It would be a long and difficult process. Annani could not do it in one sitting, and Kaia could not endure it all at once either. But since she intended to stay in the village for a while, she and Kaia could meet as many times as it took to remove Edgar's disturbing presence from Kaia's mind.

William

William shouldn't have felt anxious about leaving Kaia in Annani's hands. The goddess was gentle and caring and she was very skilled at thralling. She wouldn't damage Kaia's beautiful mind.

Furthermore, Kaia needed help.

She wasn't the type who admitted weakness easily, and the fact that she'd asked Annani to thrall away the memories plaguing her meant that she was desperate for relief.

He stood next to the bar, which was located in a convenient spot near the sliding glass door, allowing himself to watch Kaia and Annani without being obvious. The goddess had her back to him, so he couldn't see her expression, but he could see Kaia's, and she looked pained.

It doubled the size of the ball of stress in his gut.

What was Annani seeing inside Kaia's head?

Was Kaia trying to block the invasive probe?

If he'd had time to prepare her, he would have coached Kaia on how to relax and lower her mental shields. The less she resisted, the less damage her mind would sustain. But he hadn't been prepared for Annani to jump into action so quickly.

Gilbert walked up to him and looked at Kaia and Annani through the glass. "What's going on? What are they doing out there?"

Kaia hadn't shared her concerns with her family, so he couldn't tell Gilbert that the goddess was performing a sort of exorcism to free Kaia from her past life.

"The Clan Mother likes to get to know new members of her clan. She wants to talk with Kaia in private." William forced a smile. "She even kicked me out."

That had probably been the initial purpose of the talk, but when Kaia told Annani about Edgar, the Clan Mother had gone straight to work.

"So, it's not a test of some sort to see if Kaia is worthy of becoming a member of her clan?"

"Not at all. Kaia is my mate, so as soon as she transitioned, she became a member of Annani's clan."

"I see." Gilbert turned to Kian. "So, Karen and I will not become members when we transition."

"That only affects the profit-sharing in the clan's holdings. Those who are not Annani's descendants, or are not mated to them, don't get the same cut as those who are, but they are residents of the village and members of our community with all the other rights and privileges as well as duties and obligations."

"What about Toven?" Gilbert asked.

"He doesn't need a share in the profits," Kian said as he joined them. "He's richer than King Midas." He chuckled. "Toven could buy the village and all of the clan holdings and still have plenty left to spare."

Gilbert's eyes sparkled with interest. "How did he become so rich?"

"Toven is seven thousand years old." Orion walked over to the bar. "He lived at a time when humans gave gold in tribute to the gods, or the one remaining god. My father hoarded it like a dragon hoards his treasure."

As Dalhu joined their group and the conversation turned to gold and the accumulation of valuables, including artwork, William shifted his gaze to look at Alena and Karen, who were each bouncing one of the twins on their knees.

On the couch, Amanda was showing Syssi Evie's new dress, and on the floor, Idina was telling Allegra a story about a princess who was looking for her lost golden slipper.

In another corner of the room, Cheryl had commandeered an armchair and was absorbed in her phone, probably checking her Instatock feed.

It was such a homey picture, and it loosened the tension that had taken hold of his shoulders.

That was why Kaia wanted a big family, and Fates willing, she would have one.

They would have it together.

"Do you still have the expensive jewelry you bought while serving Navuh?" Orion asked Dalhu.

"I had no reason to sell it." Dalhu accepted a glass of whiskey from Kian. "But if I ever need cash in an emergency, I will. I'm not emotionally attached to those trinkets. To me, they are just inflation-proof assets."

William hadn't listened to the entire conversation, so he didn't know how Dalhu had become the owner of expensive jewelry, and he didn't particularly care.

All he cared about was Kaia and whether what Annani was doing would help free her from her demons without causing permanent damage to her incredible mind.

Kaia

When Annani released Kaia's mind and then her hands, Kaia kept her eyes closed and looked inward. Edgar was still there, but his presence was muted. It was as if he had faded into the background, or rather the intensity of his feelings and his persona had, but he was still casting a shadow over her.

It was a marked improvement, but it wasn't the complete cure she'd hoped for.

Opening her eyes, she sighed. "I feel more like myself. Thank you."

"You are welcome." Annani patted her hand. "I was careful, and I did not go as deep as I would have had to go in order to submerge the memories of your past life. Instead, I just manipulated them." The goddess smiled mischievously. "I gave them a different spin."

Kaia frowned. "Forgive me, but I don't follow. What do you mean by spin?"

"Can you still sense the traces of Edgar's resentment of women?"

Kaia closed her eyes and dove inside. She still had fragments of those memories, but the emotions they evoked were much calmer. "I don't. It's like I can remember the rejection, but I'm no longer angry about it."

The goddess clapped her tiny hands. "That is precisely what I did. I changed those memories and made them much less painful and humiliating, and on the other hand, I magnified the feelings of satisfaction Edgar had from his academic achievements. That took care of the resulting anger and resentment."

Kaia wasn't a therapist, and she couldn't understand how the goddess had erased the hatred without erasing the memories of it, but the end result was that she felt calmer and more like herself, and that was all that mattered.

What about the male urges, though? Were they still there?

It was hard to tell. Annani was beautiful, but she was so otherworldly that even Edgar couldn't have fantasized about her, and anyone with eyes could see and admire her perfection regardless of their gender or sexual orientation.

"Thank you." Kaia dipped her head, wondering whether she should get up first or wait to be dismissed. "May I join William now?" She glanced at the sliding doors, but the glass was reflective, and she couldn't see inside.

"You may, but we are not done, my dear child." Annani refilled her glass with lemonade and took a sip. "We should meet again next week and the one after that so I can continue refining those memories until there is no sting left to them."

Kaia hadn't planned on staying in the village longer than the week that Bridget had demanded, but refusing the goddess's offer would be rude.

Perhaps she could phrase it in a nonoffending way?

"I'm sure you are aware of the secret project that William and I are working on. We need to return to Safe Haven to complete the work."

Annani nodded. "Then we shall continue our sessions when you are done. How long do you expect it will take?"

"It depends. Once we are done with the initial deciphering, William can dismiss the team, and we can continue working on the journals here in the village."

"So, the main reason for returning to Safe Haven is the team members you left behind?"

Kaia nodded.

"Then the solution is simple. William should pay them what he promised them and send them home. Your uncle is transitioning, and the rest of your family is planning to move into the village in a week or two. It makes no sense for you to be over there while they are over here."

Kaia's main impetus for wanting to return to Safe Haven hadn't been the research but the two compellers who she'd hoped could help her forget her life as Edgar. But what they could do was no way near as amazing as what Annani had done and still intended to do.

Kaia inclined her head in deference to the goddess. "I couldn't agree more."

William

When Kaia and Annani walked back in, the smile on Kaia's face melted away the ball of stress that had been wreaking havoc on William's stomach.

He hadn't touched any of the fancy hors d'oeuvres that Okidu had been circulating, and he'd drunk way too much of the whiskey Kian had been pouring.

"Are you okay?" he whispered as he pulled her into a quick embrace.

"I'm great. The Clan Mother convinced me that we should stay in the village and not return to Safe Haven."

He arched a brow. "What about the research?"

"We can do it here. The team can keep working with Marcel on tasks that we assign to them, Marcel will send their results here, and you and I will assemble the puzzle pieces in your lab."

"What about the geneticist and the ethicist you wanted to hire, and the genetics lab you wanted to build there, and the people you wanted to hire for that?"

"Marcel can stay in Safe Haven and supervise a new team of humans who will build a genetics lab." She put her hands on his chest. "And you know what the best part of staying here is?"

"What?"

"No more goop for breakfast, lunch, and dinner."

He smirked. "I thought the best part was my comfortable four-poster bed."

Behind them, Gilbert groaned. "I really didn't need to hear that."

"What do you mean by goop?" Kian asked.

William turned around. "The so-called healthy food leaves a lot to be desired."

"Why didn't you say something before?"

"It wasn't important, and I didn't want to bother you with minutiae."

"I thought that you didn't want the guests to return for another retreat," Kaia added. "If they didn't like the food, they wouldn't come back."

"Why would I want that? I'll have a talk with the chef."

Annani sat on the couch between Karen and Alena, her face alight with pleasure as she looked at the children.

"What a lovely sight this is." She reached for one of the boys. "Can I hold him?"

Looking apprehensive, Karen nodded. "Of course, Clan Mother."

As Annani pulled the child onto her lap, he looked up at her with doe eyes.

"He's fascinated with your glow," Karen said. "Are you sure that it's not harmful?"

Annani laughed. "If anything, it's beneficial, right, Evan?"

How did she know who was who?

William still couldn't tell them apart.

The boy lifted his hand and touched her face. "Na-ni."

"He said my name." The goddess grinned. "Such a smart boy." She kissed his cheek. "And so sweet."

Karen relaxed. "They are both very good boys. They eat well, sleep well, and are not fussy."

Annani nodded sagely. "I think boys are easier to raise when they are little. Kian was my easiest child, but then as a young man, he went through a rebellious stage." She leaned toward Karen and whispered loudly, "He ran off and got married against my explicit wishes."

"Mother," Kian said in a warning tone. "No one wants to hear that story."

"I would love to hear it sometime," Karen said.

Annani leaned back with Evan in her arms. "I am going to stay in the village for a while this time, so we can meet for tea or lunch and share stories." Her expression turned serious. "Stay here, Karen. This is your home now. The house in the Bay Area is just a place you used to live in."

Karen swallowed and looked to Alena for help.

"My mother is right. For the longest time, I thought of the sanctuary as my home, but I realized that I feel just as much at home in the village and in Scotland as I do there. I have people I love here, in Scotland, and in the sanctuary, so as long as I have a room or a house where I can keep my things and add personal touches, I feel at home in all three places."

"Isn't it confusing?" Karen asked. "I think that we need one place to be our anchor. I can't imagine having several and feeling equally connected to each one."

Alena smiled. "You don't know until you try. You haven't stayed in the village long enough for it to feel like home, but give it another week or two, and it will."

"I need to go back and train my replacement. They have been good to me, and I don't want to repay them by quitting without notice and without ensuring a smooth transition." She chuckled. "I think that word is going to haunt me."

"You can quit if you want," Cheryl said. "You can call and say that you have a family emergency that you need to take care of, and that you don't know how long it will take to resolve. It wouldn't even be a lie. Eric is unconscious, and we don't know how long he will stay like that. You can tell your boss that you're profoundly sorry and you understand if she needs to replace you with someone else. What are they going to do? Send the cops after you and force you to go back to work? We are not in China, and this is still a free country."

"Cheryl is right." Gilbert sighed. "And we should listen to the Clan Mother's wisdom. Let's just stay."

"What about Berta?" Karen turned a pair of pleading eyes to Kian. "Is there any way we can bring her here with us?"

He shook his head. "I'm sorry. You will have to find a different solution."

As the discussion about caretakers continued, William tuned it out and began running in his head the details of conducting the research in two locations. They'd already had a system that they'd employed before Kaia started transitioning, but it had been designed as a temporary solution, and they needed to refine it.

Kaia leaned her head on his shoulder and whispered, "What are you thinking so hard about?"

"How to make it all work."

A smirk lifting her lovely lips, she turned into him and whispered directly into his ear. "I hoped that you were thinking of ways to use that four-poster bed of yours."

His mind immediately went to where she'd directed it, and as scenarios of what they could do with that bed flashed through his mind, he couldn't wait to enact them.

The problem was that with Annani there, leaving right away wasn't an option. They had to wait for her to take her leave first.

"Hold that thought," he whispered in Kaia's ear, and as his hand migrated to her bottom, he quickly scanned the room to see if anyone was watching them.

Someone was, and Annani smiled knowingly as if she'd heard their exchange, which she might have. Her hearing must be superior even to that of the immortals.

"You make such a beautiful couple and you are so well matched." Annani's eyes glowed with mischief, and William wondered what was on her mind. "The Fates have rewarded you both magnificently, and I cannot wait to preside over your mating ceremony." Annani turned to Karen. "We are going to have so much fun planning their wedding."

Gilbert opened his mouth, probably to protest, but then closed it and released a sigh. "The Clan Mother knows best."

It was nearly midnight when Annani left with Orion, Alena, and her Odus.

William and Kaia said their thanks to the hosts, escorted her family to the bridge, and then they were finally alone.

Standing on the threshold of their home, William swung Kaia into his arms, and when she laughed and wound her arms around his neck, he walked in and kicked the door closed behind him.

"Let's see what we can do with that four-poster bed, shall we?"

"Definitely. But before you carry me off to your man cave and have your way with me, I have a question."

"What is it?"

"Is McLean going to be my last name when we get married? Or can I choose any last name I want? I would like to keep Locke, but I assume that at some point I will have to fake my own death and get a new fake identity."

William smiled.

Kaia's mind never took a break. "When the time comes, you can have any name you want, and I'll adopt it as well. We can be Mr. and Mrs. $E=mc^2$."

Kaia threw her head back and laughed. "I love it." She pulled herself up and smashed her lips over his. "I love you, my prince."

"And I love you, my princess. Forever and beyond."

THE ADVENTURE CONTINUES
SOFIA & MARCEL'S STORY IS NEXT
The Children of the Gods Book 65

DARK GAMBIT THE PAWN

TURN THE PAGE TO READ THE EXCERPT—>

JOIN THE VIP CLUB

To find out what's included in your free membership, flip to the last page.

Dark Gambit The Pawn

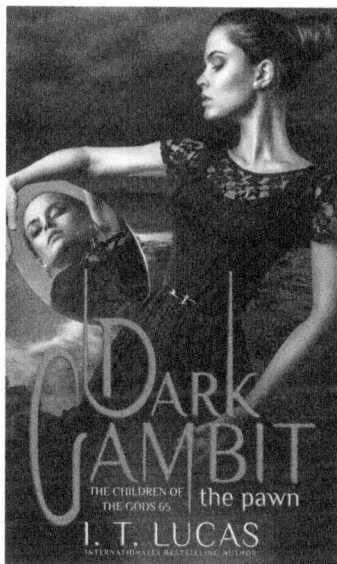

Temporarily assigned to supervise a team of bioinformaticians, Marcel expects to spend a couple of weeks in the peaceful retreat of Safe Haven, enjoying Oregon Coast's cool weather and rugged beauty.
Things quickly turn chaotic when the retreat's director receives an email with an encoded message about a potential new threat to the clan.
While those in charge of security debate what to do next, Safe Haven's first ever paranormal retreat is about to begin, and one of the attendees is a mysterious woman who makes Marcel's heart beat faster whenever she's near.
Is the beautiful mortal his one truelove?

Or is she the harbinger of more bad news?

Sofia

"You know who I am." Sofia handed the guard her identification card. "Why do you stop me every time I come home?"

"It's the protocol." Pioter smiled apologetically as he scanned her card and handed it back to her. "Are you here just for the weekend? Or are you going to stay longer this time?"

"I don't know. It's up to Igor."

Everything was up to Igor, but she shouldn't complain. At least she was allowed to leave the compound and attend university. Most of his subjects weren't as fortunate.

The founding group of pureblooded Kra-ell males were the elite of the compound and had more freedom and privileges than anyone else, but they couldn't come and go as they pleased either. Igor was a control freak who kept even his nearest and dearest on a tight leash.

Not that anyone was dear to him.

The male was cold and calculating, and if he were human, he probably would be classified as a sociopath.

The Kra-ell might have a similar opinion of him, but no one was stupid enough to voice it.

He was ruthless and cruel to the purebloods and the hybrids, but surprisingly, he wasn't a monster to the human inhabitants of his compound. Perhaps he thought of them as pets, or maybe he pitied them for their short lifespans.

Supposedly, the pureblooded Kra-ell could live for a thousand years, but no one knew how long the hybrids would live. The oldest one was in his eighties, and he looked like he was in his twenties, so they might live just as long as the purebloods.

It was frustrating how little she knew.

Igor and his cohort of close pureblooded males didn't share what they knew with anyone. Not even their children and grandchildren.

One would think that being related to Igor's second-in-command would allow Sofia access to more information or get her preferential treatment, but it didn't. It might have elevated her status just a little over the humans with no Kra-ell blood in them, but most importantly, it provided her with a little more protection from unwanted advances.

Valstar might barely acknowledge her existence, but she was thankful for whatever advantage having him as a grandfather provided her.

Her relation to a high-ranking Kra-ell was most likely the reason she'd been selected to pursue higher education in the human world. Like the other fortunate young humans who'd been granted the opportunity, Sofia was under Igor's heavy-handed compulsion to keep the compound and the existence of the Kra-ell people on Earth a secret. She had to call once a week and report her progress to him, and she also had to make the long drive from the university to the compound for a monthly face-to-face meeting with her dear leader to reinforce the compulsion. But all of that was a small price to pay for her slice of freedom.

What was Igor afraid of, though? That she or one of the other students would reveal that they were the human descendants of aliens who drank blood? Or that their leader was most likely conspiring to take over the human world?

First of all, no one would believe them, and they would be subjected to a mental health evaluation. Secondly, none of them would do that willingly and endanger their families.

Well, she wouldn't, but in truth, she couldn't speak for the others.

Her mother was a piece-of-work Kra-ell hybrid who resented her human daughter, but she wasn't horrible enough for Sofia to want her dead, and her human father was great. Sofia loved him and her two aunts. She also had friends who were dear to her. Most were human, but there were a couple of Kra-ell hybrids who she considered friends as well.

Both were males who were interested in her as more than a friend, but Sofia had no intentions of hooking up with anyone from the compound, human, hybrid, or pure-blooded Kra-ell.

She might never escape Igor's rule and live a normal life in the human world, but she could stretch out her studies for many more years and enjoy her freedom. He wanted her to learn foreign languages and master them, and that took time. Thankfully, the linguistics department of the University of Helsinki offered enough variety to keep her studying for many years to come.

After parking her ten-year-old Honda in the under-ground garage of the administrative building, Sofia climbed the stairs to the first floor, where she was stopped by a guard and her backpack was searched, and when she reached the second floor, she was stopped again by one of Igor's personal guards.

"Good evening, Gordi." She handed him her backpack for inspection. "Do you need to search me?"

She was wearing leggings and a form-fitting long-sleeved shirt that clung to her slim frame like a second skin. She couldn't hide a pin under that outfit, which was why she'd chosen to put it on. She'd hoped it would spare her a pat down.

"You know that I do." He motioned for her to lift her arms.

"Where do you think I can hide anything?" She did as he asked.

"Your hair." He motioned for her to release her tresses from the bun she had it gathered in. "You could hide a small firearm in that thing."

She rolled her eyes. "As if I would do something as stupid as that." She pulled out the pins holding the bun up, shook her long hair out, and let it cascade down her back. "Better?" She handed him the pins for inspection.

Gordi's eyes lit up with arousal. "You have such beautiful hair. Why do you always put it on top of your head like that?" He returned the pins to her.

It wasn't a style any of the Kra-ell pureblooded or hybrid females would ever adopt, which was precisely why she had.

It pissed her mother off.

"That's how I like it." She pretended not to notice the gleam in his eyes as she gathered her hair, twisted it on top of her head, and secured it with the pins. "Can I go now?"

Regrettably, the hybrids found her attractive for some reason.

Her dark hair, her height, and her slimness were traits she'd inherited from her Kra-ell grandfather, and her blue eyes and her gentle nature came from her Finn father. She was too thin to be considered attractive by human standards, and wasn't exotic enough to be attractive to the purebloods, but the hybrids found her features pleasing.

"Wait here." Gordi returned the backpack to her. "I'll check if Igor is ready to see you."

Slinging a strap over her shoulder, Sofia let out a silent breath and thanked the Mother that she was Valstar's granddaughter. If she were any other female, human or hybrid, Gordi could have commanded her into his bed, and there would have been very little she could have done to refuse him without courting severe retaliation.

Technically, it wasn't regarded as a command but as an invitation, and technically she could refuse, but in reality, no one dared to. To refuse a hybrid or pureblooded Kra-ell was to offend him, and since they held all the power in the compound, they could and would make her life and the lives of her family hell.

Gordi came out of Igor's office. "You can go in now."

"Thank you." She ducked into the room and immediately bowed her head. "Good evening, sir."

"Good evening, Sofia." Igor regarded her with his cold, calculating eyes. "How are your studies progressing?"

"Very well, sir. I receive top grades in all my classes."

It was the same exchange they had every month, and she often wondered whether Igor checked her grades by having them emailed to him.

Perhaps he had done it in the beginning, when he hadn't been sure she was up to the task, but after eight years of proven success, it would have been a waste of his time to keep checking on her.

Sofia was fluent in six languages and could converse in seven more, and she had no intentions of stopping unless Igor commanded her to quit.

He nodded. "I am satisfied with your progress. Keep up the good work."

She bowed again. "Yes, sir."

"Let's take care of your compliance with the compound's security rules, shall we?"

Sofia swallowed. Despite having gone through that once-a-month process for years, she still hated how it felt to have her will re-squashed with a ten-ton anvil.

"Yes, sir."

Emmett

"Here are all the contest entries." Riley dropped a pile of printed papers on Emmett's desk. "I'm surprised that we only got forty-two." She glanced at the stack. "Are you sure you don't want me to read through them first? I can rate them and save you some time."

"Thank you for the offer." He smiled at her. "But I will enjoy reading them myself. I'm curious to find out what we caught in our net."

It wasn't a writing competition, and Emmett didn't care how well or how badly the essays were written. All he cared about was whether they hinted at the author's paranormal talent.

The contest had been Eleanor's idea. Those who couldn't afford to participate in a paranormal retreat could submit an essay to win a free subscription to Safe Haven's newsletter. They would also get unlimited access to its extensive library of self-improvement seminars and motivational materials. It was a good way to collect the names and email addresses of potential paranormal talents. Later, they could invite those who showed promise to participate for free and continue testing their abilities.

"As you wish." Riley cast another disapproving look at the stack. "It's such a waste of paper to have them printed. You could've read the emails on your computer screen."

"You know that I'm old-fashioned." Emmett lifted the first page. "I don't like staring at screens."

Shrugging, his office manager turned on her short, sensible heel and walked out the door.

Riley, who had taken over the management of the community and the retreats in his absence, was still adjusting to his return and her perceived demotion. She didn't like it, but she needed to get over it, or he would have to replace her with someone with a more subservient attitude.

Safe Haven was Emmett's baby, his creation, and even though he was sharing it now with Kian and the clan, he had close to full autonomy to do with it as he pleased.

Eleanor was running the paranormal enclave with the government talents that she'd recruited in her former job. Marcel had replaced William at the lab the clan had built on the premises and was temporarily supervising a team of scientists. Leon was in charge of security for the entire complex, and Anastasia was helping create content for the new paranormal retreats. That left Emmett to do what he did best, which was promoting the spiritual and paranormal retreats with his guru persona and giving the place its spiritual spin.

Leaning back in his chair, he got comfortable and started reading the first essay. He found nothing of interest and put it in the *no* pile. The next five landed on top of it, and the next two formed the *maybe* pile.

The tenth one was titled: *How the Lions and the Rats became allies. A fable.*

That should be interesting.

Emmett leaned back in his executive chair, lifted his feet onto the desk, and began reading.

> *A long time ago, in a far, faraway land, there lived a ferocious lioness named Viva who led a very large pride. Many different animals lived in that land, some big, some small, but the lions ruled over them all.*
> *Viva was a proud female, and she paid little*

regard to the animals living in her territory who
were too small for a lioness to eat. But there was
one rat named Crafty, whose shenanigans were so
outrageous that they had reached even Viva's ears.
As his name implied, Crafty was cunning and
smart, and he got away with mischief that other
animals would never dare to try.

Emmett's heart thundered in his chest.

His father had named him Veskar after an animal from their home world that was similar to a rat and was known for being crafty. Only members of Jade's tribe knew him as Veskar, and Emmett knew of only two who were still alive and free, both residing in the immortals' village. The rest of their tribe had been either murdered or captured, so if this was written by one of them, it must have been submitted from captivity. Given that the first part of the fable was written from the pride leader's perspective, Jade must be the author.

The next part was written from the rat's perspective.

Crafty had a healthy respect for the lions, and he
stayed away from them whenever he could. Those
big cats normally didn't eat rats, but they might
eat a rat who was prone to mischief.
Wishing to find a place where there were no lions
and where rats were treated with respect, Crafty
left the lions' territory and never looked back.
He traveled across the lake to where the humans

lived, and he found a community of village rats
who were all very well fed.
With his cunning and his smarts, it didn't take
Crafty long to take over as the leader of the pack.
Those spoiled village rats who never had to work
hard for their scraps were now his to command.
He was the king of the rats.
Happy and contented, Crafty basked in his success,
and the only thing missing from his perfect life was
the satisfaction of showing his fellow wilderness rats
how well he had done for himself. From time to time,
he thought about swimming back across the lake to
tell his family and friends about his wonderful new
life in the human village, but it was too risky.
What if, while he was gone, another rat took over
as the leader of the pack?
What if, on the way, Crafty encountered one of
those ferocious cats and got eaten?
He stayed where he was and forgot all about those
he had left behind.

This part did not give Emmett any new clues, and he was starting to doubt that the email had been sent by Jade. There were probably many fables featuring rats and other animals. If he searched the internet, he would probably find many more that had nothing to do with him.

The next part reverted to the lioness.

One day, when the big cats were all asleep, a
massive earthquake shook the ground, collapsing

*the pride's home, killing some, and trapping the
rest under a pile of stone.*

*Not just the lions suffered. Many of the small cave
dwellers were squashed under the avalanche of
rocks. Those who survived fled through passages
and openings that were too small for the big cats to
fit through. The lions' size, the foundation of their
superiority, was now a hindrance.*

They were doomed.

*"How many survived?" Viva asked once the count
was done.*

*"Thirty adults and sixty cubs," answered the lion
who had counted the live ones.*

Viva's heart sank. "How many died?"

*"One adult female and her four cubs," the one
who'd counted the dead said mournfully. "And if
we don't find a way out of the collapsed caves soon,
we will all die here as well."*

*"Who could save us?" a lioness cried out. "Does
anyone even know that we are trapped?"*

*"Maybe the little critters who escaped through the
nooks and crannies will tell someone who will be
willing to help us," another lion said.*

*The only ones who could help were the humans,
and they didn't understand animal language.
Despondent, Viva did not say a thing. She lay
down and put her head on her paws.*

Emmett was done with only the first one out of the three
printed pages when he straightened in his chair, snatched

the phone off his desk, and called Eleanor. "Come to my office right away. It's urgent."

"On my way." She ended the call.

Marcel

Marcel didn't appreciate being called mid-morning by Eleanor and asked to come immediately to Emmett's office. If it were anyone else, he would have demanded explanations before rushing over, but Eleanor wasn't the type to get worked up over nothing.

The door to Emmett's office opened before he had a chance to knock. "Thanks for coming." Eleanor smiled apologetically. "I would have come to you, but I'm not allowed in the lab."

Normally, she would have been correct, but he would have her in if she'd called and explained her problem. As long as he was there with her and made sure that she didn't see what he and the team were working on, it would have been okay.

"What's the emergency?" Marcel closed the door behind him.

"This." Emmett waved a stack of papers. "The email arrived two days ago, but I only read it today." He handed him a three-page document. "I need Kian to see it, but I don't want to send it from here in case it's encoded, and someone can follow the email to the village. I don't know the protocol for sending secure emails, but I assume that you have a safe channel of communication in your lab, and I need you to send it to him along with a note from me explaining what's going on."

Marcel read the title. "How the Lions and the Rats become allies. A fable." He lifted a brow. "It's a children's tale. Why does it need encryption, and what does it have to do with Kian?"

"It's from Jade," Eleanor said, cutting straight to the chase. "She wrote it in such a way that only Emmett would know it's from her. It's a call for help."

"Did you read it?"

Emmett might have seen in the story what wasn't there, but Eleanor was not prone to flights of fancy.

"I did. Without Emmett's explanation, I would have thought nothing of it, but with his input, the fable becomes a coded cry for help."

"How do you know it's from her?" Marcel asked Emmett.

The guy grimaced. "My Kra-ell name is Veskar. My father wasn't happy about the birth of a hybrid son who looked too human for his taste, so he gave me an insulting name. Veskar can be loosely translated as a crafty rat." Emmett pointed to the pages in Marcel's hands. "The fable's hero is called Crafty, and he's a rat."

"I see."

Marcel sat down and read the first page. "Do those numbers mean anything to you?"

Emmett shook his head. "They don't, but I'm sure that they are not random. I just don't know what she's trying to communicate."

"How many members did her tribe have?"

"None of those numbers add up to anything that makes sense," Eleanor said. "Emmett and I already tried to figure it out, but the numbers don't match the total number of the tribe's population, not the number of males or females, and not the number of humans. Not during Emmett's time in the tribe, and not right before the attack."

Marcel nodded. "That's what I thought. The sixty-four and thirty-one or the sixty and thirty could be latitude and longitude coordinates." He read the passage. "Thirty adults and sixty cubs lived. One female and her four cubs died." He lifted his head and looked at Emmet. "Longitude is also called meridian, and the synonyms for meridian are the greatest, the uppermost, and so on. Therefore, the number of adults could represent longitude. Latitude lines are also called parallels, and some of the synonyms for parallels are secondary and kin, which means that the number of cubs could represent the number for latitude."

"Oh, that's so clever of her." Eleanor crossed her arms over her chest. "And it's even cleverer of you to figure it out."

Marcel wasn't sure that it was. If Jade was trying to communicate a secret message in an email that she knew was monitored, that wasn't clever at all. He wasn't the only one who could figure out that those numbers were coordinates. Not that he was convinced that they were. It was just a hypothesis.

"Let's check those coordinates." Marcel pulled out his phone, opened the map application, and typed in the numbers. "Sixty longitude and thirty latitude point to St. Petersburg. Let's check sixty-four and thirty-one." His brows lifted. "Interesting. It's probably a coincidence, but this set of coordinates is smack in the middle of a place called Karelia, which sounds a lot like Kra-ell. The area straddles northwest Russia and the eastern portion of Finland. The coordinates fall on the Russian side."

Eleanor turned to Emmett. "Mey said that the enemy Kra-ell male's echo she'd heard had a Russian accent."

They could be reading into the fable things that weren't there, and combining mismatched pieces of a puzzle, but Marcel was willing to suspend disbelief.

"Let's see if there are any more clues hiding in the story." He continued reading.

> *One day as Crafty was sitting on his throne and conducting pack business, a rabbit he had known from the wilderness hopped over. "Crafty, how good it is to see you. Did you hear what happened to the lions' pride?"*
> *"I did not."*

After the rabbit told Crafty about the earthquake that had trapped all the big cats underground, he sighed. "Even the cubs are too big to fit through the crevices that my family and I used to escape. They will all die in there." The rabbit shook his head. "I wish I could help, but I'm just a small rabbit, and all I can do is run."

Crafty might have disliked the lions' haughty attitudes, but they had never been his enemy, and he did not wish to see them all dead. He wouldn't leave the cubs to die of starvation.

The rabbit might be helpless, but a smart rat with a large pack could do what even the powerful lions could not.

He could dig an escape tunnel and prove the real value of rats. They weren't just parasites who lived off human scraps. They could be powerful and respected allies.

Crafty summoned his followers and told them his plan. "The pride will forever be in our debt, and we will never hunger for meat again." He stretched to his full height and lifted his paws. "We will prove to everyone that rats are not at the bottom of the food chain and that we deserve as much respect as the lions. With our smarts, determination, and cooperation, we can do what none of the other animals can."

One of the bigger rats lifted his paw. "How do we know that they won't eat us once we get to them? Lions don't usually eat rats, but they will be hungry, and they have cubs that they will be desperate to feed."

"I will tunnel through the last couple of feet alone and talk to their leader. If she swears not to let anyone of her subjects eat us, I will come back, and we will enlarge the tunnel so they will be able to get out."

"She might promise you that and then eat us after we free her," a female said. "Or she might just eat you before giving you a chance to explain."

Crafty laughed. "I would not be much of a meal, and the pride's leader is too smart to eat her only hope of survival. She's a mother, and she'll do anything to save the cubs, even if it means making an alliance with rats. She's also proud, and if she gives me her word, she will stand by it."

"What about the other cats?" the big male asked. "They will eat us for sure."

It was possible. The leader might have lost her hold on the pride, or she might be injured and weakened, and they might not listen to her, but Crafty couldn't just do nothing and let them all die.

"She won't let them. Let's go!" He singsonged that special tune that would ensure the pack's compliance. "We will prove to the world that rats are not to be sneered at."

It took the pack three days to swim through the lake and then another seven days to burrow underground, and when Crafty smelled the lions, the live ones and the dead, he made the signal for his pack to stop. "I shall continue alone from here."

413

As he dug through the last three feet, he didn't bother to make the tunnel more than two inches wide, compressing his body and squeezing through. When he emerged from the tunnel the lions were asleep, and as he scurried as fast as his paws could carry him to the largest lioness, the others lifted their massive heads and bared their teeth.

He slid between her outstretched paws. "Don't eat me! I came to save you!"

Her big feline eyes widened. "How?"

He stood up and stretched to his full height of seven and a half inches. "My name is Crafty, and I am the leader of a big rat pack. I promised my subjects that you and yours would forever be in our debt if we dug a tunnel and got you out. But you and your subjects must swear alliance to me and mine. You also need to swear that you will not eat any members of my pack and that once you are free, you will share your kills with us."

Hope surging in her heart, the leader nodded her massive head.

To save her family, she would kiss the rat on his little whiskers if that was what he demanded in payment, but all he was asking for was assurance for the safety of his pack and future scraps. It was a very small price to pay to save the weakening cubs. They wouldn't last much longer.

"I have heard of you, Crafty, and I know that you are a very smart rat. I swear it on my life and the lives of everyone in my pride that if you and your pack save us, you will never go hungry for meat for

as long as we live. My pride and I will share our kills with you and yours, and we will never eat any of your subjects or any other rats." She grimaced. "Rats were never a food source for us and never will be." Weakened from hunger, she lifted herself with effort and turned to the others. "Swear it, and let's get out of here."

After the lions repeated the vow that their leader had made, Crafty returned through the tiny tunnel he had dug for himself and told the others what was promised.

When the rats had finished digging the rest of the tunnel and freed all the lions, the leader of the pride and her subjects kept their promise. From that day on, the pride of lions and the pack of rats lived in harmony and mutual respect, and no one in that part of the world dared to look down their noses or whiskers at Crafty or any other rat.

Marcel shifted his gaze to Emmett. "Does seven or three mean anything to you or seven and a half inches?"

Emmett shook his head. "They don't. The only thing I got from the fable was that Jade and the other females were trapped, that they had children with them, and that they needed me to save them in a stealthy manner, maybe literally by digging a tunnel. Without your input, I would have never suspected that the numbers of the adults and cubs could represent coordinates."

DARK GAMBIT THE PAWN

The Children of the Gods Series

Reading Order

THE CHILDREN OF THE GODS ORIGINS

1: GODDESS'S CHOICE

When gods and immortals still ruled the ancient world, one young goddess risked everything for love.

2: GODDESS'S HOPE

Hungry for power and infatuated with the beautiful Areana, Navuh plots his father's demise. After all, by getting rid of the insane god he would be doing the world a favor. Except, when gods and immortals conspire against each other, humanity pays the price.

But things are not what they seem, and prophecies should not to be trusted...

THE CHILDREN OF THE GODS

DARK STRANGER

1: DARK STRANGER THE DREAM

2: DARK STRANGER REVEALED

3: DARK STRANGER IMMORTAL

DARK ENEMY

4: DARK ENEMY TAKEN

5: DARK ENEMY CAPTIVE

6: DARK ENEMY REDEEMED

Dark Widow

Dark Dream

Dark Prince

Dark Queen

Dark Spy

Dark Overlord

To get to Safe Haven's inner circle, the Kra-ell leader sacrifices a pawn. He does not expect her to reach the final rank and promote to a queen.

Marcel takes a big risk by telling Sofia his greatest sin. Can he trust her to keep it a secret? Or maybe it's time to confess his crime and submit to whatever punishment Edna deems appropriate?

Three miserable centuries of living with guilt and remorse are long enough.

Once the dust settles on the Kra-ell crisis, he will gather the courage to put himself at the court's mercy.

DARK ALLIANCE

68: DARK ALLIANCE KINDRED SOULS

A daring operation half a world away devolves into a full-scale crisis that escalates rapidly, requiring the clan's full might and technological wizardry to manage and survive.

Hardened by duty and tragedy, Jade is driven by a burning desire for revenge. When Phinas saves her second-in-command, Jade's gratitude quickly becomes something more.

69: DARK ALLIANCE TURBULENT WATERS

When a dangerous foe turns the tables on the clan, complicating the Kra-ell rescue operation in unforeseeable ways, Kian and his crew bet all on a brilliant misdirection.

On board the Aurora, Phinas and Jade brace for battle while enjoying a few stolen moments of passion.

Drawn to the woman he sees behind the aloof leader, Phinas realizes that what has started as a calculated political move has evolved into a deepening sense of companionship.

Jade finds reprieve in Phinas's arms, but duty and tradition make it difficult for her to accept that what she feels for him is more than just gratitude and desire.

After all, the Kra-ell don't believe in love.

70: DARK ALLIANCE PERFECT STORM

After two decades in captivity, Jade is finally free, her quest for revenge within grasp, but danger still looms large. A storm is brewing on the horizon, gathering momentum and threatening to obliterate Jade's tenuous hold on hope for a better future.

DARK HEALING

71: Dark Healing Blind Justice

The sanctuary is Vanessa's life project. The monumental task of rehabilitating the traumatized victims of trafficking doesn't leave much time for personal life, let alone dating or finding her one and only.

When Kian asks her to help the Kra-ell, she's torn between her duty to the sanctuary and a group of emotionally wounded aliens who no other psychologist can treat.

She's the only immortal with the necessary training to get it done.

The Kra-ell culture and the purebloods' nearly androgynous alien looks shouldn't appeal to her, and yet, she finds one of them disturbingly attractive.

Is it the dangerous vibe he emits?

Does it speak to her on a subconscious level?

Or is it her need to put the broken pieces of him back together?

And why is he interested in her?

She cannot offer him a fight for dominance like a Kra-ell female would, but some strange and unfamiliar part of her wishes she could.

72: Dark Healing Blind Trust

Riddled with guilt over the crimes he was forced to commit, Mo-red is ready to stand trial and accept the death sentence he believes he deserves, but when the clan's alluring psychologist offers a new perspective on his past and hope for a better future, he resolves to fight for his life.

73: Dark healing Blind Curve

Kian is still reeling from the shocking revelations about the twins when a new threat manifests, eclipsing everything he's had to deal with up until now. In light of the new developments, Igor, the other Kra-ell prisoners, and the pending trial are no longer at the forefront of his mind, but the opposite is true for Vanessa. As her relationship with Mo-red solidifies, she is determined to save the male she loves, even if it means breaking him free and living on the run.

Dark Encounters

74: Dark Encounters of the Close Kind

Convinced that her family is hiding a terrible secret from her, Gabi decides to pay them a surprise visit.

Something is very fishy about the stories her brothers have been telling her lately. Her niece, a nineteen-year-old prodigy with a Ph.D. in bioinformatics, has gotten engaged to a much older guy she met while working on some top-secret project, and if Gabi's older, overprotective brother's approval of the engagement wasn't suspicious enough, he also uprooted his family and moved to be closer to the couple.

What Gabi discovers when she gets to L.A. is wilder than anything she could have imagined. Her entire family possesses godly genes, her brothers and her niece have already turned immortal, and she could transition as soon as she finds an immortal male to induce her. Finding a suitable candidate in a village full of handsome immortals shouldn't be a problem, but Gabi's thoughts keep wandering to the gorgeous guy she met on her flight over.

Could Uriel be a lost descendant of the gods?

He certainly looks like them, but that doesn't mean that he's a good guy or that he's even immortal. He could be a descendant of a different god—a member of an enemy faction of immortals who seek to eradicate her family's adoptive clan, or what is more likely, he's just an extraordinarily good-looking human.

75: Dark Encounters of the Unexpected Kind

Who is Uriel?

Is he a lost descendant of the gods or just a gorgeous and charming human who has rocked Gabi's world?

76: Dark Encounters of the Fated Kind

As Aru and his team embark on a perilous mission, their past and present converge in a meeting that holds the key to their fate.

Dark Voyage

77: Dark Voyage Matters of the Heart

As Annani and Syssi set out to unravel the mysteries of Syssi's visions about the gods' home world, the long-awaited wedding cruise sets sail with Aru, Gabi, and Aru's teammates on board.

While the gods find themselves surrounded by immortal clan ladies eager for their affections, they soon discover that destiny has a different plan for them.

The Children of the Gods Series Sets

Books 1-3: Dark Stranger trilogy—Includes a bonus short story: The Fates take a Vacation

Books 4-6: Dark Enemy Trilogy —Includes a bonus short story—The Fates' Post-Wedding Celebration

Books 7-10: Dark Warrior Tetralogy

Books 11-13: Dark Guardian Trilogy

Books 14-16: Dark Angel Trilogy

Books 17-19: Dark Operative Trilogy

Books 20-22: Dark Survivor Trilogy

Books 23-25: Dark Widow Trilogy

Books 26-28: Dark Dream Trilogy

Books 29-31: Dark Prince Trilogy

Books 32-34: Dark Queen Trilogy

Books 35-37: Dark Spy Trilogy

Books 38-40: Dark Overlord Trilogy

Books 41-43: Dark Choices Trilogy

Books 44-46: Dark Secrets Trilogy

Books 47-49: Dark Haven Trilogy

Books 50-52: Dark Power Trilogy

Books 53-55: Dark Memories Trilogy

Books 56-58: Dark Hunter Trilogy

Books 59-61: Dark God Trilogy

Books 62-64: Dark Whispers Trilogy

Books 65-67: Dark Gambit Trilogy

Books 68-70: Dark Alliance Trilogy

Books 71-73: Dark healing Trilogy

MEGA SETS

INCLUDE CHARACTER LISTS

The Children of the Gods: Books 1-6

THE CHILDREN OF THE GODS: BOOKS 6.5-10

TRY THE SERIES ON

<u>AUDIBLE</u>

2 FREE audiobooks with your new Audible subscription!

PERFECT MATCH SERIES

VAMPIRE'S CONSORT

When Gabriel's company is ready to start beta testing, he invites his old crush to inspect its medical safety protocol.

Curious about the revolutionary technology of the *Perfect Match Virtual Fantasy-Fulfillment studios*, Brenna agrees.

Neither expects to end up partnering for its first fully immersive test run.

KING'S CHOSEN

When Lisa's nutty friends get her a gift certificate to *Perfect Match Virtual Fantasy Studios*, she has no intentions of using it. But since the only way to get a refund is if no partner can be found for her, she makes sure to request a fantasy so girly and over the top that no sane guy will pick it up.

Except, someone does.

> **Warning:** This fantasy contains a hot, domineering crown prince, sweet insta-love, steamy love scenes painted with light shades of gray, a wedding, and a HEA in both the virtual and real worlds.

> Intended for mature audience.

Captain's Conquest

Working as a Starbucks barista, Alicia fends off flirting all day long, but none of the guys are as charming and sexy as Gregg. His frequent visits are the highlight of her day, but since he's never asked her out, she assumes he's taken. Besides, between a day job and a budding music career, she has no time to start a new relationship.

That is until Gregg makes her an offer she can't refuse—a gift certificate to the virtual fantasy fulfillment service everyone is talking about. As a huge Star Trek fan, Alicia has a perfect match in mind—the captain of the Starship Enterprise.

The Thief Who Loved Me

When Marian splurges on a Perfect Match Virtual adventure as a world infamous jewel thief, she expects high-wire fun with a hot partner who she will never have to see again in real life.

A virtual encounter seems like the perfect answer to Marcus's string of dating disasters. No strings attached, no drama, and definitely no love. As a die-hard James Bond fan, he chooses as his avatar a dashing MI6 operative, and to complement his adventure, a dangerously seductive partner.

Neither expects to find their forever Perfect Match.

My Merman Prince

The beautiful architect working late on the twelfth floor of my building thinks that I'm just the maintenance guy. She's also under the impression that I'm not interested.

Nothing could be further from the truth.

I want her like I've never wanted a woman before, but I don't play where I work.

I don't need the complications.

When she tells me about living out her mermaid fantasy with a stranger in a Perfect Match virtual adventure, I decide to do everything possible to ensure that the stranger is me.

THE DRAGON KING

To save his beloved kingdom from a devastating war, the Crown Prince of Trieste makes a deal with a witch that costs him half of his humanity and dooms him to an eternity of loneliness.

Now king, he's a fearsome cobalt-winged dragon by day and a short-tempered monarch by night. Not many are brave enough to serve in the palace of the brooding and volatile ruler, but Charlotte ignores the rumors and accepts a scribe position in court.

As the young scribe reawakens Bruce's frozen heart, all that stands in the way of their happiness is the witch's bargain. Outsmarting the evil hag will take cunning and courage, and Charlotte is just the right woman for the job.

My Werewolf Romeo

The father of my star student is a big-shot screenwriter and the patron of the drama department who thinks he can dictate what production I should put on. The principal makes it very clear that I need to cooperate with the opinionated asshat or walk away from my dream job at the exclusive private high school.

It doesn't help matters that the guy is single, hot, charming, creative, and seems to like me despite my thinly-veiled hostility.

When he invites me to a custom-tailored Perfect Match virtual adventure to prove that his screenplay is perfect for my production, I accept, intending to have fun while proving that messing with the classics is a foolish idea.

I don't expect to be wowed by his werewolf adaptation of Red Riding Hood mesh-up with Romeo and Juliet, and I certainly don't expect to fall in love with the virtual fantasy's leading man.

The Channeler's Companion

A treat for fans of *The Wheel of Time*.

When Erika hires Rand to assist in her pediatric clinic, she does so despite his good looks and irresistible charm, not because of them.

He's empathic, adores children, and has the patience of a saint.

He's also all she can think about, but he's off limits.

What's a doctor to do to scratch that irresistible itch without risking workplace complications?

A shared adventure in the Perfect Match Virtual Studios seems like the solution, but instead of letting the algorithm choose a partner for her, Erika can try to influence it to select the one she wants. Awarding Rand a gift certificate to the service will get him into their database, but unless Erika can tip the odds in her favor, getting paired with him is a long shot.

Hopefully, a virtual adventure based on her and Rand's favorite series will do the trick.

Note

Dear reader,

I hope my stories have added a little joy to your day. If you have a moment to add some to mine, you can help spread the word about the Children Of The Gods series by telling your friends and penning a review. Your recommendations are the most powerful way to inspire new readers to explore the series.

Thank you,

Isabell

FOR EXCLUSIVE PEEKS AT UPCOMING RELEASES & A FREE COMPANION BOOK

Join my *VIP Club* and gain access to the VIP portal at itlucas.com
To Join, go to:
http://eepurl.com/blMTpD

INCLUDED IN YOUR FREE MEMBERSHIP:

YOUR VIP PORTAL

- Read preview chapters of upcoming releases.
- Listen to Goddess's Choice narration by Charles Lawrence
- Exclusive content offered only to my VIPs.

FREE I.T. LUCAS COMPANION INCLUDES:

- Goddess's Choice Part i
- Perfect Match: Vampire's Consort (A standalone Novella)
- Interview Q & A
- Character Charts

If you're already a subscriber, and you are not getting my emails, your provider is

SENDING THEM TO YOUR JUNK FOLDER, AND YOU ARE MISSING OUT ON **IMPORTANT UPDATES**, **SIDE CHARACTERS' PORTRAITS, ADDITIONAL CONTENT, AND OTHER GOODIES.** TO FIX THAT, ADD isabell@itlucas.com TO YOUR EMAIL CONTACTS OR YOUR EMAIL VIP LIST.

Check out the specials at
https://www.itlucas.com/specials

Printed in Great Britain
by Amazon

56967929R00245